HER PERFECT HUSBAND

JACK STAINTON

ALSO BY JACK STAINTON

A Guest To Die For

You're Family Now

Mother

Last One To Lie

He Is Here

The Boss's Wife

Dead Ever After

Truth Lies Beneath

PART I

DAY ONE

1

HIM

As soon as the finca came into view, I instinctively knew something was wrong. It was too dark, too quiet… too empty. Checking my watch, it was barely two hours since I left her. A stupid quarrel over something I'd already forgotten.

Increasing my pace, I stumbled down the unkempt footpath, the coarse gravel loose beneath my unsteady feet. The local beer—cold but strong—had gone down far too easily, and combined with the relentless Andalusian heat, it left my head fuzzy and my movements lethargic. Chain smoking ten cigarettes hadn't helped, only adding to my dizziness. Sweat trickled down my neck, clinging to the back of my shirt. Finally, after negotiating the final sharp bend on the dirt track, I squinted down at the silhouette of the finca against the burning sun beyond. The white walls were prominent, but the windows were dark, like closed eyes. Why was there no sign of life?

I paused at the front door, leaning against the frame, and

fumbled with the key. "Laura?" My voice trembled slightly as I finally pushed it open.

The air inside was stifling. Why hadn't she put the air-con on?

"Laura?" I called again, my voice louder this time, echoing along the dark and deserted hallway.

No answer.

Something was wrong. I knew it.

A strange sense of unease crept over me as I moved through the finca. The living room was untouched, the cushions on the sofa still plump and perfectly arranged. The kitchen was empty, the work surfaces bare except for the two glasses we'd used earlier and the welcome basket to keep us going for a while. No sign of her phone. No handbag. My breath caught in my throat.

I headed to the bedroom, nearly tripping on the rug as I went. The door was ajar, and I pushed it open with my shoulder, blinking against the dark. The shutters were closed, and I reached for the switch and winced as the overhead light flared on, momentarily blinding me.

The bed was neatly made; our suitcases were on top, exactly as we had left them. Mine was open, but Laura's remained zipped. Still packed. Her straw hat sat next to it.

A chill rushed over my skin like I'd stepped into a freezing shower.

"Laura!" I shouted, my voice cracking.

I checked the en suite, throwing the door open. Empty. The shower stall was dry, the towels untouched.

Where the hell could she be?

Maybe she'd gone for a walk? But she wouldn't have just left. Not without saying something. Not without a note or a text. It was just a pathetic argument. We'd had far worse. Besides, she'd never walk along that terrain alone. Especially not in that heat. And certainly not without her hat.

Stumbling back into the main room, I tripped over a small step connecting the hallway to the living area. I cursed loudly as I caught myself against the edge of the sofa, my bare shin throbbing in protest.

"Where on earth are you?" I muttered under my breath, rubbing the sore spot as I staggered towards the sliding glass doors that led to the pool. Stepping outside, the heat hit me once more, doing nothing to sober me up. The property was silent, eerily so, except for the faint rustle of wind through the nearby olive trees. Even the cicadas had ceased making their incessant din.

My eyes scanned the perimeter, searching for any sign of her. Nothing. No movement, no sound.

Then, a high-pitched noise broke the silence.

A car alarm.

I straightened, my ears straining to pinpoint where it was coming from. It wasn't far away. I turned, my gaze taking in the landscape. The neighbouring houses were barely visible, their faint, whitewashed walls scattered across the hills as if built with toy bricks. Miguel had said the closest property was a kilometre away, but the car alarm... it sounded nearer than that. He mentioned there was a neighbouring finca, but as far as he knew, nobody ever used it.

"Laura?" I called again, my voice threatening to break.

Moving around the side of the property, the gravel crunched loudly beneath my feet. But as I reached the driveway, my breath caught in my throat.

Our car was gone.

How did I not notice on the way in?

I grabbed the edge of the wall to steady myself. Laura wouldn't have driven. She hated driving, especially on roads like those—narrow, winding, with sheer drops at every turn.

Would she?

A thousand thoughts flooded my mind, each more frantic

than the last. Maybe she'd gone for help. Had she hurt herself? Maybe she was angry and wanted to get away from me for a while. But why wouldn't she have left a note?

"She wouldn't," I muttered to myself, shaking my head. "She wouldn't just leave."

But the empty driveway told a different story.

I turned back towards the house, my head pounding as the alcohol began to leave my system, only to be replaced by the inevitable onset of a headache. The finca suddenly felt too big, its boundary walls and iron gates resembling a prison more than a holiday home.

The chirp of the car alarm came again, closer this time. Or was it my imagination? I squinted into the distance, but the landscape offered no clues, just the dark silhouettes of hills and trees. It could have been miles away, given the terrain and desolation of the surroundings.

I needed to think, to clear my head, but the alcohol muddled my thoughts. I stumbled back inside, flicking on lights as I went, illuminating every corner of the house in a desperate attempt to find some clue, some explanation.

What had happened here before I stormed off to the bar?

I leant against the kitchen counter, my hands gripping the edge as I tried to steady my breathing. The memory of her earlier words echoed in my mind: *"Take as long as you want."*

Had she meant it as a warning? A signal that she'd planned this? Or was somebody else involved; had she been taken against her will?

Another sound outside—a faint rustling, followed by the distant rumble of an engine. My head snapped up, and I ran to the window, peering into the wilderness.

Again, nothing. But I'd definitely heard a car somewhere.

I grabbed my phone and called Laura's number. It went straight to voicemail.

"Damn it!" I cursed, slamming it down on the worktop.

My thoughts raced. If she'd taken the car, she couldn't have gone *that* far. Not with how steadily she would be driving.

But the reasons she might have left churned in my mind.

She couldn't know. Could she?

I stared outside, the faint hum of the car alarm still ringing in my ears.

2

HIM

HOURS EARLIER

THE MOMENT we left Madrid behind and hit the vast emptiness of Castilla-La Mancha, doubt settled in my chest.

The drive would be long—almost six hours according to the satnav—and oppressive with heat that the car's air conditioning couldn't quite seem to keep at bay. The roads shimmered under the relentless sun, stretching endlessly ahead, and the silence in the car was thick, weighted with something unspoken. It sat between us, pressing against my skull like an oncoming migraine.

I kept my hands on the wheel, my eyes fixed on the road, but my mind wouldn't relax.

I recalled how much Laura hated those roads.

She'd hated them the last time we drove through the mountains, flinching at every tight bend, muttering for me to slow down. I could still hear her voice, tense and curt. *"For God's sake, James, you're taking the corners too fast."* I sensed her fingers tightening around the door handle, knuckles white.

But this time, there was nothing. No sharp intake of breath, no complaints in hushed tones. Just silence.

I swallowed, shifting in my seat again.

Outside, the landscape changed, the flat plains giving way to rolling hills, jagged peaks rising against the horizon. The olive groves stretched in perfect lines, endless rows of silvery-green. Now and then, we passed a town clinging to the hillside, the kind of place where time seemed to stand still. Clusters of whitewashed houses hugged the slopes, no doubt their streets too narrow for anything but foot traffic and the occasional battered scooter.

Eventually, the satnav guided me off the main road, directing me deeper into the mountains. The tarmac grew narrower, winding upward, holding onto the cliff side in a way that made my stomach lurch. The guardrails, where they existed, looked flimsy, barely more than a suggestion.

I eased off the accelerator, my fingers curling on the wheel.

I could almost hear it. *Careful, James.*

But the silence pressed in harder. Still no words.

A sharp bend loomed ahead, the road curving tight around the rock face. As I steered into it, I spotted a twisted gap in the guardrail, metal bent outward as if something had crashed straight through it.

For a split second, I imagined it too vividly—skid marks streaked across the tarmac, the screech of tyres, the sickening drop.

I swallowed hard and forced my eyes back onto the road. Just a guardrail. Just another turn.

The sun hung high in the sky, a ruthless white-hot glare beating down. Heat waves rippled off the tarmac, distorting the edges of the highway, making the horizon blur and shift.

The road was almost deserted, as if we'd left civilisation miles behind. The car's air conditioning wheezed in protest, struggling to keep up. A burst of static crackled from the radio before cutting out entirely, leaving only the low whir of the engine and the rhythmic click of the indicator as I followed the satnav instructions.

We were close.

The small town came into view; a scattering of white buildings perched on the hillside, their walls bathed in the midday glow. There was something unreal about it, a postcard from another time.

As we reached the first houses, it was as if we'd arrived in the middle of the night. They all looked empty, the windows shuttered. A cat slinked between two buildings, pausing briefly to watch as I rolled past before disappearing into the shadows.

Carmen's bar was exactly where the directions said it would be, on the outskirts of town, half-hidden behind a cluster of trees.

But we already knew that.

A low, squat building with a faded awning sagging above the entrance, the paint on the sign had peeled away, the letters barely legible.

I pulled into the dirt lot, dust kicking up in the heat as the engine sputtered into silence.

For a moment, I didn't move.

The car ticked softly as the metal cooled, settling into the hush of the surroundings, not wanting to intrude on the peace and quiet. I could hear the hum of cicadas, and watched as a pile of dry leaves was disturbed by a slight breeze.

I turned my head slightly, glancing towards the bar. The windows were dark, the door barely ajar.

A prickle ran down my spine.

I exhaled, rolling my shoulders, willing away the stiffness that had crept in from the hours of driving.

Sighing, I reached for the door handle. "Okay," I said sarcastically. "I'll go see if he's inside, should I? Leave it to me."

Still, I hesitated.

The silence in the car was unbearable.

I paused for the briefest of moments before stepping out. The dry heat hit me immediately, pressing against my skin, thick and unmoving. I shut the door behind me, listening to the echo of it in the near-empty lot.

It was too quiet.

I glanced back at the car, at the passenger seat.

Then, before I could think too hard about it, I turned and headed to the bar.

3
____

HIM

AFTER NODDING AMICABLY towards the patrons sat at metal
tables outside, shaded by large parasols advertising what I
presumed was the local beer, I made for a huge wooden door
with *Bienvenido* painted crudely across it.

Inside, the bar was dimly lit and smelled of stale body
odour and cigarettes. The inaudible murmur of conversation
stopped as soon as the door swung shut behind me, as if
someone had flipped a switch. It wasn't gradual; it was
sudden. Although there were no more than a dozen people
inside, all eyes settled on me, a mix of curiosity and something
harder to define. Suspicion? Recognition?

I hesitated in the doorway, considering turning on my
heels. I wished Laura had accompanied me.

The locals sat hunched over stools along the bar—an elon-
gated stretch of highly polished wood—their postures rigid as
they stared. It was like walking into a scene from a horror
movie, where the newcomer is the only one who doesn't yet
know they've walked into a trap.

The bartender emerged from behind the bar. In her mid-forties, she was confident in that quiet, controlled way some people have when they know they own the room.

"Hello," she said knowingly. "Welcome to Carmen's bar. How can I help you?"

Of course she knew I was English.

"Hi," I replied, forcing a polite smile. The group of men at the bar didn't stop staring, their eyes following me as if I were an actor in a play, waiting for their cue. I tried to ignore them, but the way their silence filled the room caused my skin to prickle.

"Er… hi…" I paused. "James."

She just smiled, enjoying my nervousness.

"I'm here to meet…" I trailed off, letting it hang. "Someone. He's taking us to our accommodation."

Her smile flickered, only for a second. A barely there moment that made my pulse skip. Maybe it was nothing. Maybe it was. Her gaze slipped—just briefly—towards the locals, then back to me, a little too quickly. And like a curtain being drawn, the room stirred again. Glasses clinked. Someone laughed. The spell broke.

"Hello, James," she said, her voice lighter now. "Can I get you a drink while you wait?"

"A beer, thanks."

She nodded and turned, pulling a glass from under the bar. Her movements were casual, not rushed. She didn't need to impress me, but somehow, she still did.

I watched her pour. She didn't look at me again, not until she placed the beer on the bar. Our eyes met for the briefest moment. Should I smile?

I paid, took the glass, and moved to a table near the door. I sat facing the entrance, one eye on it, the other conscious of the stares behind me.

But it wasn't the locals I could sense.

I sipped the beer, the icy liquid doing little to ease the tightness in my chest. I worried about Laura, wondering if the trip would end up a complete waste of money. But I was determined. It was obvious from the moment we woke that morning that she didn't relish being there as much as me; ironic, really, considering she booked the whole thing. Did she believe our marriage was already beyond repair? She'd accused me of all sorts over the past few months while burying her head in her work.

Her work. *Her bloody work.*

She wouldn't let it go. She treated her patients with more respect than she showed me. Still, I was determined to fix things. I'd already had one failed marriage, and I wouldn't allow another to go the same way. And now, after the girl who Laura nurtured as if she were her own daughter, had taken her life... I thought maybe, finally, she'd come up for air.

Surely a week away from it all—away from the stress, the grief, the guilt—was exactly what we needed?

Several minutes passed, though it felt much longer, before the door creaked open.

A man entered, his presence shifting the energy in the room once more. The locals fell silent again, although this time, they resumed their animated conversation considerably sooner. Unlike me, I gathered they must have recognised him.

He spotted me immediately—the only non-local in the bar —and his smile was wide. He was short and stocky, with thinning hair slicked over his head, and a sweat-stained shirt that clung to his back. Despite the oppressive heat, the room suddenly felt colder.

"Welcome, welcome," he said, his English heavily accented. "I am Miguel. I show you the finca, yes? Very beautiful. Very quiet."

I shook his hand, trying to hide my unease. There was something about him that set me on edge, but I couldn't put my finger on it. Maybe it was the way his eyes flicked over me, like he was assessing me, or the way he kept glancing at the door as if expecting someone else to walk in.

"Sounds great," I said, forcing a smile. "We're ready when you are. My wife is in the car."

He nodded and headed for the exit. I downed the last of my beer, suddenly wishing I had time for another, before turning to gesture my thanks to Carmen.

Her gaze lingered—friendly, yet suspicious.

There was something in her expression I couldn't place. As though she saw straight through me and was recalling what I was pretending to forget.

Did my body language give me away?

Following Miguel outside, again the heat slammed into me like a wall.

I climbed into the driver's seat, starting the engine as Miguel jumped into his own vehicle, an old, battered Land Rover. He waved for us to follow, pulling out onto the road with a cloud of dust trailing behind him.

As I began to drive, I suddenly wondered who we were actually following. I hadn't asked for any ID. I hadn't seen the need, it had seemed unnecessary, but now I wasn't so sure.

Because the truth was, once I'd thought about it, I wasn't entirely certain who we were following up into those hills.

$$4$$

____

HIM

MIGUEL'S TOUR was thankfully brief as he spoke of the finca's history and something about his family's legacy. But my mind had been elsewhere. Every so often, I thought I heard something—a soft rustle, the faintest sound of footsteps just out of sight.

We moved around the property, Miguel suddenly taking his time as if he had nowhere else to be. He gestured towards things I could clearly see for myself—"the terrace," "the outdoor shower," as though I were blind.

His voice had that low, easy rhythm people use when they think they're being charming. But it grated.

I nodded along, barely listening, resisting the urge to check my watch. I just wanted him gone.

What was there to show us, really? It was a holiday home. Walls, roof, a pool. We'd figure it out.

But Miguel lingered. Let his gaze rest on things too long. On me too long.

He smiled as he spoke, but it didn't quite reach his eyes. I felt myself tensing when he stepped too close.

Eventually, we found ourselves in a corridor with heavy wooden doors on either side. All were open, apart from one at the end, and I could see the three bedrooms, all immaculate. Then we came across the closed one. Miguel didn't offer to open it.

"What's in there?" I asked, gesturing to it with a nod.

Miguel hesitated, just for a second. "Storage," he said. "Nothing interesting."

I let it go, but my fingers twitched at my side.

We finally stepped into a room that looked like a study. An antique desk stood in the centre, its surface bare. A single chair sat near the large window overlooking the valley below.

Miguel moved to the window, his hands resting on the sill. "Beautiful, no?"

For a split second, my knees felt weak, and I had to steady myself against the desk. The room spun slightly, my vision tunnelling before I forced myself to take a slow, deep breath.

Not now. Not here.

I straightened, swallowing the bitter taste rising in my throat.

"Sir?" Miguel said carefully. "Are you all right?"

I nodded quickly. "Yeah. Just tired."

Miguel studied me again, that same unreadable expression on his face. "Perhaps you need rest. This place… you look unsettled."

I forced a chuckle. "Yeah. Maybe that's it."

But I didn't believe myself either.

As we stepped back into the corridor, I heard it again. The faintest sound. A whisper? A sigh? A breath?

It was close.

I turned quickly, my eyes darting through the study window.

Nothing.

Miguel raised an eyebrow. "Something wrong?"

I forced a smile. "No," I lied. "Just thought I heard something."

Miguel chuckled. "The finca is old. It makes noises."

I nodded, but as we continued walking, my skin prickled with unease. Because the sound I had heard wasn't the creak of an old house. It wasn't the groan of wood shifting. It was something more deliberate. Like fabric brushing lightly against a wall.

I kept my eyes forward and followed Miguel to his car.

"It's completely secure," he said as he opened the door. "All new locks installed last month."

"Thanks," I replied, just wanting him gone.

Miguel waved his hand vaguely out to the horizon. "You've got peace and quiet out here. Nearest house is a kilometre away."

I nodded, but something made me glance over my shoulder—at the bend in the track where it led farther down the hillside.

I couldn't see anything through the olive branches, but I stared for a second too long before turning back.

"And you walk into town from here, I presume?" I asked, being polite.

Miguel smiled, but there was something off about it, like he was reciting instructions he didn't trust himself. "Yes. Follow the track uphill about ten minutes; you'll pass an old ruin. There's a path on the right. It's a shortcut through to Carmen's bar. Town's just past that."

His answers were clipped, suggesting he'd already mentally checked out.

Still, his directions were accurate. After he left, I went back inside, and we argued again—not about anything important, just one of those stupid, spiralling things that escalates before either of you knows why. Afterward, I asked if she fancied a drink. She didn't. That suited me just fine.

Where the hell was she?

An hour had passed since I returned from the bar, my panic rising by the minute, by the second. At least that bloody car alarm had ceased, the owner finally realising how damn annoying it was.

I'd looked everywhere despite our own car being missing. She was gone. But more importantly, of her own free will, or taken?

I played over the events since early that morning. The argument before we left our apartment in Madrid. The deafening silence of the journey into the mountains. Arriving at the bar. Leaving it to me to meet the owner of the finca.

The owner! I should call Miguel, see if he'd spotted her after I left. Maybe she called him to ask about something. And then what?

Shit.

But I couldn't call him. I didn't know his surname or have his contact details. Only Laura knew, and now she was gone.

The distant hum of an engine stirred me from my spiralling thoughts. I was in the living room, nursing my third cup of black coffee. My head pounded, but I needed caffeine. I had to sober myself up, compose myself in case I needed to call somebody and explain my wife was missing. If I stank of alcohol, what would they think? Fearful somebody might accuse me of...

Don't go there, James.

Standing, I stepped to the open patio doors, straining my ears. The sound was faint, barely audible, but a vehicle was definitely getting closer. My heart jolted.

Our car. It had to be our car. With Laura driving.

I bolted outside, my feet crunching over the gravel as I ran to the edge of the driveway. The sultry evening air clung to me once more as I squinted into the distance. At least I was sobering up.

The sound grew louder, the engine climbing in pitch as it navigated a steep incline. Then, suddenly, headlights appeared, weaving in and out of view as the car wound its way down the tight bends of the hillside road. I held my breath, hope surging through me.

It was Laura. It had to be.

I stumbled forward, stopping at the edge of the driveway where the dirt track began. The gravel shifted under my weight as I stood there, my chest rising and falling in ragged breaths. The car grew closer, the engine groaning. I shielded my eyes with one hand.

The engine rumbled louder, closer, and finally, the car emerged from the shadows. But as it rolled to a stop, my stomach sank.

It wasn't our car.

The vehicle, a dark, battered SUV, idled in front of me. I stood there, deflated, my pulse hammering in my ears. It must be bad news. Somebody's found her, or the car at least.

The driver's door creaked open, and she stepped out.

5

___

HIM

CARMEN. The bar owner.

She was shorter than me, maybe five and a half feet. Her dark hair spilled over her shoulders, and her eyes, sharp and watchful, locked onto mine. She wore casual clothes: jeans that hugged her figure and a lightweight jacket thrown over the same white T-shirt she had worn earlier in the bar. I'd barely spoken to her then, just ordered my beer and returned to a table outside where I could drink and smoke in peace. As she approached, I couldn't help but notice the curve of her lips, the effortless confidence in her stride. She was beautiful, undeniably so.

"James," she said, her tone soft but laced with concern. "Are you okay?"

"Where is she?" I blurted, stepping closer, trying to peer inside the back of her vehicle. My voice cracked, the question tumbling out before I could stop it.

Carmen's brow furrowed into deep creases. "What? Where's who?"

"Laura. My wife. She's—she's gone. I thought..." My words faltered, and I pointed feebly at her SUV.

Carmen shook her head slowly. "I don't know what you're talking about," she said. "I saw you when you left the bar and noticed you'd had a few drinks. I wanted to make sure you got back okay. That footpath is precarious."

I gave a slight nod, as if her explanation made perfect sense. Maybe it did. But the fact she'd gone to that kind of effort—when the bar was still open—gnawed at me. I pushed the thought aside. I couldn't fret about Carmen right now. There were much bigger things to worry about.

I rubbed my temples, the weight of the growing panic pressing down on me. "You didn't see her? On the road? See our car?"

"No," she said firmly. "James, what's going on? You look really shaken."

"Please," I said, gesturing to the house. "Come inside. I'll explain."

Carmen hesitated for a moment, her dark brown eyes studying me carefully, before nodding.

She followed me into the kitchen, her gaze sweeping over the space. "You need water," she said, more a statement than a suggestion. She moved without waiting for a reply, opening cabinets until she found a glass. She filled it from the tap and handed it to me, her expression unreadable. "Drink," she instructed, her tone leaving no room for argument.

I obeyed, gulping it down in uneven swallows. The water was cold, and I felt it reach the pit of my stomach, but it did nothing to steady my nerves.

"She's gone," I said finally, putting the empty glass on the counter. "Laura. My wife. And so is our car. I don't... I don't understand why."

Carmen leant against the surface, crossing her arms. "Slow down, James. Start from the beginning," she said.

I hesitated, running a hand through my thick brown hair. As soon as I began, the story sounded ridiculous, even to my own ears. "We had an argument," I admitted. "It wasn't... it wasn't serious. But then I went to your bar. I needed some air, some space. When I came back, she was gone."

"Are you sure that's the only reason you came back to the bar?" she asked, a glint of mischief in her eyes.

"Yes," I snapped. "Of course it is." I stared at her, desperate for her to listen.

"Okay," Carmen conceded. "Gone how? Did she leave a note? A message?"

"No. Nothing. Just... gone."

Carmen's eyes narrowed slightly. "And your car? You said it's missing too?"

I nodded, my throat tightening. "Yes. But she wouldn't drive on these roads. She hates driving at the best of times."

Carmen studied me for a long moment, her gaze unwavering. "James," she said carefully. "Are you sure you didn't misunderstand something? Maybe she just needed some space, like you did."

"I'm not imagining it," I replied, my frustration spilling over. "She wouldn't just leave without saying something."

Carmen held up her hands, palms outward, her expression calm. "Have you called the police?" she asked.

"No," I admitted, my anxiety only multiplying. The police? So soon? "Do you think I should?"

Her reply came quickly. "No," she said, shaking her head. "Not yet."

I frowned, unsettled by her haste to suggest it, yet equally quick to dismiss the idea. Carmen must have noticed my hesitation because she softened her tone, adding, "It's still very soon. Laura's only been missing for, what, three hours or so? Maybe four?"

"Closer to three," I admitted, though the knot in my stomach didn't ease.

"Exactly," Carmen said, offering a faint smile. "She could've gone to get food from the supermarket or even driven down to the coast to unwind. That's where the closest large shops are."

"That doesn't make sense," I said, shaking my head. "She'd never drive on these roads. She hates driving."

Carmen tilted her head, as if considering my response, then countered gently, "If I had an argument with my partner and he went to the bar for the afternoon, I would want some time to myself too." She smiled. That same smile that would turn any man's head. And her words stung more than they should've, probably because they carried an element of truth. Laura could easily have been upset enough to leave, but something still didn't sit right. I shifted my weight, glancing at the window as though Laura might materialise outside.

"It kind of makes sense," I muttered reluctantly. "But... it's not like her. Maybe we should call the—"

Carmen cleared her throat, halting me mid-sentence. Her dark eyes studied me intently. "James," she said gently. "We're quite isolated up here in the mountains. The police don't patrol this area often; there's just no need. Their main presence is down on the coast, where the larger resorts are. They deal with the serious incidents. Up here, it's... quiet." She paused, as if considering her words. "Calling them now would probably just lead to a lot of unnecessary questions and stress for you. Let's wait a little longer. See if she comes back."

Her reasoning was plausible, and yet I couldn't shake the feeling there was more to it. Still, I nodded, forcing myself to accept her logic for now. "Thanks," I murmured. "I appreciate you checking on me."

Carmen smiled faintly, the tension between us dissipating

slightly. "Of course," she said. Then, as if sensing the awkward silence, she gestured to the room. "Nice place."

"It is," I replied. "This was meant to be a break from everything. A proper reset." I forced a short laugh. "But so much for that."

She didn't respond right away, just offered a small smile. I couldn't help noticing how comfortable she looked. Not in a way that suggested ownership, but how easy she found my company.

"How's the bar?" I asked eventually, unsure of what else to say. If she didn't know where Laura was, then I didn't want her to stay. It might only complicate things further, the local bar owner in my finca, only hours after my wife disappeared.

Her eyes flicked back to mine, her smile shifting, softening. "Busy," she said. "But manageable. I've always preferred it that way."

"Do you have any other staff?" I asked, realising I needed to shut up but unable to stop myself.

"Nobody permanent." Her voice had a note of pride. "A few people help out here and there, but mostly, it's me."

I nodded.

Carmen tilted her head slightly. "But it suits me," she added.

I glanced down and noticed her hand—no ring. Not that I'd expected one, but still.

"You're not seeing anyone?"

Her laugh was light, but she nevertheless paused before answering. "No. Some of us choose to stay single, you know."

I gave a half smile. "Still surprises me."

"Maybe it shouldn't," she said, her eyes holding mine. "Sometimes, it's just simpler."

Before I could think of anything else, she glanced at the clock behind me. "I should head back. Can't disappear too long. Eloisa will wonder where I am."

Having become temporarily lost in her presence, I suddenly remembered my predicament. "If you see Laura, please let me know." She nodded. "Thanks for checking up on me."

We exchanged numbers, and I walked her to the door. She lingered for a second, as if debating whether to say something else, then simply nodded and left. I stood on the gravel, watching until the dust from her tyres had settled, until there was nothing remaining but silence.

I returned indoors, aware of the emptiness once more.

Where the hell was my wife?

6

HER

Darkness.

Not just the kind that comes when you close your eyes. This was much deeper. Thicker. A darkness she'd never known before.

And the heat. God, the heat.

It clung to her like a second skin, thick and stifling. The air was stale, her flesh was damp, slick with sweat, her vest clinging to her back.

Her vest.

She frowned. That wasn't all she'd put on that morning.

Her hands roamed over herself, fingers brushing against her bare arms. She had worn a blouse. Linen. She'd chosen it deliberately—light, soft, easy to wear. She remembered buttoning it up, smoothing the fabric flat, thinking it was perfect for the journey. But now it was gone.

Her breath hitched.

She felt her legs. Denim. Shorts. Still there.

Shoes? Her toes curled inside. Converse. Her favourite pair. Still on her feet.

But the blouse.

Where was it?

Her fingers dug into her skin, as if trying to convince herself she was still clothed, still covered. But she knew. Whoever put her there had also taken her blouse.

Who? When? Why?

A sickening thought hit her. What else did they do?

She pressed her hands against her stomach, searching for anything else out of place. Her skin felt unmarked, but that didn't stop the icy wave crawling up her spine. Whoever had put her here… had touched her. Undressed her.

She shifted slightly, her head throbbing as she moved. A sharp pain flared at the back of her skull. Instinctively, she reached up, her fingers brushing against something sticky. Blood. Dried, crusted blood.

She swallowed hard, her throat raw. Her mouth was dry, her tongue sticking to the roof like Velcro, and her limbs ached as if she'd been lying still for an eternity. How long had she been here?

But more importantly. Where was here?

Slowly, she stretched out a hand, feeling nothing but empty air at first. Then—wood. Rough, uneven. Not cold like metal. The grain scraped against her fingertips. She moved her hand along it, testing, searching. It was solid. Sturdy.

Her other hand pressed down beneath her. Wood again.

She inhaled deeply, steadying herself as she moved, crawling forward inch by inch. Her palms skimmed the surface, splinters biting into her skin. The space was small but not cramped. She could move, but not freely. It reminded her of something—

A shipping container.

But not metal. No cool steel against her hands. Wooden

walls, wooden floors. Some kind of crate. A prison made of timber.

Her breath quickened.

She forced herself to crawl, feeling as she went, mapping the space in the dark. Her hands hit another wall sooner than she expected. A sharp turn. She followed it. Another. And another. Four walls, completely enclosed. No windows. No doors—

No way out.

Her heart pounded in her chest, a slow, heavy rhythm.

Think.

She squeezed her eyes shut, forcing herself to push past the pain in her skull, past the heat pressing down on her. She had to remember.

The last thing she remembered…

Packing.

The suitcase—she had packed it neatly, folded each item with careful precision, knowing exactly how much space she had to work with. Then she waited until he loaded it into the car.

Yes. That was it.

She frowned, gripping onto the memory.

It was fuzzy, shifting away from her the harder she tried to grasp it.

Then. James.

James hated how the patients became embroiled in their lives. He always said, "you bring your work home with you," that "she cared more about her subjects than she did for him." But how could she not? She had seen people broken, desperate. She had heard their stories.

And she had tried to help.

It was her duty to help.

She exhaled sharply, resting her forehead against the wooden wall.

James.

She could still hear his voice, raised and sharp. She had seen the anger in his eyes.

He could be so controlling. Possessive.

She forced herself to push the thought aside.

It doesn't matter about him. Not yet. I have to get out first.

She braced herself against the floor, the darkness pressing in like a living thing. Trapped. Alone.

But she wasn't going to stay there.

She had to find a way out.

7

———————

HIM

I SAT OUTSIDE on the tiled patio, the weight of everything pressing down on me. Darkness had fallen, and I felt more isolated than ever before. The silence was deafening, broken only by the faint hum of cicadas. It wasn't soothing; if anything; it irritated me, wanting them to shut the fuck up. On the table in front of me sat a half-empty bottle of cheap red wine. I clutched the glass in one hand, my other hovering near the overflowing ashtray brimming with stubbed-out cigarettes. As I exhaled, the smoke curled in the humid air, before vanishing into the night.

Earlier, I'd emptied the welcome basket that Miguel had left in the kitchen: bread and olives plus milk, cheese and some vacuum-sealed meats in the fridge. Just enough to get by for a day. I wondered if that was why Laura had really left— to find a supermarket. But as the time passed by, that notion became more and more ridiculous.

I checked my watch—9:13 pm. How long had it been now? Seven hours? Maybe more. Far too long for a simple errand, even if Carmen had been right about the closest large shops being down at the coast. My mind churned, running through every possible explanation, each one adding to my growing anxiety. Had she had an accident on the winding mountain roads? Those narrow curves were treacherous, even in daylight.

I picked up my phone and called her for what felt like the hundredth time. Her name—Laura—glowed on the screen as I held it to my ear. The ringing echoed in the suffocating quiet, dragging on until, predictably, it went to voicemail.

"Laura, it's me again," I said, my voice cracking under the weight of suppressed panic. "Can you just let me know you're okay? Please. I don't care if you're angry, just call me."

I hung up and stared at the screen, willing her to reply. Opening our text thread, I typed another message:

> Please, Laura. Just tell me you're safe.

The messages remained unread. Frustration clawed at my chest as I tossed the phone onto the table, running a hand through my hair. Something was definitely wrong.

The night deepened further, shadows stretching across the patio from the outside lighting. I poured another glass of wine, trying to drown the growing unease. But sitting there, stewing in my own thoughts, wasn't helping. I had to do something— anything.

Slipping my phone into my pocket, I stood, wobbling slightly as the alcohol hit me harder than I anticipated. I swore under my breath, steadying myself before heading along the gravel path in the direction of the bar.

The trek was rougher than I remembered from earlier. The uneven track seemed to shift beneath my feet, and I stumbled more than once, catching myself on a branch of a tree lining the way. My phone torch offered little help, but enough for me to complete the journey. By the time the warm, yellow glow of the bar came into view, sweat clung to my skin.

I pushed open the heavy wooden door, greeted by the familiar scent of cigarettes and stale beer. The place was nearly empty, apart from two locals perched on stools at the far end of the bar. Just as before, their eyes snapped to me as I entered, their expressions unreadable but uncomfortably intense.

Carmen appeared from the back of the bar, her gaze softening when she saw me. A faint smile tugged at her lips, but there was something else in her eyes—sympathy, maybe—that made my stomach twist.

"You're back," she said, her voice carrying an inevitability. "I thought you might be."

"I didn't know where else to go," I admitted. "Laura hasn't come home. She's not answering her phone. Not reading my messages."

Her brow furrowed slightly as she glanced at the two locals. They muttered something to her in Spanish. Carmen's expression hardened as she responded sharply, her words cutting through the air like a knife. Whatever she said worked —they downed their drinks, tossed a few euros on the counter, and shuffled out without another word.

As soon as the door clicked shut, Carmen secured it with a firm twist. Her gaze shifted back to me, steady and calm. "Come with me," she said, heading to the side door.

I hesitated but followed, my feet dragging as we stepped outside into the humid night air. She locked the door behind her and gestured towards her SUV.

"Get in," she said.

I slid into the passenger seat, the tension in my shoulders refusing to ease. Carmen started the motor, the headlights slicing through the darkness as we pulled onto the uneven road.

The drive was quiet at first, the hum of the engine and tyres on tarmac the only sounds. I stared out of the window, searching the mountainside, unsure what I was really looking for, scared by what I might see.

"She'll turn up," Carmen said suddenly, her voice calm and confident. "But you need to be there when she does."

I glanced at her. She had one hand on the wheel, the other resting casually on the gearstick. The soft glow of the dashboard illuminated her face.

"You think so?" I asked, my voice barely above a whisper.

"Yeah," she said, her tone leaving no room for doubt. "She's just got the hump with you."

Then, unexpectedly, she reached over and rested her hand on my thigh, just beneath the hem of my shorts. The warmth of her touch sent a jolt through me, my body stiffening in surprise.

I froze, unsure how to respond. Carmen didn't look at me, her focus fixed on the road, but a faint smile played on her lips, as though she could sense my discomfort.

Her hand lingered for a moment before she withdrew it, returning it to the wheel as if nothing had happened. I stared at her, my mind clouded by wine and confusion.

She turned off the main road onto the dirt track leading back to the house; the SUV bouncing over the uneven terrain.

When the finca came into view, she pulled into the driveway and killed the engine. She turned to me, her eyes meeting mine in the dim light.

"You'll see," she said softly. "Everything will be fine."

Her words hung in the air. How could she be so confident? She didn't even know Laura. My instincts screamed that something was off, but I didn't know what. I'd begun to think beyond an accident—surely somebody would have seen the car? Abduction seemed the most likely. Somebody must have snatched Laura, taken her against her will, and used our car as the getaway. Carmen's unwavering smile did little to placate my growing unease.

We climbed out of the SUV and walked up the gravel driveway together, the weight of her presence beside me almost suffocating. At the door, I hesitated, glancing back at her. She gestured for me to go inside before taking a long look over her shoulder.

PART II

DAY TWO

8

____

HIM

I DIDN'T SLEEP. The entire night, I either paced the bedroom or lay on top of the bed, staring at the fan on the ceiling. Every so often, I'd stop and strain my ears for any sound—gravel under Laura's tyres, her footsteps on the path outside. But there was nothing. Just the oppressive silence of the finca. It was overbearing, the night holding secrets you never even consider during daylight hours.

Carmen had taken the spare room. At least, that's where I thought she'd gone. I heard her moving around during the night, her footsteps light. Once or twice, I thought I heard whispering—the same whispers I thought I heard when Miguel showed us around—but every time I pressed my ear to the door, the house fell into an unnatural stillness.

I rose early and when the first light of dawn filtered through the kitchen windows, Carmen emerged, looking far more composed than I felt. Again, I couldn't help but admire her beauty and the way she moved with her usual confidence, gathering coffee, milk, and a chipped ceramic mug as if she owned the place. Watching her, I inevitably recalled her hand reaching out and resting on my leg during the drive back.

"You need this," she said, handing me the mug.

I took it without a word, the aroma of the coffee hitting me hard. I sipped it, the intense taste snapping me out of my state of exhaustion.

By mid-morning, after three cups of thick, bitter coffee that only seemed to make my nerves worse, Carmen insisted I shower. "It'll help," she said. I knew it wouldn't, but I complied. What else could I do? My mind was in shambles, the prospect of what had happened to Laura making me feel more and more nauseous by the hour.

The bathroom was humid and faintly fragrant. I turned on the Italian shower, its huge, rounded head releasing a powerful cascade of steaming water.

As it soaked into my skin, I scrubbed shampoo into my hair and lathered my body, trying to cleanse more than just the physical grime. I needed to wash away the oppressive guilt that clung to me. I should've supported Laura more after the suicide case, but she wouldn't let it go. As hard as it sounded, the death of Megan Walsh was supposed to be the beginning of a fresh start for us. I even planned to discuss her getting a new job, away from the cases she forever buried her head in, and away from Doctor Sarah Chen, her mentor, who she bloody doted upon. But now Laura was gone.

The thought hit me hard, my breath hitching in the hot mist. I stood still for a moment, letting the water run over me, eyes closed. And that's when I heard it—the unmistakable click of a door.

My eyes flew open, jand I rubbed a circle into the fogged glass of the shower, peering out into the steamy bathroom.

"Laura?" My voice sounded strange, muffled by the rush of water.

No response.

"Carmen?" I tried again, louder this time. "Is that you?"

Nothing.

I shut off the shower, the abrupt silence almost deafening, and stepped onto the mat. Water dripped from me as I reached for the towel, the cool air clinging to my wet skin. My hand froze as I noticed the door. It was slightly ajar.

I could've sworn I'd closed it.

I cursed myself for not locking it, a wave of unease washing over me. Drying myself quickly, I wrapped the towel around my waist and approached the door slowly, the wooden floorboards creaking beneath my feet.

"Hello?" I called, my voice shaky.

The hallway was empty and silent.

Quickly, I ducked into the bedroom and yanked open the drawer where I'd unpacked my underwear and socks. I grabbed a pair of boxers and dropped the towel, eager to get dressed and shake off the unsettling feeling creeping over me.

When I turned back to the doorway, I nearly jumped out of my skin. Carmen was standing there, watching me.

"Jesus!" I exclaimed, desperately trying to cover my modesty. "I didn't hear you."

She didn't apologise or even look embarrassed. Instead, she smiled—a slow, knowing smile—and her eyes flicked over me without shying away. "I have to get back to the bar," she said, her tone as casual as if she'd just walked into a café. "I'll close up around four and come back to check on you."

Before I could muster a response, or ask the burning question of whether she'd been the one who opened the bathroom door, she turned and walked away. Her footsteps faded into the distance, and then I heard the distant hum of her car starting.

I sat on the edge of the bed, barely noticing my goosebumps as the air conditioning whirred away. My mind raced with questions. Why had she been standing there? Had she come into the bathroom? And why hadn't she averted her eyes, the way most people do in awkward situations? Instead, it felt as if she'd been assessing me, not just physically but emotionally too.

After her car disappeared down the gravel driveway, I put on a fresh T-shirt and shorts before looking out of the window. The Andalusian sun appeared relentless, its heat already climbing into the low thirties. I wondered where Laura could be and how she could cope with the humidity. Hesitating, I stepped outside.

The contrast hit me immediately. The dry, searing heat was like a slap, momentarily sucking the breath from my lungs. My skin prickled under the unyielding sun, and the shimmering pool beckoned, but I ignored it. How the hell could I act as if nothing had happened?

The gardens stretched out before me, a maze of twisting pathways lined with lush, manicured plants that shouldn't have survived that kind of heat. Thin black irrigation tubes wound through the undergrowth, hidden but just visible enough to remind me that even the beauty was artificial.

"Laura!" I called, my voice breaking the stillness. The echo bounced off the mountains, fading into the valley below.

I retraced my steps from when we'd first arrived, walking along the narrow footpaths that twisted through flowering bushes and the occasional olive tree. The cicadas' incessant chirping rose and fell, filling the air with their relentless symphony.

"Laura!" I shouted again as I reached the perimeter of the property. The valley stretched out below, dotted with olive groves and a winding dirt road that led to a few whitewashed houses.

The cicadas stilled, just for a moment, as if they too, were waiting for a reply.

Nothing.

I turned back towards the finca, the climb uphill making my legs ache, my throat dry. Sweat clung to my back as I trudged through the gardens.

And then it happened.

A car alarm pierced the air, sharp and jarring. My heart leapt, the sound much closer than I'd expected. Was it the same alarm as I'd heard the day before?

I froze, every muscle tensed, my breath catching in my chest.

The only other property was the finca just along the track. Miguel had confirmed it was always empty, so why did it sound like the alarm was coming from there?

9

————

HIM

The sun pressed down hard, and my shirt clung unpleasantly as I trudged down the dirt path. I kicked up dust with each step, and I couldn't shake the feeling of being watched, as if somebody were mocking me for the situation I was in.

Just under twenty-four hours. That's how long it had been since Laura disappeared. How long should I wait before involving the police? Was it different in Spain?

But what kind of questions would they ask? How deep would they dig? We'd been arguing a lot at home. We even argued before we set off for Andalusia. Would the police want to know *all* the details?

As I approached the nearest neighbours, Miguel's vague comment echoed in my mind. *"There is another finca just down the hill, but nobody ever uses it."*

Miguel. Why hadn't I asked Carmen who he was and where he lived? Laura had his details, but it appeared to be a very close-knit community, so everybody should know everyone else. I made a mental note.

I'd brushed Miguel's comment off at the time. How would he know who used the property, and how often? As far as I knew, we would have no neighbours at our finca. That's what made it so appealing. But now, standing in front of the tall wooden gates, I felt unease settling over me. Dense bushes and high fences hid the house, an almost deliberate attempt to keep the world out. It wasn't just privacy; it was fortification.

Years of relentless sun had weathered the gates, cracking and bleaching the wood. A brass bell hung beside it, the only sign that it wasn't entirely abandoned. I pressed it, the sound ringing faintly from somewhere within. I waited, ears straining for any sign of movement. Nothing.

I pressed the bell again, longer this time, the chime echoing. Still nothing. My heartbeat quickened, the questions in my mind gaining weight. Was it empty, after all?

But then something else. Was Laura in there? Hurt, trapped, or worse? My fists clenched at the thought.

"Hello?" I called, my voice sounding far too loud against the silence of the valley. "Is anyone there?"

No response.

Then, from nowhere and with a soft creak, one of the gates swung inward, revealing three figures standing on the other side. A car sat in the corner of the yard, no doubt the reason for the alarm.

It took me a moment to process what I was seeing. I was certain nobody lived there, yet here they all were, as though they'd materialised together.

Nobody is supposed to live here.

The man stood slightly to the front, his frame lean and wiry, with a mop of blond hair tied loosely at the back of his neck. He wore a faded, open shirt that revealed a sun-darkened chest and a string of beads that looked homemade. His face was long and angular, with piercing blue eyes that locked onto mine.

The woman beside him could have been his mirror image in many ways—blonde, thin, and effortlessly tanned. She wore a loose sundress that flowed down to her ankles, patterned with swirls of orange and green. Bangles jangled softly on her wrists, her head tilted slightly to the side. Her hair, though similarly sun-bleached, was wild and unkempt, cascading over her shoulders like it hadn't seen a brush in weeks. Her gaze was softer than the man's but no less unsettling; it lingered on me just a little too long, as if she were studying something about me that only she could see.

And then there was the boy.

He couldn't have been more than ten, though his expression carried the weight of someone far older. He stood a little off-centre, one hand loosely clutching the woman's dress. His build was thin too, almost fragile, but his posture was unnervingly stiff. His hair was the same pale blond as the adults', falling in uneven strands across his forehead. But it was his eyes that caught me—they were an icy, almost translucent blue, and they stared at me with an intensity that sent a chill straight through me.

Unlike the adults, the boy didn't even attempt to be polite. His head tilted slightly as he studied me, a small smirk tugging at the corner of his mouth. It wasn't a child's grin—it was something far colder, far more knowing. I recalled the whispering in our garden and inadvertently took another step back. And then, without breaking eye contact, he said something under his breath.

The woman shushed him softly, her bracelets jingling as she placed a hand on his shoulder. The boy didn't flinch, didn't look at her—his gaze stayed locked on me, the smirk still in place.

"Can I help you?" the man asked, his voice even, though

his accent added a strange rhythm to the words. He sounded Dutch. I'd worked with a Dutch guy before, and the man before me sounded uncannily similar, an almost rhythmic intonation to his voice. And even though he only spoke a handful of words, his English was impeccable. It stirred memories of the guy I used to work with and how he flipped between the two languages with ease.

I cleared my throat, feeling suddenly ridiculous for being there. "Uh, yeah. Sorry to disturb you. I just… I'm looking for my wife."

They didn't react immediately. The woman exchanged a glance with the man, who raised his eyebrows a little, as though weighing my words. The boy remained silent, though his smirk widened ever so slightly, like he'd just heard a joke that I wasn't privy to.

10

———————

HIM

"YOUR WIFE?" the man repeated, his tone flat and detached, already letting me know he had no intention of helping.

Apart from the child giving me the creeps, the two adults were already pissing me off with their laid-back attitude. They stood there, side by side, like some absurd painting, the man with his sun-bleached curls tied back and the woman with her wild, unbrushed hair spilling over her shoulders. Both of them looked more annoyed than concerned, as if I was just some idiot disrupting their day.

"Yes, my wife," I said, my voice sharper than I intended. "We're staying at the finca just up the hill. The first one you come to. And shortly after we arrived—"

My voice faltered as I noticed them exchange a glance, their expressions unreadable but undeniably dismissive. The woman's lips twitched, as if attempting to suppress a smirk. The man scratched his chin and gave a slow shrug. I could sense my hands clenching in and out of fists.

"I wondered if you'd seen anything." I desperately tried to

48

keep my tone neutral. Besides trying to contact Miguel, they were most likely my best hope. "Or heard anything?"

The man shook his head, his hand already reaching for the gate. "No. I'm sorry. We didn't hear anything." He began to push the gate towards me, the motion slow yet final, as if the conversation were over.

"You haven't even asked when it happened," I snapped, stepping closer. "How can you be so sure you didn't hear or see anything if you don't even know when I'm talking about?"

The woman sighed, a sound so light and disinterested it made my skin prickle. "When did she disappear?" she asked, her English just as fluent as the man's, but with an air of impatience that grated. She didn't smile, didn't even attempt to soften her expression, and it baffled me. If a stranger knocked on my door, clearly desperate, I would at least try to show some empathy, even if I couldn't help.

"Yesterday," I said, my voice faltering again as I realised just how long it had been. "Soon after lunch. We'd driven from Madrid, you see, and I went to the local bar, and—"

"I said," the man interrupted, his voice low and firm. "We didn't see or hear anything. Now, if you don't mind."

He pushed the gate further closed, and for a moment, I thought he was going to slam it in my face.

"How long have you lived here?" I asked, placing a foot forward.

The couple exchanged a glance.

"Why do you ask?" the woman asked.

But words failed me. I couldn't say why I was so interested.

As the guy pushed the gate closer, the boy stepped forward. Still he clung to the woman's dress, as if the touch somehow gave him confidence. His pale, almost translucent eyes locked onto mine with an intensity that made my stomach lurch. His hair looked like it had been hacked at with dull scissors.

"Maybe she's in the pool," he blurted, his voice high-pitched and sing-song, like he was talking about a lost toy instead of a missing person.

"Stop it," the woman snapped, grabbing his arm. Her bracelets clinked together as she pulled him back, but the boy didn't flinch. His gaze stayed fixed on me, unblinking, his lips curling into a faint smile.

I took a step back, unsettled. "What did he mean by that?" I asked the adults, trying to keep my voice steady.

"He's just a child," the man said sharply, his friendly façade slipping for a moment. "He doesn't know what he's talking about."

But the boy kept smiling. "She screamed," he whispered, just loud enough for me to hear.

"What?" I demanded, my heart hammering.

"I said stop it!" the woman barked, yanking him away. She glared at me as if I were the one to blame for what he was saying. "I think it's best if you leave."

"Look," the man said, his tone softening as he pushed the gate farther still, leaving only a narrow gap between us. "I understand you're upset, but we really can't help you."

Then something behind the woman caught my eye. A clothesline stretched across the yard, swaying gently in the breeze. It was dotted with sun-bleached dresses, faded T-shirts, and worn-out shorts—clothes that had clearly been endlessly washed and rewashed.

But at the far end of the line, something stood out.

A blue blouse.

Unlike the rest of the clothes, it wasn't faded or worn. It looked new, stark against the muted colours around it. My breath caught in my throat as recognition washed over me. The blouse wasn't just similar to Laura's. It was hers, wasn't it? The one she wore on the morning we travelled.

"I—" I started, but the gate slammed shut in my face, the metallic clang echoing in the still air.

"Goodbye," the man said from the far side, his tone final.

I stood there, frozen, staring at the closed gate as the boy's words echoed in my head.

She screamed.

I banged on the wood again; the sound reverberating across the valley. "Hey!" I shouted, my voice strained. "What's that on your washing line? Open the bloody gate!"

Nothing. Not a sound.

I stood for another minute, my fist hovering in the air, knowing deep down that it was futile. They weren't going to answer. They were probably standing just out of sight, smirking to themselves, or worse, whispering about me. I tried to picture the washing line, the blue blouse wafting gently in the breeze.

It was Laura's. I was certain of it.

I didn't care what excuses they'd given, how disinterested they'd acted, or even how creepy the child had been. The blouse was all I cared about. The thought of it made my stomach churn. Was it just a coincidence? No. No, it couldn't be. My instincts screamed it wasn't.

But what could I do? I couldn't break down the gate, and banging on it like a lunatic wouldn't help. I turned away, my heart pounding, and started back in the direction of my finca.

The walk felt longer than on the way there, my legs heavy. The surrounding landscape blurred into the background as my mind raced. The blouse. Laura. That bloody kid. His hideous grin while his voice echoed in my head: *Maybe she's in the pool…*

By the time I reached the finca, I was boiling over. I slammed the door shut behind me and grabbed my phone, dialling Carmen's number before I could change my mind.

"Hi, James," she answered with a smile in her tone. "Has Laura turned up?"

"I need the police," I said, trying to keep my voice steady. "Now."

"Whoa, hang on," she said. "What on earth has happened?" There was apprehension in her voice.

"I'm telling you, I've found something," I snapped. "There are neighbours. The place is supposed to be empty, but there's a family there. They know something."

There was a pause, as if Carmen was weighing up my words. "Are you sure you want to involve the police so soon, James? It's still only twenty-four hours since—"

"Yes," I interrupted. "I've seen something. I need someone here."

"Okay. I'll call Detective Isabella Santos. She's a friend of mine," Carmen replied, her tone steady. "Based in Torrox. It's about thirty minutes from here. Down by the coast. She'll come and talk to you. She's good at what she does."

"You know a detective?" I asked, trying to process the idea.

Carmen replied. "It's a small community, James. Everyone knows everyone."

I wanted to press her on it, to ask why she hadn't mentioned it before. But the thought of involving someone official, someone who could actually help, pushed those doubts aside. "Fine," I said. "Please, make it quick."

11

HIM

It wasn't long before Detective Santos and Carmen arrived. I hadn't expected Carmen, but I guess it made sense. She knew where I was staying, and as she'd said, the detective was a friend of hers.

Santos was tall and slim, with sharp features and dark, piercing eyes. Her long black ponytail accentuated her no-nonsense demeanour. As soon as I gestured them to come inside, Santos followed Carmen, and the air in the room suddenly shifted. Her very existence somehow made every-thing feel more real, more dangerous. I felt an inexplicable urge to explain the whole situation before she'd even spoken.

Once the introductions were out of the way, we moved to the lounge. Asking me to sit, Santos remained standing, her towering presence only adding to my unease at what was happening. She took out a small notepad and licked the end of a pencil, soon poised over the next blank page. Carmen perched on the arm of the couch, resting her hand on my shoulder to give support. She quickly removed it when Santos cleared her throat to speak, leaving me to stare at the empty space she'd left behind.

"Okay, Mr Blackwood," Santos said, her voice clipped. "Let's start from the beginning. Tell me everything."

"Call me James, please," I said, my voice faltering under her sharp gaze. I glanced briefly at Carmen, who gave me a faint, reassuring smile. Then I launched into the story, recounting everything I'd already told Carmen.

"We had an argument," I admitted without looking up. "It was trivial. Stupid, really. That's why I didn't call anyone sooner. I thought she'd just come back. And Carmen said it was difficult to get the police here."

"I see," Santos said, her tone measured. "Resources here are limited up in the mountains, James. But Carmen was right to call me." She glanced at Carmen, who offered a half smile in return. "Now, if I'm going to help you, I need complete honesty. Now, continue."

I took a deep breath. "I went to the bar to cool off. When I came back, she was gone. And our car too."

"And you're sure the argument was trivial?" Santos asked, her tone sharp.

"Yes," I said firmly, my eyes narrowing at her opening line. "We argue sometimes, as all couple's do. But it wasn't anything serious." I could feel sweat prickle underneath my arms, and the palms of my hands were sticky.

Santos tilted her head slightly. "Nothing serious," she repeated, her voice probing. "No escalation? No... physical altercation?"

The question hit me like a slap. "What? No! Of course not," I said, my voice rising. "Are you kidding me?"

"Very," she replied, her expression unreadable.

Frustration bubbled up inside me. The conversation was heading exactly where I'd feared it might. Maybe the reason I'd agreed with Carmen not to involve the police too soon.

"We don't have a history of that," I retorted. "We argue, sure, but who doesn't?"

Santos tapped her pencil against her notebook, her gaze never leaving mine. "What was the argument about?"

"It was nothing," I said, exasperated. "She asked if it was too much trouble for me to help unpack the suitcases. I was already stressed, and I snapped. It escalated from there."

Her pencil stilled. "You seem under pressure. Is that fair to say?"

I hesitated. "Who isn't?" I replied defensively. "Work's been stressful. Budgets are tight. Layoffs are happening. It's been a lot."

"And Laura?" she asked. "What does she do?"

"She's a trauma specialist," I faltered, not wanting to discuss Laura's work. "She works with complex cases. It's draining work. Her mentor, Doctor Sarah Chen, thought this trip would help her unwind." I immediately cursed myself for bringing Doctor Chen into it. I didn't want to mention any names, involve anybody else. It was supposed to be a missing person case, and I just needed them to find Laura.

"And this Doctor Chen," Santos pressed, her tone unreadable. "Did she recommend this finca too?"

"Yes," I said. "Well, no. Laura knew it too. It's quiet, isolated—perfect for a break."

"Isolated," Santos echoed. "Indeed."

I continued, recounting our arrival in town and meeting the owner of the finca, Miguel.

"That man who you met in my bar isn't the owner of this finca," Carmen interjected suddenly.

I turned to her, confused. "What?"

"The owner is Enrique Gálvez," she said. "I've met him once or twice. He lives in Málaga. That man who met you wasn't Enrique."

The room seemed to tilt. "Why didn't you say anything

earlier?" I demanded, trying to stand. Carmen rested her hand on my shoulder once more, and as with the leg touching incident, I felt the electricity shoot through me, despite everything that was happening.

"I assumed he was new," Carmen said, her tone defensive.

Santos's gaze sharpened. "And his name?"

"Er," I floundered. "Miguel. I'm sorry, I didn't get his last name."

Santos and Carmen exchanged a glance I couldn't read.

"Do you have his details? A phone number, perhaps?"

I stood, this time Carmen allowing me, and the room suddenly felt much hotter than it should have done with the air-con on.

"No. Laura had his details. She booked the holiday, arranged it all."

Santos frowned, her pencil hovering over her notebook. "And I suppose you've tried contacting your wife?"

"Of course I bloody have," I snapped, my frustrations growing by the second. Everything felt out of my control.

"Okay, calm down," Santos said, before turning to Carmen. "We'll track down Enrique Gálvez. It will be easy using the property listing online. Meanwhile," she said, closing her notebook and looking me in the eye, "I believe your wife is fine. With the car missing, and no reported cases of any accidents, I'm assuming she's taken herself off to give herself some breathing space. It appears you've both been under a lot of stress recently."

I opened my mouth to respond, to demand she did more than just dismiss the entire thing as a domestic blip, but I stopped myself. She was most probably right, but I still needed Laura back.

"There's another thing," I added, desperate not to mention the nearby finca, yet unable to stop myself. "I believe the family down the hill are hiding something."

12

———

SANTOS

Detective Isabella Santos paused by her car, one hand resting lightly on the roof while the other hung loosely at her side. She turned back towards the finca, her eyes scanning the scene. The midday sun scorched the dry landscape, casting long shadows from the tall chimney on top of the property. The place seemed ordinary enough at first glance, yet something about it made her uneasy. She couldn't quite put her finger on it.

The husband—James Blackwood—had been jittery and defensive during their brief conversation. Tall, with thick, wavy brown hair cut close at the sides and a broad frame softening around the edges, he looked the kind of man who was once athletic, although now dulled by stress and routine. His blue eyes had flicked between her and the ground as he spoke, as if scanning for an escape route. He'd insisted his wife had vanished without a trace, but Santos had seen enough to suspect there was more to the story. People didn't just disappear in quiet places like this, not without some reason. She adjusted her sunglasses, looking beyond the finca to the jagged hills and sparse vegetation that stretched into the horizon. If Laura Blackwood had wandered off, she might have got lost. Or worse. The thought tugged at her, but she pushed it aside. And, she'd taken the car; it appeared more of a domestic dispute, nothing else.

It wasn't the first time Santos had been called out to investigate a missing person. After almost three years with the local police department in West Andalusia, she'd seen her share of these cases. Most of them resolved themselves within a day or two, the missing person either sulking at a friend's place or drowning their sorrows in a cheap hotel. Still, something about this case didn't sit right with her, and it wasn't just James Blackwood's hesitation when she asked about their relationship.

He'd faltered at her questions about their home life, his words sporadic, as if trying to avoid giving too much away. Santos could read people well—body language was her forte —and the slight twist of his face when he mentioned Laura's boss, a Doctor Sarah Chen, hadn't gone unnoticed. There was tension there, jealousy maybe. Men like James always thought they were harder to read than they actually were.

So, had Laura Blackwood really walked out on her husband? Or was there another explanation entirely?

She exhaled slowly. She'd been an outsider since the day she started, and cases such as this didn't make her job any easier. Replacing Antonio Vargas, the long-serving detective she'd succeeded, had been a challenge from the outset. Vargas was a local hero, with two decades of impeccable service and an easy rapport with the community. Santos, on the other hand, was a divorced woman in her mid-forties, born and raised in Cádiz, but with years spent living in England after graduating from university. That made her different. Too different, as far as her colleagues were concerned.

She'd tried to fit in, but it wasn't easy. The locals had whispered about her failures, particularly the unsolved disappearance of a young boy down on the coast during her first year. It had been a nightmare, one that still haunted her. No leads, no suspects, no closure for the family. And then the missing woman from these parts just over a year ago. Another investigation left unresolved. Now, every fresh case felt like a test she was destined to fail.

The shoplifters in Nerja, the major tourist town on the coast, weren't helping either; a gang of petty thieves who seemed hell-bent on making her life miserable. Dealing with them felt beneath her, but they kept slipping through the cracks, adding another layer of frustration to her already strained days.

And now this: another missing person.

Santos leant against the car and closed her eyes for a moment, letting the heat seep into her skin. She had little sympathy for men like James Blackwood. Guys who let their jealousy fester until it poisoned everything. She'd seen it too many times, and she'd lived it too. Her ex-husband had been a charmer, the kind of man who could talk his way out of anything—until he couldn't. His infidelity had shattered their marriage, leaving her with little patience for men who made their partners miserable.

She sighed. She needed to look into the finca down the hill —who owned it, who stayed there, and whether there was any history of trouble associated with the property. Then there was this Miguel guy, the supposed owner of the finca, but Carmen knew the actual owner, an Enrique Gálvez. Santos underlined his name in her notebook and knew she must track him down first. She also needed to dig into James and Laura's lives. He said they currently lived in Madrid. If Laura had walked out on her husband, there might be a trail leading up to it—bank records, messages, anything.

And what about this Doctor Sarah Chen? Santos tapped her pen against the notepad, frowning. The way James had said her name, as if it left an unpleasant taste in his mouth… it was worth following up on.

Whether Laura Blackwood had left of her own accord or something darker was at play, it was her responsibility to find out. She pushed herself off the car and looked down the dirt track in the direction of the neighbour's finca.

"There's another thing," he'd added. *"I believe the family down the hill are hiding something. Something I spotted on the washing line…"*

"A fucking blue blouse," she said to herself with a wry smile.

13

SANTOS

S*ANTOS GRITTED* her teeth as she made her way down the dusty path in the direction of the neighbouring property. The midday sun was relentless, and she could already feel a thin sheen of sweat forming beneath her blouse. But that wasn't what irritated her. It was James Blackwood.

The way he'd practically ordered her to go there. The way he'd insisted she drop everything and march straight down to confront his neighbours, as if she were his personal errand girl.

Another chink in his armour.

Santos was already sceptical of him. He was too reactive, too forceful—as if trying to control the direction of her enquiries. Santos wasn't sure what unsettled her more—that Laura might have left voluntarily, or that James might know exactly where she was.

She cast a glance behind her. Sure enough, James was following her, trailing a few paces back with his hands clenched into fists at his sides. Why *was* he so bothered about her visit to the neighbours?

"Stay where you are," she called over her shoulder.

He stopped, glaring at her like a petulant child. "You need to ask them—"

"I'll ask what I want," she snapped. "You called me here. You wanted me to check out the neighbours. That's what I'm doing. Alone."

James muttered something under his breath but stayed put.

Santos turned back towards the finca, rolling her shoulders to shake off the tension.

The wooden gates loomed ahead, tall and sun-bleached, their heavy iron hinges rusted with age. She took a breath, knocked firmly, and stepped back.

There was a moment of stillness. Then, a scrape of wood on stone as the gates creaked open.

Three figures stood before her, framed in the archway like something out of a staged portrait.

A man, tall and wiry, with shoulder-length blond hair tied back in a loose knot. He was shirtless, strands of beads around his neck, his skin golden from the sun; a woman, equally tanned, her wild blonde curls streaked with silver, dressed in a loose sundress. Santos could see she wore nothing underneath, as if she'd thrown the dress on just for her benefit. And between them, a boy of about ten, pale and thin, his almost white-blond hair hanging unevenly over his forehead. There was something about him that drew Santos, and she had to force herself to detach her eyes from his eerie stare.

"Good afternoon," the man said, his voice smooth, his Dutch accent subtle but noticeable. "Can we help you?"

Santos kept her posture relaxed, but authoritative. "Detective Isabella Santos. I'm investigating the disappearance of a woman staying at the finca up the hill. I believe her husband spoke to you earlier?"

The woman pressed a hand to her chest. "Yes, of course. The poor man. He seemed very upset."

That's one way of putting it, Santos thought.

"He was angry," the man added with a small, apologetic shrug. "Shouting. Accusing us of things. We wanted to help, truly, but he wasn't very… approachable."

Santos didn't miss the pointed dig, and unfortunately, it only fed into the picture James was painting for himself.

"I understand," she said neutrally. "He's distraught, understandably. But I wanted to follow up myself."

The man nodded solemnly. "We are Maarten and Elise van der Veen. And this is our son, Willem."

"Nice to meet you, Detective," Willem said suddenly, his voice high-pitched and strangely formal. He gave a small, deliberate smile, and something about it made Santos' skin prickle. She noticed his mother tap his arm.

Santos forced herself to focus. "When the husband came earlier, you mentioned not seeing or hearing anything unusual. I wanted to ask again—are you sure?"

Elise shook her head regretfully. "We've been here for a month this time, just us. We come whenever we can, which isn't often. We don't have visitors. We keep ourselves to ourselves while on vacation."

Santos studied their faces. They looked concerned, but was it genuine? They certainly weren't what she was expecting, following James' insistence that she called straight away. The van der Veen family were sympathetic without actually offering anything useful.

She let the silence stretch, watching them. Eventually, Maarten sighed. "Would you like to take a look around?"

Santos raised an eyebrow. "You wouldn't mind?"

"Not at all." Elise stepped aside, gesturing into the property. "We have nothing to hide."

Santos proceeded through the gates, taking in the hippie-type paradise before her.

A wide-open courtyard, partly shaded by old wooden beams, was littered with mismatched furniture: sun-bleached cushions on rickety chairs, a large hammock swaying lazily in the breeze. Incense burned from a terracotta dish on a low table, the scent earthy and thick.

To the left was a small outdoor kitchen, complete with a stone oven and baskets of dried herbs hanging from hooks. A battered radio sat on the counter, playing soft, hazy jazz.

Beyond that, Santos noticed a makeshift greenhouse—nothing fancy, just some warped timber and patchy plastic sheeting held down with bricks. She glanced back at Maarten and Elise, who made no move to stop her.

The heat hit her like a wall. Inside, the space was cluttered: empty seed trays, cracked pots, a watering can tipped on its side. A few tomato vines and wilted basil clung to life in the back corner. Nothing out of the ordinary.

But near the entrance, tucked between a couple of crates, she spotted the remains of a joint—just a burnt-out end, flattened and forgotten. Another one sat in an ashtray perched on an old, upturned crate.

She raised an eyebrow, then let out a dry little snort. So that's what they liked to wind down with. Nothing heavy. Nothing worth reporting.

She moved on, stepping towards a covered patio area where a large wicker laundry basket sat in the shade.

She stopped.

Santos crouched down and flipped open the lid. Inside, a heap of freshly washed clothes—dresses, shirts, children's shorts.

Her pulse quickened. She pushed aside the top layer, fingers sifting through the damp fabric.

And then—nothing.

No blue blouse. No sign of anything out of place.

Santos let out a slow breath.

She could almost feel James up the hill, pacing, waiting, expecting them to come out handcuffed.

She straightened and turned back to the family. "Thank you," she said coolly. "I appreciate your cooperation."

Elise smiled, that same unreadable expression. "Of course."

As Santos stepped towards the exit, Willem spoke up again.

"I hope you find her," he said sweetly. "It must be so sad when someone disappears."

Santos met his gaze, holding it just a little too long.

"Yes," she said quietly. "It is."

14

HIM

"She doesn't believe me, does she?" I said, watching Santos disappear up the hill. "She thinks I had something to do with it."

Carmen didn't answer right away. She stood beside me, arms folded, eyes also fixed on the detective's retreating car.

We were by the pool at my request—I needed air. Inside the finca, I felt stifled, trapped, as if the walls were closing in. Santos had found nothing. The washing was gone, the blue blouse nowhere to be seen, and then she had the audacity to tell me Maarten and Elise were "a nice family" who just wanted to be left alone. Still, in retrospect, not finding anything could be determined as a blessing.

I clenched my jaw, shaking my head. "She thinks I'm bloody guilty of making my own wife disappear."

Carmen exhaled through her nose, tilting her head. "She's under a lot of pressure, that's all." But the words sounded forced, defensive of her friend.

"Pressure?" I laughed bitterly. "What pressure? She's not the one whose wife is missing."

Carmen turned to me then, forehead creased. "Are you absolutely sure Laura didn't give you Miguel's number?"

"Yes." My reply was sharp. "If I had it, don't you think I would have called him by now?"

She studied me for a moment. "You don't think they arranged something?"

I frowned. "Who? Laura and Miguel? They'd never even met before we got here."

Carmen's lips pressed together. She hesitated, then shook her head, as if she didn't even believe her own thoughts. "I doubt it. But maybe… maybe she needed space. Maybe Miguel suggested somewhere she could go."

Something about the way she said it made me uneasy. I wasn't sure if she was testing me or trying to convince herself. But then, before I could respond, she reached for my hand. Her fingers curled around mine, warm and deliberate. "Come on," she said, giving me a gentle tug.

I peered down at our hands. I should have pulled away. But I didn't.

It wasn't just the physical contact, it was something about her presence, the way she moved, the way she looked at me. Every time she touched me, it was as if she held me in a trance.

I let her lead me to the car.

She slid into the driver's seat and turned the key. As the engine hummed to life, her tone was light, casual. "Get in," she called out. "We need to get you a hire car, so you're not completely cut off down here."

I barely responded. I just climbed in beside her, and stared out of the window, my unease curling tighter in my stomach.

. . .

An hour later, I pushed my empty plate aside.

Carmen had insisted on making me lunch—an omelette and salad, quick, efficient. Now she moved around the bar, completely at ease in every space she occupied.

Outside, my hired estate car sat parked in the dusty lot. I hadn't even negotiated the price. Carmen had done that for me.

"Special rate," she'd said with a wink.

Of course she knew the owner. Carmen knew everyone. Everyone knew everyone. A town where time forgot.

She poured me another drink, listing off directions to the supermarket in town, then the hypermarket by the coast.

"The coastal one's bigger, but you'll have to drive the bends," she said, watching me. "Better off sticking to town in your state."

I nodded, only half listening. How much food should I even buy? Enough for a day? A week? Should I shop for two, just in case Laura came back?

I muttered a thanks.

Then, before I could react, Carmen leant in and kissed me on both cheeks.

Slow. Deliberate.

A couple of locals at the bar watched, one muttering something in Spanish, before they both laughed. They didn't bother hiding that it was about me. I looked at Carmen, but she only smiled. I gave myself a moment to reflect on her generosity, the way she checked on me so quickly after Laura vanished. The way she touched me without hesitation.

And then I remembered it.

The bathroom door.

The way it had been ajar.

The way she had watched me as I dressed.

My skin prickled.

What did she want from me? But more worryingly, why wasn't I doing anything to stop it?

Despite Carmen's instructions, the town car park was exactly where I knew it would be. Just one sharp turn after leaving the bar, and the road twisted into the centre before opening into the main square. It was a small place, nigh on impossible to get lost, even if you didn't know it. I noticed a couple of estate agents, and two small bars that doubled as restaurants.

Carmen said parking was free except on market days. Apparently, on a Wednesday and Saturday, the place was chaos. It was hard to imagine, seeing it now. The town was almost deserted.

The compact supermarket sat directly across from the square and I grabbed a red plastic basket with wheels, pulling it behind me through the open doors.

Inside, the air conditioning struggled. Heat leaked in from the street. I glanced at my watch. Two o'clock. Siesta time? The place felt lifeless.

I moved through the first aisle, grabbing fruit, vegetables. Then the second aisle—

And I stopped.

Was someone watching me?

Just for a second, before whoever it was darted out of view.

A sharp jolt ran through my spine.

I pulled my basket behind me, quickening my pace, reaching the end of the aisle—but there was no one there.

I doubled back. Still nothing.

The supermarket only had four short aisles, shelves stacked high, boxes half-unpacked. Picking up speed, I paced between them, checking every corner.

Nothing.

The cashier at the till stared at me, wide-eyed, unblinking. I forced a smile. She didn't return it.

Then I heard voices—outside.

I turned sharply, heading back to the fruit and veg section, looking through the open doorway. A man stood there, staring across the market square.

"Did you see someone?" I asked, hoping he understood me.

He turned. He must have been in his late sixties, maybe early seventies. And thankfully, British.

"Yeah," he said. "She bumped into me on the way out. Didn't even apologise."

She?

My pulse heightened.

I stood there, frozen. I couldn't make out a face, not even a clear outline, just the shape of someone walking away, soon swallowed by the narrow lane that led out of the square.

By the time I started forward, it was pointless. They were gone.

The old man muttered something behind me, but I barely heard it over the sound of my heart hammering in my chest.

I didn't know who it was.

But they'd seen me. Of that, I was sure.

15

HIM

UNSURE WHETHER TO RETURN TO the bar and tell Carmen about the fleeing shopper, or call Santos and explain, I ended up doing neither. I drove back to the finca reluctantly, realising I had nothing concrete to say. It could have been anyone—someone genuinely leaving the store after deciding against buying anything. The more I thought about it, the more irrational it seemed that the figure was someone I knew.

Who would I possibly recognise here, in Andalusia?

Laura was the only person, and if it were her, why would she run from me?

I chalked it up to a desperate imagination grasping for anything that might lead me to my missing wife.

Back at the finca, I unpacked the shopping in silence, changed into a clean T-shirt, and wandered the property aimlessly. I wasn't sure what I was looking for—signs of her, clues, something—but keeping busy helped keep the panic at bay. I found the washing machine tucked inside a small utility room, along with detergent and a bag of wooden pegs. I caught myself smiling at the discovery, proud of my basic domesticity—then immediately felt sick. Laura would've laughed at that. Or rolled her eyes.

The thought of her hit like a punch to the chest.

The outdoor kitchen was the property's crown jewel—a long wooden table flanked by eight chairs, a barbecue, food prep area, and glass-fronted cabinets stocked with crockery and utensils. The kind of space made for celebrations, lazy evenings, shared meals. It should have been perfect.

Instead, it felt hollow.

I grabbed a bottle of water from the outdoor fridge and sat at the table, staring at nothing. Trying to piece it all together. Trying to justify why Laura might leave of her own accord—if she had.

Yes, she'd been under pressure. The Megan Walsh case had consumed her. I'd told her, more than once, not to get so involved.

"She's just a patient, Laura," I snapped, days before Megan's suicide. "You shouldn't bring work home with you."

But Laura wouldn't back down. "It's more than that," she said. "She's struggling, and she's too vulnerable to be left alone."

I lost my temper. "That's because of all the fucking drugs she takes. She's probably spent everything on dealers."

As usual, Laura stormed out, muttering under her breath.

Then Megan died. And everything changed.

Doctor Sarah Chen had practically ordered Laura to take a break, even reminded her about the finca. All she wanted was our travel dates, so she could arrange cover at the practice.

So Laura booked it. At the time, it felt the right thing to do. A fresh start. Space to reset.

God knows I needed the break too—not that Laura ever asked about my pressure.

. . .

After throwing together a stir-fry with the veg I'd bought earlier, I opened a bottle of wine and settled outside in the same spot as the night before. From there, I could see the winding track that curled down the hillside to the finca. I kept my eyes fixed on it, watching for headlights—any sign she might be coming back.

But after more than thirty-six hours, the hope of Laura's return was thinning like smoke. I clung to it, but it was slipping through my fingers.

I smoked my last cigarette and immediately cursed myself for not buying more. Holding the wine bottle up to the moonlight, I saw it was almost empty too. I knew I'd had too much, and although the chances of being stopped up there were practically non-existent, the last thing I needed was trouble with the police. Santos already didn't trust me. One more strike and I'd resemble exactly what she suspected—a husband falling apart, hiding something.

I stubbed the cigarette into the overflowing ashtray and stood up to get another bottle from the kitchen. If sleep wasn't coming naturally, I'd drink until it did.

Then I heard it.

A sharp rustle. Movement. Somewhere down past the pool, near the edge of the garden.

"Who's there?" I called out, wincing as I detected the slur in my voice.

I held still. Listened hard. The cicadas droned on, and a breeze whispered through the olive trees, brushing the dry leaves against one another. But underneath it all, I knew I'd heard something—someone.

My heart began to race, a cold bloom of fear spreading in my chest. For the first time since arriving, I felt the true weight of the isolation. The finca was beautiful, yes, but so remote it may as well have been on another planet. The nearest lights shimmered on the far side of the valley—distant, unreachable. I thought about the houses along the track back to the bar, but what would I do? Bang on someone's door and beg to be let in?

Carmen. I could call her. Ask her to come.

But what would I say?

Hi, I heard something rustling in the bushes and now I'm scared. Can you tuck me in?

The thought made me laugh, a short, bitter sound. It could've been anything. A fox. A rabbit. A stray cat. Even a snake—they had those in the mountains, I was sure. And I'd been drinking. Too much. Again.

I turned back towards the finca, shaking my head at my own paranoia. Reaching for the door, I pushed it open.

And froze.

A sound drifted out of the darkness. Faint. Unnatural. A voice—high, soft, and singing.

It wasn't coming from the garden where I'd heard the rustle, but from farther down the hillside.

It was a child's voice.

Singing.

The melody was broken, as though whoever it was kept forgetting the words, stopping to correct themselves, then starting again. A lullaby, maybe. Or something from school. But I didn't recognise the tune, and there was something off about it. The way the notes hung in the air, slightly off-key, just a breath too slow.

I stood there, one hand still on the doorframe, the other gripping the neck of the empty wine bottle. The sound moved through the night like fog, curling around me, seeping into my skin.

And then, as though they knew they had my full attention,

the voice slowed. The final notes stretched out, eerie and thin, until they faded into silence.

No footsteps. No rustle. Just silence.

I didn't move. Didn't breathe.

And for the first time since Laura vanished, I truly felt I wasn't alone.

16

———————

HIM

SOMEHOW, the silence was worse than the singing.

I stood there, hand still gripping the doorframe, heart pounding in my chest. The finca was too quiet now, the stillness pressing in from all sides. The cicadas had resumed their mechanical hum, and the olive trees swayed gently in the night breeze. But it was all just background noise, meaningless against the echo of that voice still lingering in my ears.

I wasn't drunk enough to be imagining it.

It was that kid.

That little bastard from the Dutch finca. Why was anybody staying at *that* finca?

It had to be him.

He was playing games with me, taunting me, making a fool of me. A fresh spike of anger flared in my chest as I put the empty bottle on the table and turned in the direction of the hill that sloped down to their property.

Did they think they could just mess with me? But more

important, did they know something? Had they found something, and now they were messing with me?

Storming down the uneven hillside, I moved too quickly, my shoes slipping on dry grass and loose dirt. My breathing came sharp and fast, anger fuelling my every movement. Finally, I made out the wooden gates at the bottom, blending into the darkness beyond.

By the time I reached them, my knuckles were already white from clenching my fists. I slammed my palm against the heavy wood with a force that sent pain jolting up my arm.

"Open up!" I shouted, my voice echoing into the dark.

Nothing.

I banged again, harder this time, the impact reverberating through the night.

"I know you're in there! Where's your child?"

Silence.

A slow, creeping unease unfurled in my stomach, but I ignored it. I rattled the gate once more, frustration clawing at my insides. They had to be inside. It was almost nine o'clock. They hadn't seemed the socialising type, but still, there was no movement, no sign of life.

Were they deliberately ignoring me?

Or… had they heard the singing too?

That thought made something cold slither through me.

I stepped back, scanning the property, but the high wooden fence blocked everything from view. I needed to see inside.

An old olive tree stood nearby, its twisted trunk thick and gnarled. I knew if I climbed high enough, I'd be able to glimpse over the fence.

Fuelled by frustration, I grabbed the rough bark and pulled myself up, the dry wood scraping my hands. My foot slipped on loose bark, but I clung on, muscles straining as I climbed higher, past the lowest boughs. A thorn snagged my arm, sharp enough to make me hiss in pain, but I barely noticed.

When I reached the highest point I could safely manage, I looked down into the finca's courtyard. But everything was dark. No porch light. No glow from the windows. It was as if the entire house had been abandoned, just as I imagined before we even arrived.

I frowned, my breath shallow. Had they even been here at all?

Then I saw it.

A shadow.

A tall, thin silhouette in the upstairs window.

I froze, my grip tightening on the branch. It was motionless, almost blending into the darkness of the room behind it. But it was there.

Watching.

My pulse thundered in my ears as I stared. Was it a trick of the light? A coat rack? A curtain swaying in the breeze?

No.

Because it moved.

A slow, deliberate tilt of the head.

A prickling sensation crawled up my spine, the kind of instinctive terror that precedes a nightmare.

Then—a sound behind me.

A sharp rustling.

Close.

Too close.

I twisted around so fast I lost my footing, my balance slipping as the branch beneath me cracked. My stomach lurched as I tumbled down the embankment, landing hard, twigs and gravel digging into my palms.

I gasped, hands shaking as I scrambled to my feet. My pulse roared in my ears, but I didn't stop to look back. I didn't want to. Instead, I ran.

Scrambling back up the hillside, my legs burned, my breath came in ragged gasps, but I didn't slow down. The darkness behind me felt thick and alive, something just out of reach, something unseen but present.

By the time I stumbled into my finca's courtyard, sweat clung to my skin and a new kind of nausea twisted in my gut. I grabbed the table, steadying myself, trying to slow my breathing. The night pressed in around me, the distant hum of the valley stretching out into nothingness. That was when I saw it.

My phone.

Sitting on the table.

A fresh wave of unease gripped my chest as I reached for it. My fingers trembled against the screen.

Three missed calls.

Withheld number.

A lump formed in my throat as I stared at the glowing phone. My breathing turned shallow. I swallowed, pressing my thumb against the screen, but my fingers were too slick with sweat and a familiar nausea curled in my stomach.

No.

Not now.

I squeezed my eyes shut, gripping the edge of the table, trying to ground myself. But the dizziness was coming fast; a wave rising from the depths.

My knees buckled. I tried to steady myself, to breathe, but the bitter taste of bile coated my throat.

No, no, no—

The world tilted, the finca blurred, the night stretched and swallowed me whole.

And then—

Nothing.

17

HIM

I WOKE to a crushing weight behind my eyes, the familiar dull ache of dehydration pressing against my skull. My limbs were stiff, my mouth dry, my stomach queasy. The air in the finca felt thick and stale.

I blinked up at the ceiling. The wooden beams above me blurred in and out of focus. The couch.

I was on the couch.

How did I get there?

I tried to sit up, but a sharp sting ran through my hands. I winced, lifting them to find angry red scrapes across my palms.

The hill. The finca.

The kid in the window.

The singing.

It came back in pieces, broken fragments stitched together by flashes of sensation. Banging on the gate, climbing the embankment, seeing someone in the upstairs window. And then… a noise. Behind me.

I squeezed my eyes shut as a sharp pulse of pain flared in my skull. Something had happened after that. But the memory felt just out of reach, buried beneath the haze of exhaustion.

Then I heard voices. Low murmurs from the kitchen. I turned my head towards the sound, grimacing as a fresh wave of nausea rolled through me. Footsteps approached, soft but deliberate, and then Carmen and Santos appeared in the doorway. Carmen smiled. Santos didn't. Instead, she studied me. What was she looking for?

Carmen stepped forward, a glass of water in her hand. She knelt beside me, her free hand finding the small of my back. Her touch was slow, calculated.

"Here," she murmured, gently lifting me as she pressed the glass into my fingers. Her hand lingered, rubbing gentle circles against my back. Then, unbelievably, she lifted the bottom of my shirt and continued to rub in the same circular motion against my bare skin. It felt so wrong, yet I did nothing to stop her. The sensation was strangely soothing, almost hypnotic. I should have pulled away, but I didn't.

Before I could say anything, Santos cut through the moment.

"Carmen found you an hour ago," she said, her tone clipped. "She called you a few times, but you didn't answer. So she drove down here. You were lying outside on the ground next to the table."

I frowned, my sluggish brain struggling to process. "Outside?"

"You don't remember?"

I took a slow sip of water, wincing as the coolness hit my dry throat. "No," I admitted, my voice hoarse.

Santos folded her arms. "There was an empty bottle of wine."

I let out a sharp exhale, but even that movement sent a fresh pulse of pain through my head.

"You think I drank myself unconscious?" I muttered.

Santos didn't blink. "I think you're not helping yourself, James."

I wanted to argue, but my head ached too much. Instead, I forced another sip of water.

Santos moved to the opposite side of the room, one hand resting on her hip. "I've news about Enrique Gálvez. The finca owner."

I dragged a hand through my hair. "And?"

"It's not good news."

My breath hitched. What the hell could she mean?

She didn't waste time. "I've tracked him down. Carmen was right. He lives in Málaga. He said he just leaves changeovers to a local agency. He barely even remembers the place half the time. It's not the only property he owns."

"Okay…" I said, not seeing where she was going.

"So, I called the agency," she continued, her tone measured, authoritative. "And they told me they're short-staffed. Said some of their employees have started sub-contracting some of their work to 'trusted locals' to handle the changeovers when they're too busy. No background checks, no oversight. Just whoever can get the job done."

I stared at her, feeling a sinking weight in my stomach. I recalled the drive from Carmen's bar to the finca…

I suddenly considered who we were actually following. I hadn't asked for any ID. I hadn't seen the need, that it had seemed unnecessary. Because the truth was, once I'd thought about it, I wasn't entirely sure who we were following up into those hills.

"But surely whoever sub-contracted him must have his details?"

Santos shook her head slowly. "Unfortunately, we've hit a dead end there too. He could easily have advertised himself on social media, or some listing site. We haven't found anything, but that doesn't mean he used his real name if it was all underhanded." She paused. "How did you get in? Did Miguel have a set of keys?"

I thought back to when we arrived. "Yes. But I never asked for any ID."

Santos sighed heavily.

"So you're telling me he could have been anyone?" I asked, sitting up straighter. "That Miguel could be any nutter showing people to their holiday accommodation?"

"Exactly," she said, not even trying to soften the blow. "And you're sure only Laura had his phone number?"

I nodded sheepishly.

"So that means we're at a dead end. Carmen had never seen him before either, and she knows everyone."

I exhaled sharply, running a hand through my hair. "Unbelievable. So, that's it? We just… what? Wait around for something to happen?"

Santos raised an eyebrow. "We keep digging," she said. "But, yes, this complicates things."

I could feel my frustration bubbling up again, but I forced it down. I glanced at Carmen, who was still rubbing slow, absent circles against my back. If she realised she was doing it, she didn't show it. I tried to stand, and Carmen released her hand from underneath my shirt, but only to rest it on my shoulder to prevent me from getting up. A brief silence descended amongst us. Were the police really at a dead end? No other leads to go on?

And then Santos cleared her throat. "There's another thing, James. The locals have been talking."

Something in her voice made me sit up straighter. "About what?"

Santos exchanged a glance with Carmen, who kept her

hand on my shoulder. If anything, her fingers pressed slightly deeper into my skin.

"About Laura," she said.

A chill spread through me. "And?"

Santos hesitated, then said, "Nobody saw her."

I frowned. "What do you mean?"

She inhaled slowly, choosing her words carefully. "Yesterday, when you arrived, when you met Miguel, nobody saw Laura."

My breath caught.

"That's because she waited in the car," I said, forcing the words out.

Santos didn't flinch. "That's what you say."

I shook my head. "That's what happened."

She studied me for a long moment. "Only you say she was in the car. But the locals saw you. Alone."

A slow, crawling unease slithered through me.

"That doesn't mean anything," I snapped. "She didn't have to come into the bar. She just wanted to wait outside."

But even as I said it, my own certainty faltered.

Santos tilted her head. "Could have," she agreed. "But nobody saw the car, either."

I blinked at her, pulse thudding in my ears.

"That's ridiculous," I muttered. "We were there. She was there. The car was there. How else would we have got from Madrid without a fucking car?"

Santos held my gaze. "Are you sure?"

A sharp pulse of frustration shot through me. "Of course I'm sure!"

I swallowed, the dryness in my throat suddenly unbearable.

I thought back to arriving at the finca. To Laura beside me, staring out of the car window as I went inside to meet Miguel.

My head spun.

"What are you saying?"

Santos watched me carefully.

Carmen finally pulled her hand away from my shoulder, and for the first time since she'd entered the room, her touch was gone.

Santos' voice was quiet, but each word sent ice through my veins.

"I'm saying, James… are you sure Laura ever came to the finca at all?"

18

———————

SANTOS

THE NIGHT STRETCHED WIDE and empty around the finca, the air cooler now, but the weight in Santos' chest had nothing to do with the temperature.

She stepped outside, letting the wooden door swing shut behind her, muffling the inaudible murmur of voices from inside. She barely registered them. Her mind was already working through everything that had just unfolded.

Was this just a simple missing person case?

Santos took a deep breath, staring up at the sky. As usual, in the height of summer, it was a clear night, stars scattered like glitter on a black card. The valley below stretched into the distance, nothing but rolling hills and the occasional house, their lights offering an orange glow. She tried to imagine Laura Blackwood standing where she was now—if Laura had ever stood there at all.

James was inside. But for a moment, Santos pictured him out here instead, hunched over the same rail, trying to piece together a version of events that made sense. Trying to convince himself of something. Or maybe trying to forget.

When she'd brought up the locals not seeing Laura when they arrived the previous day—no one spotting the car—his reaction hadn't merely been confusion. It had been anger. Just a flash. That could be guilt, sure. But it could also be grief, or fear. A man whose wife had disappeared should be angry. That wasn't the problem.

It was what came after—the way his face changed. As if he was doing the math in his head and didn't enjoy the answer.

And Carmen finding him earlier... that stuck with her too.

She'd called Santos straight away, said she found James slumped at the outside table, passed out cold. One bottle of wine, she'd said but Santos doubted that was all. James didn't look like a man battling a hangover. He didn't have the usual signs—no clammy skin, no sickly hue, no avoidance of light or movement. Instead, he seemed fogged over. Blank in places.

Could he be a heavy drinker? Maybe. Or was it part of a pattern? Could he be blacking out without realising?

And if so... then what could he even recall about Laura's disappearance?

Santos reached her car and leant against the door, rubbing her temples. The notepad she carried everywhere dug into her side, and she pulled it free, flipping to the page she'd scrawled on earlier.

She glanced down at the note mentioning James' scratched hands. They weren't superficial, certainly not the kind you'd get from simply keeling over drunk at a table.

They were deeper. Angled. Abrasions, as if he'd slipped down an embankment, or climbed through rough terrain. Something steep.

Her gaze lifted again, following the slope down towards

the trees. In the daylight, you could make out the path to the Dutch family's finca below. At night, it was nearly invisible. Had James wandered in that direction, in a daze or worse?

If he'd gone down there… what had he seen?

Or what had he done?

He'd been adamant they knew something. The blue blouse. But Santos had found nothing untoward with the Dutch family. And she'd checked. They did own the property, and they used it very infrequently. It stood empty for months at a time.

She shivered. A sudden breeze blew through the valley, scattering dry dust into the air. The sound was soft but constant, akin to something brushing past her shoulder. She turned sharply, scanning the dark. But there was nothing. Just the night sky, silent and endless.

Still, she moved faster now, wrenching open the car door and climbing in. She locked it without thinking.

This wasn't a straightforward case. It wasn't even a clean one. It was a mess and she could feel it slipping out of her grasp if she let it linger. It was still less than forty-eight hours since Laura Blackwood disappeared, but it already felt more than a domestic dispute.

She dropped her head against the steering wheel for a moment, exhaling hard, then grabbed her notebook again.

One name stared up at her.

Doctor Sarah Chen.

Underlined.

Santos tapped her pen against it.

James had mentioned her with a sour twist, like saying the name left a bad taste in his mouth. Not just another doctor. Not just someone from his wife's world. There was history there. Resentment, maybe. Mistrust that had taken root long before Laura vanished.

And Santos had done her own digging.

On paper, Chen was solid. Reputable. No major complaints. A respected psychiatrist with a specialty in difficult, high-profile patients—the kind of professional who avoided publicity at all costs, for the sake of her clients. No scandals. No lawsuits.

Whichever way, Santos had to start somewhere.

Santos started the engine. Her headlights cut across the dark gravel, illuminating the edge of the track.

She would call Doctor Chen in the morning.

And she would be listening carefully, not just to what the doctor said…

But what she didn't.

PART III

DAY THREE

19

———————

HIM

MORNING CAME, sluggish and heavy, as though it too had barely slept. I lay still, eyes open, watching the faint light creep in through the gap between the shutters, casting thin, pale lines across the ceiling. I felt as if I hadn't slept at all.

Because how could I?

I couldn't stop thinking about Miguel. Who was he? Where was he?

And what that meant for me. But much more importantly, for Laura.

I pushed a hand down my face, scrubbing at the exhaustion weighing on me. I hadn't shaved since I'd arrived, stubble clinging to my chin. The moment Carmen had found me by the outside table and subsequently called Santos, I'd felt a shift. She already doubted me, but now she had reason to.

And I knew what that meant.

I'd seen the flicker of doubt in Santos' eyes when she questioned me. The careful way she watched my reaction, cataloguing every word, every change in my expression. Did she really think I had something to do with it? That I'd somehow taken matters into my own hands?

I would never hurt Laura. But I had a history of blacking out, and I knew how it looked.

I exhaled sharply and sat up, rubbing my temples. My head throbbed, my limbs heavy with exhaustion, but the thought of lying there any longer, letting my mind keep circling the same tracks, was unbearable.

Pushing the covers aside, I got up, moving stiffly to the kitchen. My throat felt dry, my body sluggish, but even as I moved on autopilot, other thoughts started creeping in.

Carmen.

She'd left minutes after Santos, but I could still feel the warmth of her hand on my back, the way she'd pressed her palm against my skin—soothing, slow.

The way she'd rubbed small, circular motions, just beneath my shirt.

I hadn't stopped her.

I should have, but… I didn't.

And the strangest part? It had felt good.

Even then, standing alone in the kitchen, I could recall the way my muscles had eased under her touch, how her fingers had traced patterns against my spine, how hypnotic it was.

What did she want from me? What did I want from her?

I shook the thought away and reached for the coffee, pouring a cup so strong the bitterness stung my tongue. It helped—just a little.

I needed to keep my head straight. Because otherwise, I was in trouble.

I swallowed hard, forcing the coffee down, then turned to the window. Outside, the world looked unchanged, but every-thing felt different.

Returning to the bedroom, I decided to make myself

useful and lifted Laura's suitcase onto the bed to unpack. Unsure what it would achieve, it still felt right.

Hanging her items in the wardrobe in some semblance of order, I paused when I noticed a diary or journal tucked away at the bottom of the case.

Retrieving it, I sat on the bed and flipped through the pages. None of it made much sense to me. Notes about work. Patients names. An array of dates and times, obviously all representing something to Laura yet meaning nothing to me.

Losing patience, I flicked to the back and on the last page was a list of phone numbers, some circled, some not. But right there, second from the top, was Doctor Sarah Chen's name, followed by what I presumed was her mobile number. With my finger tucked into the appropriate page, I hurried into the kitchen to retrieve my phone and tapped in Sarah's number. It only took two rings for her to pick up.

"Hello?" she said. "Doctor Chen."

"Hi, Sarah." My voice quivered and my hand trembled. "It's James here. James Blackwood, Laura's—"

"Husband," she interrupted. "Is everything okay with the finca?"

"Yeah, yeah, the finca is fine..." I trailed off, cursing myself for not rehearsing what I might say.

"What's wrong, James? Is it Laura? Is she okay?"

Does she know?

"Well, that's just it. She's disappeared. Has she tried to—"

"Disappeared? What do you mean, disappeared?"

Struggling to keep my temper in check, I resisted telling her to shut the fuck up and let me talk. I'd barely spoken to Sarah Chen in the past. She had been to our house a couple of times, me inadvertently returning home early and finding her and Laura deep in conversation over coffee. But apart from a 'hello' or a 'how are you?', I'd never needed to speak with her at length, yet I still remembered her clearly.

There was something about her that was hard to forget. She had an air of quiet authority, the kind that filled a room without needing to raise a voice. She was petite, with sleek black hair cut in a sharp bob that framed her heart-shaped face perfectly, as if every strand had been placed deliberately. Her skin was pale and smooth. Her eyes were dark, almond-shaped, and unflinchingly direct.

As soon as I heard her voice, I recalled that gaze on me. It wasn't confrontational, just... piercing, as though she were cataloguing me, deciding what to make of me, while I stood there, unsure if I should leave the room or sit down and join them.

There was a faint scar along her jawline, just visible when the light caught it. It didn't belong on someone so immaculate. I'd noticed it the second time she'd come over, distracting me for a moment before I remembered to return her polite smile. Whatever had caused it, she didn't seem the type to offer an explanation.

And then there were her hands. I remembered how they moved when she motioned to something Laura was saying. Long, slender fingers, nails painted a soft pink. I'd been struck by how delicate they looked—surgeon's hands, Laura had once called them—but there was something unnerving about the way she used them. She gestured sparingly, deliberately, as though every motion carried the same weight as her words.

I hadn't realised it at the time, but even those brief, forgettable encounters had left an impression. Sarah Chen wasn't someone you could easily ignore, even if you tried.

"Soon after we arrived. I went to the local bar, and when I returned, she had gone, along with our car. You haven't heard from her, have you?"

The line went silent for a split second. "No. I haven't heard a thing..."

"You don't seem convinced," I replied.

"Well," she continued, each word carrying the same weight. "I'm not that surprised, James."

I lifted the phone from my ear and stared at it for a few seconds, unable to comprehend what she'd just said. "What do you mean, you're not surprised?"

"Far from me to say it, but do you think she's taken herself off? She had mentioned how unhappy she was. Told me that your marriage was becoming an everyday struggle…" She paused. "I wouldn't be surprised if she's left you, James."

20

HER

THE STENCH WAS UNBEARABLE.

She had tried to block it out, to separate herself from the filth that was creeping into every part of her existence, but there was no avoiding it. The air inside the container was thick and humid, acrid with sweat, and something worse. She'd even taken to drinking her own urine and the smell clung to her skin, to her hair, seeping into her lungs with every breath.

She'd stopped trying to sit in one place. No position was comfortable. The floor had hardened beneath her like solid rock, the soles of her feet raw from her pacing, the constant shifting, curling into herself when the exhaustion became too much. But she hadn't slept properly. Because every time she closed her eyes, the darkness became something else.

Not just the absence of light, but a weight pressing down on her chest, creeping under her skin, twisting inside her bones.

She didn't know how long it had been now. Two days?

Three? Her body felt hollow, her throat scorched from thirst. She could feel herself weakening, her limbs heavier than they should be, every slight movement costing more energy than it should.

She swallowed, wincing. How much longer could she last?

A wave of dizziness rolled through her, and she pressed her forehead against the wooden wall, focusing on the rough texture beneath her skin. She couldn't let her mind slip.

She exhaled slowly, trying to think.

Doctor Sarah Chen.

She had been angry about the Megan Walsh case. She was her patient, after all.

So had Chen followed her to Andalusia?

That didn't seem possible. Or at least, it shouldn't have been. But what did Doctor Chen know?

Laura had been careful—so careful—but Chen was smart. Observant. Too perceptive for her own good.

Had she guessed?

Had she figured it out?

No.

No, she couldn't have.

Her chest tightened.

Megan Walsh.

Dead.

A suicide.

Laura had told Sarah she would attend the funeral. No need for both of them to go. *We're too busy, overwhelming case load.* It was a logical excuse. True, even.

Doctor Chen hadn't questioned it. She had simply nodded, gone back to work.

But was she really content? Did she know something?

Not suspicion exactly, but something colder. A quiet detachment.

She squeezed her eyes shut, forcing herself to stop. It

wasn't helping. She couldn't waste her energy thinking in circles, trying to untangle a web that didn't matter if she didn't get out of that place. She had to focus on the present. And the present was the container, the dark box, the suffocating, putrid tomb.

She clenched her jaw, blinking rapidly as another wave of nausea hit her. The air was thick, unmoving. She hadn't eaten, hadn't drunk anything in days, but the smell alone was enough to make her stomach churn.

I can't stay in here.

She had to find a way out.

She had searched the walls before, run her fingers along every seam, every crevice, every joint in the wooden panels, but it was solid. No gaps. No loose slats.

She shifted onto her knees, forcing herself to move, to try again. Even if it was useless. Even if her body screamed at her to stop.

Her fingers traced the lower edges of the wall, her breath coming faster, panic starting to press at the edges of her mind.

And then—

Something small.

Metal.

Cold.

Her heart lurched as her hand curled around it, a sharp spike of adrenaline cutting through the exhaustion.

It was no bigger than her thumb, but it was jagged—one edge uneven, snapped off from something larger.

A hinge? A bracket?

It didn't matter.

It was something.

Her pulse thudded in her ears as she turned it in her fingers, adjusting her grip.

She pressed it against the wooden wall.

Scraped.

The sound was faint. Almost nothing.

But it was something.

She clenched her teeth and scraped again, pressing harder this time, feeling the resistance of the wood beneath her fingers.

It was slow.

So, so slow.

But it was movement.

It was progress.

She had to keep going.

Because if she stopped, if she let herself believe for even a second that this was hopeless, she was as good as dead.

21

HIM

I shouldn't have called her.

As soon as I hung up, I regretted it.

Sarah Chen. Why had I done it?

To cover my tracks? To make it seem as if I was doing everything I could to find Laura? Or had it been something else? A desperate attempt to grasp onto anyone who might have answers, even if I despised them?

I let out a breath through gritted teeth, my jaw so tight it ached.

I'd never liked her.

I continued to hang Laura's clothes in the wardrobe as my mind mulled over what Chen could possibly know.

She had always overworked Laura, always needed her for one more case, one more urgent situation, one more addition to the impossible workload. And Laura had let her. Doted on her. Like Chen could do nothing wrong. Like she had to be obeyed by her constant demands.

And now she had the audacity to suggest Laura had left

me? I bit the inside of my cheek before stepping outside, needing the air. That's when I heard the laughing.

But it wasn't like a child's laughter—light and innocent. Instead, it was wrong. A broken chuckle that rose and fell unnaturally, stretched out, warped. As if it was mocking me; someone imitating how a child should sound but getting it slightly off.

A shiver prickled along my spine.

Then it stopped.

Cut off so abruptly that the silence was almost overbearing.

I turned my head slightly, just enough to glimpse a figure darting between the olive trees at the edge of my property. It was the boy from the Dutch finca, skipping along the dirt track in the direction of his house.

Goosebumps rose across my skin despite the heat.

She screamed...

And then I remembered the blouse. Had I really imagined it? Convinced myself it could have been Laura's?

It made no sense.

How on earth could they possibly have it?

But Santos had found nothing.

I forced myself to look away, shifting my focus to the dirt track beyond the trees. It stretched out in both directions, disappearing around the bends of the hills. I looked down towards the Dutch family's finca, hidden behind thick bushes and wooden fencing. I couldn't get in, but I knew I had to.

Exhaling sharply, I started walking, keeping my pace even, natural, as if I had no real purpose. Just a man taking in the Andalusian scenery.

I reached their gates without breaking stride, resisting the urge to turn my head towards the house.

No sound.

No movement.

Just the faint creak of wood shifting in the breeze. So where was the child? He'd only skipped past a few moments before. Laughing. At me.

Knowing it was futile to hang around outside their property, I kept walking, pushing forward for another ten minutes. The terrain grew steeper, the incline making my legs burn, and then I saw it—the quarry.

It stretched before me like a scar in the landscape, a vast, abandoned pit swallowed by time. The entire perimeter appeared fenced off, high wire barriers marked with faded warning signs. The metal had rusted in places, sections sagging, curling at the bottom, torn open in spots where the fence had long since given up.

I stepped closer, placing my fingers through the holes in the wire, gripping it lightly as my eyes swept the terrain below.

Rocks. Crumbling earth. And something else.

Halfway down, wedged into the slope between the carcasses of a couple of ruined buildings, stood a wooden structure. The others were barely structures anymore—charred beams, twisted metal, and walls eaten by time and weather. But the wooden unit looked in far better condition. Not quite a shed. More like a container.

A strange unease crept over me.

And then—

A noise behind.

I spun, my heart slamming against my ribs. Loose stones shifted as if disturbed by someone running. The boy?

I scanned the track behind me, but there was no one there. The wind stirred the trees, but otherwise, silence.

"Who's there?" I called, my voice shaky.

Nothing.

I lingered, my pulse hammering in my ears, then glanced back at the quarry one last time. The wooden container sat still, untouched, like time had forgotten it.

I turned and headed back up the hill, my pace quicker now, my feet moving instinctively towards the Dutch finca's gates. I waited outside, listening. Where was the child?

I leant slightly closer, straining my ears, but the house was silent. No voices. No movement.

Just emptiness.

I lingered, breathing in the dry air, but if someone was watching me, they gave no sign of it.

I forced myself to turn away, making my way back to my own finca.

But as soon as I realised I'd left the door unlocked, I instinctively felt something was wrong. I paused at the threshold, listening. Nothing. Then I stepped inside, alert now, each movement measured. The air felt different—disturbed.

I found myself in the bedroom, barely aware of how I'd got there. And that's when it hit me.

Something was off.

I frowned, scanning the room, my skin prickling, but there was nothing obvious. Everything was in its place. And yet, I knew something was different. Then my eyes landed on the wardrobe.

More specifically, the empty space on top. The place where I'd left Laura's suitcase. But now it was gone.

A sharp jolt ran through my body as I took a step forward, yanking the wardrobe doors open.

I stared inside, my heart pumping. There was nothing but empty hangers, mocking me. All of Laura's clothes were gone, the very ones I'd unpacked only an hour before. Everything.

A hollow, creeping dread curled in my stomach.

I stepped back, rubbing a hand over my jaw, my breath shallow.

Had I moved them?

No.

No, I would have remembered.

Wouldn't I?

I turned, scanning the room as if expecting to find the Dutch boy standing there, laughing at me.

But of course he wasn't there, so if it wasn't the child, then who else?

A worse thought struck me.

Had Laura come back? Taken her stuff? Had she slipped in while I was out, grabbed her things, and left again?

But why? She would have waited for me.

I swallowed hard. I needed to think. I needed to figure out what the hell was happening.

And most of all—

I needed to find Laura.

22

SANTOS

Santos adjusted her grip on the phone, rolling her shoulders back as she paced outside her office. The lunchtime air was thick and humid. She listened to the traffic as an endless row of cars made their way down to the beach for the afternoon.

She had spent the morning pulling at loose ends, trying to untangle the increasingly knotted mess that was Laura Blackwood's disappearance. A missing woman, an evasive husband.

And still, nothing added up. Which was exactly why she was there, phone pressed to her ear, waiting for them to pick up. Finally, the line clicked, flooded by a smooth, professional voice. "Doctor Sarah Chen speaking."

Santos stopped pacing.

"Doctor Chen. My name is Detective Gabriela Santos."

There was a pause—brief, but noticeable. Then, evenly measured: "Yes?"

"Where are you?"

"In the UK. Is that important?"

Santos didn't waste time. "It's about Laura Blackwood."

Another pause. This one was longer.

"Laura?" Chen's tone was neutral. Too neutral.

Santos narrowed her eyes.

"Yes, Laura. She's missing."

A beat.

Then, the faintest inhale before Chen replied.

"What? When?"

Santos felt it immediately. The delay. The calculation.

She didn't buy it. Chen already knew.

Santos let the silence stretch, listening carefully. When Chen didn't elaborate, she finally said, "She disappeared shortly after arriving in Andalusia with her husband. She hasn't been seen in three days."

Another measured pause. Then: "That's awful."

Santos wasn't convinced. Not concerning. Not horrifying. Just *awful*.

She kept her voice calm, steady. "When did you last speak to her?"

"Last week, perhaps?" Chen's response was too smooth. "We haven't been in regular contact lately."

Bullshit.

But Santos didn't react. Instead, she let the silence settle, waiting to see if Chen would fill it. She didn't. So Santos pressed on. "I assume you know her husband, James?"

"Barely. We've met a handful of times."

Barely. Handful. A deliberate way to distance herself from him?

Santos tapped her fingers against her thigh, shifting the weight on her feet. "What do you think could have happened to Laura, Doctor Chen?"

There was the slightest hesitation before Chen answered. "I wouldn't know."

Santos smirked faintly. There it was again. No concern, no genuine curiosity, just that cool, measured voice, the sort of tone people use when they'd rehearsed their answers a dozen times already.

Time to test the waters.

"Let's talk about why you suggested Laura and James take a break," she said, almost casually.

A pause. Just long enough to register.

"One of Laura's patients, if you can call them that, took her own life a few weeks ago. Laura took it badly."

"Okay," Santos replied, a little disappointed by what sounded a perfectly plausible reason. "What was the name of this patient?"

"Megan Walsh," Chen said.

"Megan Walsh?" Santos repeated. "And did you know her too?"

"Not really," Chen said. "Megan was Laura's case. I wasn't involved."

Santos tilted her head, pen tapping lightly against her notepad. "But surely you supervise all the cases in your clinic, don't you?"

A quiet moment passed.

"To an extent," Chen replied smoothly.

"To an extent?" Santos asked.

Chen didn't respond immediately. The silence drew out a little longer this time.

"I trust my staff," she said eventually. "Laura was more than capable."

Still not an answer. Not really.

Santos let that settle before continuing. "So this suicide case was Laura's last case before she came here? Is that right?"

A soft exhale over the line. "That's correct."

Santos nodded to herself, jotting something meaningless in her notes. "Right."

Then Chen cleared her throat, and Santos waited. "You do realise Megan Walsh took her own life, don't you, detective? That can be a pretty traumatic experience for all involved."

Santos didn't react immediately.

"Okay," she said softly. "And do you think that's relevant to Laura going missing?"

"No," Chen said after a moment. "Although grief can have all kinds of effects on people."

Santos stared at her notepad, blank beneath the scribbles, a slow tic building behind her eyes. It was true, no one really knows how death affects a person, except the one living through it.

There was a shift on the other end of the line.

Chen wasn't enjoying being questioned.

Her voice was lighter now, an attempt at pleasant dismissal. "Detective, I'd love to continue this conversation, but I have a patient waiting."

Santos knew what that meant. She was pulling away. A controlled retreat, a way to cut the call before she slipped up. And then—something changed.

A noise in the background.

It was faint, but instantly familiar. Santos frowned, her ears straining. She knew that sound. It was something she had heard all day, right outside her own office.

An ambulance siren, loud and shrill.

Santos' pulse kicked up a notch. She knew from living in England that ambulances didn't make the same sound, their sirens were quite distinctive. And that meant Chen was in Spain. Hadn't she just claimed she was in the UK? Santos lowered her voice. "Sorry, where did you say you are, Doctor Chen?"

A split second of silence.

Then, light, clipped: "Sorry. I have to go."

Santos pressed, "Doctor—"

But the line clicked dead. She lowered the phone slowly,

staring at the screen. The faint wail of the ambulance still rang in her ears, slowly fading. She scanned the street across the car park.

Santos gritted her teeth, a slow wave of certainty creeping over her.

Doctor Sarah Chen was hiding something.

And finally, Santos knew where to start looking.

23

HIM

I KNEW I should call Santos.

That was the logical thing to do, the responsible thing, the action of someone who had nothing to hide. Laura's suitcase was gone. All of her clothes too. That wasn't normal. That wasn't something that could be brushed off.

But as I stood in the bedroom, staring at the empty space where her clothes should have been, phone in hand, ready to dial, I hesitated.

And I didn't call.

Because part of me didn't trust what might come next.

I needed Santos to find Laura, but I wasn't sure I wanted her digging too deep. There were places I wasn't ready for her to look. Questions I wasn't ready to answer. Things that could be used to paint a version of me I wouldn't recognise, but that others might believe.

Especially her.

The day before, when she'd turned up after Carmen reached out, there'd been something off in the way she looked at me. Not quite accusatory, but not open, either. A narrowing of the eyes. A quiet cataloguing of details.

"You think I drank myself unconscious?"

"I think you're not helping yourself."

I couldn't win with her. She didn't see a grieving husband—she saw a suspect. And if she'd already spoken to Sarah Chen—if Chen had said what she'd said to me, that Laura might've left me of her own accord—then whatever fragile benefit of the doubt I'd been clinging to would've snapped in two.

Santos wasn't just looking for Laura.

She was watching me.

I exhaled slowly, flipping the phone over in my palm. If I told her about Laura's missing suitcase, would she even see it for what it was? Or would she tilt her head slightly, cross her arms, and say something like, *"So now all of her belongings are gone too? How convenient."*

I didn't trust her.

And right then, I needed to talk to someone I could trust.

Without thinking too hard about it, I scrolled to Carmen's name and called. She answered after two rings, her voice carrying that easy warmth she always seemed to have, the kind that made everything sound just slightly less terrible. "James."

I hesitated for a second before speaking. "Can you come over?"

A pause. Then, a slight tease in her tone. "What is it?"

I pinched the bridge of my nose, exhaling slowly. "I just don't want to be alone right now."

A beat of silence. Then, softer this time. "I'll get someone to cover the bar. I'll be over later, okay?"

I lowered the phone and stared at it for a moment, then at the empty wardrobe.

I didn't know if it was the right choice. But I knew it was the easier one.

She turned up just after seven with her arms full. She carried two bottles of wine and two fresh pizzas. Not exactly subtle, I thought, but I hadn't eaten since lunch and my stomach rumbled as she placed them on the kitchen counter and turned the oven on as if she owned the place.

"You shouldn't have gone to so much trouble," I said as I uncorked the first bottle.

Carmen smiled, shaking out her hair as she reached for two glasses. "You sounded as though you needed it on the phone."

She moved around the space with familiarity, as if she had always been part of my life and it was just another evening, a casual meal between friends. Except that wasn't what it was, and I think we both knew it.

I watched her as she took the bottle from me and poured the wine, studying the way she carried herself, how effortlessly she slid into my space, how she had this quiet ability to unsettle me without ever appearing threatening.

She had done it before, but I had tried to ignore it with all that was going on. Then the way she had rested her hand on my leg in the car, just for a second too long. The way she had stood in the doorway of my bedroom, watching me dress, not bothering to look away when I caught her. And then, of course, there was the way she had rubbed my back, slow and deliberate, right in front of Santos, as though she was marking some kind of territory.

I took the glass from her without a word, and we retired to the outside table.

Before I knew it, the first bottle had disappeared. We ate pizza and then the second bottle seemed to go even quicker.

At one point, she laughed at something I said—something I barely even remembered saying—and I found myself laughing too, except the sound felt distant, like it belonged to someone else.

The warmth of the evening, the heaviness of the alcohol, the slow, creeping fog in my brain—it all blurred together, stretching time, dulling the edges of the night.

Carmen reached for my hand at one point, her fingers brushing over mine, light at first, then pressing more firmly, tracing circles absently against my palm.

I knew I should have pulled away. But I didn't.

Morning hit like a hammer. A dull, throbbing ache pulsed behind my eyes, my mouth dry, my limbs heavy and uncooperative.

And then I became aware of it.

The weight beside me.

The warmth of another body.

My stomach lurched.

I turned my head slowly, heart pounding, a deep, sick feeling curling in my gut before I even looked.

Carmen.

Lying beside me.

In my bed.

Her breathing was deep, even, completely at ease, her arm draped lazily over the sheet.

My mind snapped into full awareness. How the hell had we ended up there? As panic gripped me, I pressed a hand to my forehead, trying to force the night into focus.

Had we—?

I swallowed hard and glanced down at myself. At least I was still in my boxers.

I turned back to Carmen. Her bare shoulder was exposed,

but the rest of her was hidden beneath the sheets. But that didn't tell me anything.

I sat up too quickly, my pulse hammering against my ribs, my body protesting the movement. I had no memory of getting into bed. No memory of anything after that second bottle, or did we open a third?

I looked at her again, waiting for something—for her to stir, for her to look at me, for some kind of answer. But she didn't move. Instead, she looked so comfortable, like she belonged there. Like she wasn't at all surprised to be there.

And that was the part that unsettled me the most.

PART IV

DAY FOUR

24

HIM

MESMERISED, I stood at the edge of the bed, watching her.

Carmen was sleeping like a baby, her body gently curled beneath the sheets, her breathing deep and steady. Strands of her dark hair spilled across the pillow, a sharp contrast against the white linen.

Finally, she stirred, shifting slightly before her eyes flickered open. The moment she saw me standing there, she smiled, soft and slow, as if she had been expecting it.

"What are you doing?" she murmured, stretching lazily.

I didn't answer right away.

She patted the empty space beside her. "Come back to bed."

Her tone was smooth, inviting, but something in me recoiled.

"No," I said, my voice sounding too sharp, too certain. "This is a mistake, Carmen."

Carmen let out a small sigh and rolled onto her back, blinking up at the ceiling as if considering my response. Then, without hesitation, she threw back the sheets and stood up. She was completely naked.

I froze.

I knew I should have turned away, but I couldn't. It was similar to watching a car crash—that awful, involuntary pull, something you know you shouldn't watch yet impossible to look away from.

She moved across the room with the same effortless grace she always had, seemingly unfazed by my reaction. When she reached the bedroom doorway, she paused, one hand resting lightly against the frame, her bare hip jutting slightly as she turned to look at me.

"Calm down," she said with a smirk, before disappearing out of view. A second later, the shower started.

I exhaled sharply, rubbing a hand over my face.

What the hell was happening?

I had no memory of how we ended up in bed together. The wine, the food, the blurred edges of conversation—I could recall all of that. But nothing else. Had we actually done anything?

Even if we hadn't, the intimacy of it—of waking up with her like that, of seeing her like that—it was enough to make my skin crawl.

And yet, it wasn't just discomfort I felt.

Something deeper gnawed at me.

I turned and walked out of the bedroom, making my way to the kitchen, trying to shake off the lingering unease.

I needed coffee. Something strong, something to pull me back into myself.

As I filled the machine, my mind churned.

What did Carmen really want from me?

Even if the previous night had been innocent—though there was nothing innocent about waking up next to her naked—it still didn't make sense. She had seen me vulnerable. She had seen me drunk.

She had seen me naked.

And now I had seen her.

It wasn't normal.

None of it was normal.

I'd arrived in Andalusia four days previously. My wife had gone missing and none of the other stuff should have happened either. Carmen, Miguel, the fucking weirdos in the finca down the lane and then Doctor Chen suggesting Laura wanted out of our marriage.

Four days.

It had been four days since Laura vanished, and there I was, drinking wine, sharing a bed with another woman.

It didn't matter if nothing had happened.

If Carmen was feeding any of that information back to Santos, then the story practically told itself—James Blackwood didn't care that his wife was gone.

The coffee finished brewing. I poured a cup, gripping it too tightly as I took a sip.

The sound of running water stopped.

A few minutes later, Carmen appeared in the doorway.

She was wrapped in a towel, hair damp, skin flushed from the heat of the shower. She didn't seem uncomfortable in the slightest. In fact, she looked perfectly content.

She poured herself a coffee and stood across from me, lifting the cup to her lips without a word.

I watched her, something uneasy settling in my chest.

Finally, I spoke. "What do you want?"

She raised an eyebrow over the rim of her cup. "Coffee," she said lightly.

I shook my head, frustration creeping into my voice. "I mean, what do you really want, Carmen?"

She sighed, setting her cup down. "We're doing this already?"

"Yes. We are."

She leant back, watching me carefully. It was the way she always looked at me—as if she knew something I didn't.

"What's really going on?" I asked. "Why did you stay?"

She tilted her head slightly. "You asked me to come."

"I mean before that. The very first day I arrived. You were checking on me within hours. Why?"

Carmen shrugged. "I told you. The path's dangerous. You'd had too much to drink. I wanted to make sure you were okay."

Something in my stomach twisted.

She had an answer for everything.

I nodded in the direction of the bedroom. "And what about last night?"

She didn't flinch. Didn't look away.

"Nothing happened," she said smoothly. "You were drunk, you looked vulnerable. I stayed."

"You stayed," I repeated. "Next to me, naked."

She smirked. "I sleep naked. It's not a crime."

I let out a sharp breath, raking a hand through my hair. She was playing with me. But before I could say anything else, she walked over, leant forward, and pecked me lightly on the lips.

It wasn't deep. Wasn't demanding. Just enough to make a point.

"Chill out, James."

I stared at her. "You think this is normal?"

"I think you need to relax."

She retreated to her original position and sipped her coffee like it was any other morning.

Then she tilted her head slightly. "Can I ask you something?"

I hesitated, then gave a reluctant nod.

Her gaze sharpened. "What was the real reason you called me over last night?"

I swallowed.

There was something different in her tone now.

I opened my mouth to respond, but for a moment, I didn't know what to say.

The answer should have been simple.

But it wasn't.

Carmen waited, watching me, letting the silence stretch.

Finally, I exhaled and muttered, "Laura's suitcase is missing. All of her clothes too."

Carmen's expression didn't shift.

She just nodded slightly. "And why didn't you mention that the second I got here?"

I frowned. "I don't know. I got caught up. The wine. The food."

"The wine," she echoed, a flicker of amusement in her eyes. "That's what made you forget that your missing wife's clothes had disappeared?"

I tensed. "That's not what I meant."

She smiled faintly, then stepped forward and touched my hand—just briefly, just enough to unsettle me.

Then she placed her mug on the counter, stretched, and turned towards the doorway.

Pausing for only a second, she glanced back and murmured, "Don't you try to blame all this on me, James Blackwood. I bet you couldn't wait to come to the finca."

25

HIM

CARMEN TOOK her time getting dressed, leaving the bedroom door open and slipping her clothes back on with an ease that only heightened my discomfort. She hummed softly as she moved through the kitchen, slicing thick pieces of bread, arranging cheese and olives on a plate as though this was just another lazy morning, not the aftermath of something that shouldn't have happened.

I sat at the table, watching her, my head still clouded with the remnants of sleep and last night's wine, my thoughts tangled in knots I couldn't begin to unravel. But still I did nothing to get her to leave.

I needed to go into town.

The thought struck me suddenly, as if my mind was desperate for something tangible to focus on, something practical and necessary. The fridge was nearly empty, my supplies dwindling, and if I didn't restock, I'd be left with nothing but black coffee and the stale remains of the bread Carmen hadn't claimed for herself.

But it wasn't just about groceries, was it?

I needed air, distance, a moment away from it all—from the strangeness of Carmen, from the suffocating weight pressing down on me, from the growing realisation that I had no idea what I was supposed to do next.

And yet, I still hadn't called Santos.

Carmen had been right about that. If I had been thinking clearly, if I had truly believed I was an innocent man just searching for his wife, then Santos should have been the first person I called the moment I saw Laura's clothes were missing. Just as I should have followed up on the Dutch family and the strange kid mocking me. And how to get into their property to check.

But instead, I had hesitated, weighed the consequences, convinced myself that the detective already suspected me, that she would twist my words into something incriminating. And so, rather than reach out to the one person who was actually investigating Laura's disappearance, I had picked up the phone and called Carmen.

Had it been a mistake? Or just an excuse? Or was it something more? Not wanting Santos to delve too deep?

I barely heard Carmen as she set the plate down in front of me, giving me a knowing smile before pouring herself another coffee.

"You can call me anytime, you know."

I said nothing, but she didn't seem to mind.

She stepped closer, her voice lowering just slightly as she leant in, her breath warm against my skin. "I had a wonderful night," she murmured, her lips barely brushing my cheek.

I stiffened, my fingers curling around the edge of the table.

Then, just as she was pulling away, she whispered, almost playfully, "And by the way, you have a wonderful body."

She grabbed her bag, strolled to the door, and before I could react, she was gone.

I followed her outside, watching as she climbed into her SUV, rolling the window down before flashing me a final, lazy smile.

"Try not to overthink everything, James. Maybe this is meant to be. Perhaps it always was."

The engine rumbled to life, the tyres kicking up loose gravel as she turned onto the dirt track. I followed her onto the road and stood there, watching her go, waiting as the dust cloud billowed behind her vehicle, waiting until the last trace of her had disappeared beyond the hills, until the road was silent once more.

Only then did I turn back towards the house and stop dead in my tracks.

A jolt shot through my spine, my breath catching in my throat.

Standing just a few feet away, positioned slightly off the track, were three figures.

The Dutch family.

Just standing there.

Watching me.

A prickle of unease crawled up my arms. I hadn't heard them approach, but how was that even possible?

The valley was quiet, the kind of quiet where sound travelled effortlessly; the crunch of gravel underfoot, the rustling of dry leaves, even the distant hum of cicadas was amplified in the stillness. You couldn't move out there without making *some* noise.

So how hadn't I heard them?

I swallowed, my throat suddenly dry.

"What do you want?" I asked, forcing my voice to stay steady.

They didn't answer.

The man and woman stood motionless, their expressions unreadable, neither curious nor concerned. It was as if I weren't even there, like they were looking through me rather than at me.

But the boy—

The boy was grinning.

That same awful, unsettling grin I had seen before, his lips stretching just a fraction too wide, his eyes locked onto mine, glinting with something I couldn't place.

Something wrong.

Something taunting.

My hands clenched involuntarily.

A surge of something intense, something primal and ugly, burned beneath my skin. I wanted to shake him. I wanted to grab him by the shoulders, shake the smirk off his face, demand to know what the hell he was playing at. I wanted to drag him into the pool and hold his head under until that grin dissolved into panic.

They walked past me.

Slow, deliberate steps.

Neither adult acknowledged me as they moved by, as if I were nothing more than a passing shadow. But the child—

His body kept moving forward, but his head turned. His face stayed locked onto mine, his expression never faltering, the grin never slipping, his eyes never blinking.

A chill slithered down my spine.

Then, in a voice that was almost casual, almost amused, he said, "Did you enjoy the quarry?"

The breath left my lungs in a sharp, uneven exhale.

I took a step back, heart pounding. "What?"

But he just kept walking, his head finally snapping forward again as if he had never spoken at all.

I watched them, my body rigid, my pulse thudding against my skull.

How did he know?

Had he followed me after I followed him? But why hadn't I seen him?

The air felt thick, the valley's silence pressing in around me. I stood there, frozen, as the family disappeared over the hill, their figures swallowed by the dry brush, their presence lingering long after they were gone.

I turned back to the finca, the unease curling deep in my stomach.

The silence no longer felt like silence.

It felt like something was listening, and somebody was waiting.

26

———————

SANTOS

Santos sat in her car outside the station, fingers drumming lightly on the steering wheel as she listened to the call ring through.

Doctor Sarah Chen wasn't picking up, but that didn't surprise her.

After the previous day's phone call, something wasn't sitting right. The way Chen had hesitated at key moments, the clipped, measured answers, and—most of all—the background noise.

The ambulance siren.

Santos was done playing games.

She hung up, flipped through her notepad, found the number she needed, and tapped into her phone. It rang for a few moments before a woman answered, her voice clear and professional.

"Clínica Chen, buenos días." Although she spoke in Spanish, Santos immediately picked up the English undertone.

"Yes, hello. This is Inspector Gabriela Santos with the Andalusian police. I need to speak with Doctor Chen."

A pause. Then, slightly hesitant: "Doctor Chen isn't available at the moment. May I take a message?"

Santos frowned. "When will she be available?"

Another pause. "I... I'm not sure. She hasn't been in the office. She's out with a patient."

Santos' pulse quickened. So Chen wasn't in the UK. Why lie? "Do you know *exactly* where she is?"

A longer hesitation. "She didn't say."

Santos narrowed her eyes. She could hear it in the woman's tone—uncertainty, reluctance.

She decided to push. "What's your name?"

A brief silence. Then: "Rebecca."

"Rebecca," Santos repeated, her voice firm but calm. "I understand that patient confidentiality is important, but this isn't about a patient. This is about Doctor Chen herself."

Rebecca didn't respond.

Santos took a breath, adjusting her approach. "I'm investigating a missing person's case. A British woman disappeared from her finca four days ago. I need to confirm whether Doctor Chen has had any contact with her recently."

Still, Rebecca hesitated. Loyalty. Santos could hear it, feel it. This woman was loyal to Chen.

"Listen," Santos continued, her voice lower now, more urgent. "This woman is possibly in danger. If there's anything you know, anything at all, you need to tell me."

Rebecca sighed, a soft exhale over the line.

"Rebecca. The missing woman is Laura Blackwood."

Then, finally. "Laura Blackwood?"

Santos sat up. "Yes."

A beat of silence. Then Rebecca's voice, softer now. "Laura Blackwood, who works here? At the clinic?"

"Yes. That Laura Blackwood. Now, can you help me, please?"

"Yes," Rebecca replied, and for the first time, Santos noticed an element of fear in her voice. "She... she came here about a year ago to work with patients."

Santos grabbed her notebook. "What kind of clinic is this, exactly?"

A brief pause. Then, reluctantly: "It's a trauma centre. We specialise in cases involving women from the UK; vulnerable women, high-risk cases, mostly domestic abuse survivors or those in protective relocation. Many of them are sent here under special circumstances, given safe housing in the city."

Santos scribbled notes furiously. "And Laura came here to work?"

"Yes. She was due to go back home soon, but she stayed because of one particular patient."

Santos already knew the answer before she asked.

"Megan Walsh?"

Rebecca hesitated, then, quietly said, "Yes."

Santos leant forward. "Why couldn't Doctor Chen look after Megan?"

Rebecca stalled, and for a second, Santos thought she might refuse to answer. Then, a small sigh.

"Well, she was. But Doctor Chen had to leave," Rebecca admitted. "Her mother fell ill in the UK. Terminal cancer. She had no choice but to go."

Santos frowned. Hadn't Chen said she barely knew Megan Walsh? "And she left Megan in Laura's care?"

"Yes. But she didn't want to. Doctor Chen was... hesitant. Very hesitant."

Santos tapped her pen against the notebook. "Why?"

A long pause.

Then Rebecca said something that made the hair on the back of Santos' neck rise.

"Because she was attached to her."

Santos blinked. "Attached?"

"Yes. Doctor Chen and Megan... they had a strong bond. A very strong bond."

Something in Rebecca's tone made Santos pause. "Are you saying it was inappropriate?"

"No, not like that," Rebecca said quickly. "But Doctor Chen was... invested. More than usual."

Santos felt a flicker of something—an opening, a weak spot in Rebecca's loyalty.

"She was reluctant to leave Megan," Rebecca continued. "She almost didn't. But her mother was dying. There was no choice."

"And when she came back?"

There was another silence.

"Megan refused to transfer back to her."

Santos stilled, although her own investigations had already told her as much. But why did it matter? "Refused?"

"Yes."

That wasn't normal. Vulnerable patients didn't refuse transfers. The doctors made the decisions, not them. But Megan Walsh had insisted on staying with Laura. Why? Santos pressed the heel of her hand to her temple, thinking. Laura had taken over Megan's care. Chen had returned two months later, expecting to resume control. But Megan didn't want her back. Instead, she stayed with Laura. And then, not long after...

Megan killed herself.

Santos exhaled, allowing the weight of the information to sink in.

Rebecca must have sensed her train of thought because her voice softened. "Doctor Chen took it hard. So did Laura."

Santos nodded slowly. "Of course they did. Megan Walsh's suicide must have been devastating for them."

Silence. A long, stretched silence. Too long.

Santos' grip on her phone tightened. She didn't enjoy long silences. Long silences meant something wasn't being said.

Rebecca inhaled, as if she was about to speak, then, suddenly, a noise in the background.

A muffled voice. Someone else in the room with her.

Rebecca's voice changed. "I… I have to go."

The line went dead.

Santos sat motionless, the words "something was never quite right" circling in her head, wrapping around her like a vice. She stared at the phone, jaw clenched, fingers drumming against the steering wheel as her mind raced.

Megan Walsh's suicide. Doctor Chen's attachment. Laura's involvement. Not forgetting the strange behaviour of James Blackwood himself.

Something was wrong. Very wrong.

27

HIM

I COULDN'T STAY in the finca. It felt too silent, too isolated. Besides, I needed provisions.

Twenty minutes later, I walked through the town, letting my feet lead me nowhere in particular. The midday heat had settled in, thick and oppressive. Even in the shade of the whitewashed buildings, the air clung to me.

The small town was built into the hillside, its streets steep and narrow, winding their way between homes stacked precariously above one another. Cobbled paths twisted, dipping into alleys so tight I could stretch my arms and touch both sides.

A few families passed by—locals, judging by their easy pace and the way they greeted each other. There were tourists too, standing in the doorways of ceramic stores, their sunburned faces peering at painted tiles and overpriced trinkets.

I kept walking. I just wanted to clear my head. Away from the finca. Away from the Dutch family, with their too-quiet house and the strange boy who stared too much.

I thought about him again.

She screamed.

That's what he'd said.

And then—*Did you enjoy the quarry?*

I frowned. What the hell did he mean? He followed me there, but why?

And although desperate to get into their finca, it was like a bloody prison. But surely they would have said if they knew anything?

I reached the town square, an open courtyard surrounded by cafes and tapas bars, their chairs spilling out into the shaded corners. At the far end, tucked away from the main path, I spotted a small bar with a faded blue awning. Quiet. No tourists. That was good enough for me.

I stepped inside for a pack of cigarettes, ordered a drink, then took a seat outside, settling under the wide shade of a sun-bleached parasol. The waiter—a short, tanned man with sweat on his brow—brought me my beer. I lit up a cigarette, inhaling deep, then exhaled slowly, watching the smoke drift into the thick air.

The Dutch boy's voice still echoed in my head.

She screamed.

I should have called Santos. Tell her about the kid, the things he'd said. But I didn't want to. I didn't like her. I just wanted her to go away. Wanted someone else to find Laura so I could be done with it all. No more questions. No more fishing.

I took another drag, then noticed a shadow falling over the table. When I looked up, a man was pulling out the chair opposite me. He sat down and placed his fresh beer on the table between us. Just like that.

I clenched my jaw. There were plenty of empty tables. He could have sat anywhere. But instead, he sat right fucking opposite me. I nodded stiffly, then flicked ash from my cigarette.

The man smiled; yellowing teeth, framed by a white beard. His hair was long and unkempt, curling around his ears. Beneath the overgrowth of facial hair, his skin was weathered, tanned deep from years under the Andalusian sun.

I tried to ignore him, lighting another cigarette and blowing the smoke away from us both. That should have been enough to keep him quiet, to make him realise I was in no kind of mood to socialise. But then he spoke in broken English.

"Have you found your wife yet?"

I froze, and my stomach twisted.

The way he said it—so casual. He may as well have been asking about the goddamn weather.

Annoyance prickled up my spine. Carmen was right. Everybody here knew everybody else's business.

I exhaled through my nose, forcing calm. "What's it got to do with you?"

The man just smiled again. Not unkind. Not mocking. Just… knowing. He leant back, stretching one arm over the back of his chair. "Small town."

I didn't respond.

"People talk," he continued. "They watch."

I picked up my beer and took a slow sip, letting the bitterness settle on my tongue. Trying to decide if I should just get up and leave. But something about him kept me in place.

He tapped his fingers against the table. "Name's Fabián."

I didn't offer mine.

Fabián lifted a hand and signalled the waiter. "Another beer for my friend," he said in Spanish.

I shook my head. "I don't want another beer."

He chuckled. "You might."

The waiter brought a fresh one anyway, setting it down with a nod. Fabián wrapped his fingers around his own glass, lifting it slightly. "Salud."

I didn't touch my drink. Instead, I leant forward, resting my elbows on the table. "What do you know?"

Fabián's smile faded slightly. He studied me for a long moment, as if weighing something. Then, finally, he spoke. "You do know your wife isn't the first woman to go missing around here, don't you?"

Fuck.

A slow chill crawled up my spine. I sat back. Blinking. Processing.

"What?"

Fabián took a sip of beer, then wiped his mouth with the back of his hand.

"Women," he said simply. "They disappear. Sometimes they come back. Sometimes they don't."

I stared at him. I didn't know if he was fucking with me or not. My pulse thumped in my ears. I glanced around the square—at the families, the tourists, the old men playing cards under the shade of the church wall. Nothing about the place felt dangerous. But then again, hadn't I already felt it? That undercurrent of something unspoken. I swallowed, my throat suddenly dry. Leaning in, I kept my voice low. "When?"

Fabián didn't answer right away. He took another sip of beer, licking the foam from his lips.

Then, finally: "About a year ago."

Fuck.

I looked up at Fabián. "Who? Tell me."

He tilted his head slightly. "First, tell me something."

I exhaled sharply. "What?"

He watched me, his eyes darker now. "You know people think it's you, don't you?"

My blood ran cold. I didn't answer. Couldn't answer.

Fabián just smiled. And then he said softly, almost amused. "You should be careful, amigo."

28

HIM

IN A WAY, it felt good.

Good, that I wasn't alone. Good, that it had happened before. A year before. And Fabián hadn't mentioned a body being found. Therefore, it could have nothing to do with me, just as with Laura.

But if there was a pattern, why wasn't Santos chasing that?

I rubbed a hand across my mouth, suddenly tasting the insipid tang of beer and cigarettes. I needed to get out of there. Fabián had left as soon as he'd told me to be careful, leaving his beer barely touched. The town square was still busy, families lingering over late lunches, children weaving between tables, the scrape of cutlery against plates. The normalcy of it all made me feel out of place, an intruder in someone else's life.

I turned away from the square, heading back to my car. I'd promised myself I'd pick up a few things from the supermarket, but it could wait. I needed something stronger than groceries.

Carmen's bar wasn't far, just a short drive along the winding road. When I pulled up outside, the afternoon sun was still beating down, painting everything in a golden light. The bar was quiet. A few locals were at the counter, an older couple sitting by the window with a small jug of wine between them. The music was soft, the overhead fan humming lazily.

Carmen was wiping down glasses behind the bar, her dark hair pinned up, loose strands curling at her neck. She looked up as I slid onto a stool.

"Hi, you," she said, setting the glass down.

"Beer."

She raised an eyebrow but poured one, anyway. When she set it in front of me, I said, "Please. Come and sit with me."

Carmen hesitated, glancing at the kitchen, then at the door. "I can't…"

"Just for a minute."

She sighed, then reached for a bottle of water and gestured towards the back corner. "Fine. But not here."

We moved to a quiet table, away from the bar. I took a long sip of beer before speaking. "I just met a guy in the town square."

Carmen's expression didn't change, but something about her posture did. A slight shift. A tightening.

"Fabián, he said his name was."

She didn't blink, but I kept watching her. She stayed quiet, forcing me to continue. "He says women go missing around here. That Laura isn't the first."

Carmen exhaled slowly. "Fabián talks a lot."

"That wasn't a denial."

She picked at the label on her bottle. "You're listening to town drunks now?"

"Not a drunk. Just a guy who happened to find me, as if he'd been waiting for me."

She shook her head. "James, this is a small place. People gossip. They make up stories."

"So he's lying?"

She hesitated. Too long. Then, finally said, "I don't know."

I sat back. "I thought everybody knew everybody around here."

"They do."

"So how come you haven't heard about it?"

Carmen's fingers stilled on the bottle. Then, just as suddenly, she changed course. "I have," she admitted. "I just dismissed it at the time."

I narrowed my eyes. "Why?"

Carmen sighed. "Because it was gossip, James. It was some British woman, a tourist everyone presumed, who arrived one day to do some hiking. My guess is that she moved on somewhere else."

I frowned. That wasn't how Fabián made it sound. "So you've not heard of anybody being found?"

Carmen shrugged. "As I said, people talk. It was over a year ago. If anything had actually happened, don't you think the police would've been all over it?"

I didn't answer, but she had a point. The same point I'd considered myself.

Carmen watched me for a second. Then, casually, she said, "What about Doctor Chen?"

I blinked. I hadn't expected that. "What about her?"

She looked down at her bottle, running her thumb along the rim. "Santos is looking into her, isn't she?"

I tensed.

Carmen wasn't asking; she was fishing. I forced my expression to stay neutral. "Why do you care about Chen?"

Carmen's gaze flicked up. "I don't."

"You just brought her up."

Carmen exhaled through her nose, shaking her head. "Forget it. I just meant that you mentioned Chen before, when we are at your finca with Santos."

I didn't like how the conversation was turning, so I changed the subject again.

"Why do you do that?" I asked.

Carmen's brow furrowed. "Do what?"

"Backtrack."

She stiffened slightly. "I don't."

"You do."

"I just don't think it matters, James."

"It does if you're lying to me."

She exhaled, rubbing her forehead. "I'm not lying. You're just..." She shook her head. "Look, I get it, okay? You're desperate. You're looking for answers everywhere. But chasing rumours and listening to people like Fabián Vargas isn't going to help you find Laura."

I studied her. She was saying all the right things, but something felt off. The conversation was going round in circles, as if we were both playing a game neither of us knew the rules to. I finished my beer and set the glass down. "Can I stay at yours tonight?"

The words were out before I could think them through. I wasn't sure why I even asked. I just didn't want to go back to the finca. Not that night. But was there something more?

Carmen blinked. "What?"

"Just for the night," I said. "I don't want to go back there."

She didn't answer right away. Then, too quickly, she said, "That's not possible."

I frowned. "Why not?"

Carmen grabbed her bottle and stood up. "I'll come to you instead."

I stared at her. It wasn't an answer, but she walked off before I could say anything else, disappearing into the back of the bar.

I sat there for a long time, turning the conversation over in my head. The way she clammed up. The way she shut down the idea of me staying at hers so quickly. Like she needed to be in control of the situation. Like there was something at her place she didn't want me to see. I left the bar without another word.

When I drove to the supermarket, the streets were quiet, the town settling into that stillness that only usually came after dark. For a split second, I had an urge to turn back, to ask Carmen more questions, but then I heard a sound behind me, soft, deliberate footsteps on stone.

I spun around.

Nothing.

Just the empty street.

A breeze rolled through, gently rattling the loose signs above the shops. Maybe I imagined it.

Or maybe someone was following me.

29

HIM

IT WASN'T REAL. It couldn't be. That's what I told myself as I drove back from town, forcing my grip to relax on the wheel, easing my foot off the gas when I realised I was going far too quickly, given the terrain.

The paranoia had started before I entered the supermarket, but it really cranked up the second I left. First, the feeling of being watched, then the way I kept catching glimpses of someone in the corner of my eye. A woman in a green dress.

Laura's dress.

I'd turned too fast once and nearly walked straight into an elderly couple, their tanned faces startled as I mumbled an apology and hurried past. It wasn't real. Just my mind playing tricks. Just as with the blue blouse on the Dutch family's washing line.

By the time I reached the finca, the feeling had dulled, now a lingering headache. I cut the engine, and sat for a second, letting the air inside the car settle. And then a strange sensation fell over me. It was always silent down there, but that day it was different. The place felt... wrong.

I stepped out, the heat pressing down like a weight, and turned instinctively to the track. The Dutch finca sat just below, its high fences stark against the dry earth. But there was no sound. No sign of life. Were they still out?

I pulled the bags from the car, four of them loaded into my arms, and made my way in the direction of the house. But as I reached the front door, something stopped me.

A sound. From inside? I froze, my heart hammering.

It hadn't been loud, just the faintest sound, like something being moved. Or someone shifting their weight.

Slowly, I set the bags down, even the rustling plastic loud in the silence. My breath felt too thick, my heart slammed against my ribs. The door was locked, but that meant nothing. There were windows. Other ways in. And I had a habit of leaving things open.

I moved along the side of the building, each step cautious, as if someone could jump out on me at any moment. The ground crunched beneath my feet, dry gravel shifting under my weight. I reached the corner and hesitated. My fingers curled against the rough plaster.

Then, slowly, I leant out.

Nothing.

The footpaths vanished between clusters of trees and dry brush as they meandered down the garden. The cicadas sang, but nothing else. Not a sound.

I exhaled, stepping out fully, scanning the area, my nerves still wired tight. Then I saw them.

Footprints.

Wet, fresh.

They led from the pool steps, dark smudges evaporating at the edges, tracking along the hot stone until they disappeared down one of the sloping paths into the garden. The pool rippled under the late sun, blue and disturbed, wavelets brushing against the sides.

My mouth went dry as I tried to swallow and take a step forward. Then another.

I didn't want to follow them. Every part of me screamed to turn back, to leave it alone. But my feet moved anyway, carrying me forward, my pulse a heavy thud in my ears.

It was the Dutch boy. It had to be.

But were they home? Their finca was silent, dark, when I looked, but then again, it always was.

The path twisted down through the trees, the scent of dry earth and warm pine thick in the air. I followed the footprints until they faded completely, the ground too parched to hold any trace.

I stood there, scanning the undergrowth, waiting—for what? Someone to step out? To laugh? To tell me I was imagining things?

Finally, I backed slowly away, retracing my steps until I reached the finca door. I forced myself to keep my breathing even. It was fine. I grabbed the shopping bags and made my way inside, locking the door behind me.

The air conditioning hummed, sending a wave of cool air over my skin, but it did nothing to slow my heartbeat. I unpacked the bags mechanically, my hands moving without thought—milk, bread, fruit, wine. Every few seconds, my eyes flickered towards the window, back to the pool.

Who the hell had been in it?

After I finished, I made coffee, the act grounding me, bringing some sense of normalcy back. I took the mug to the bedroom, ready to lie down for a while, let my head clear.

Then I saw it.

Laura's journal.

It sat on the bed, open, its pages slightly curled at the edges from the humidity.

I stopped in the doorway, staring at it. I was sure… I was sure I'd put it away. I'd put it in the bedside drawer the last time I looked through it.

I stepped closer, my breath shallow, my fingers twitching at my sides. Then I saw what was on top of it.

A photograph.

A chill ran down my spine.

Before I even picked it up, I recognised the two people in it.

Both laughing. Arms around each other.

Laura.

And Doctor Sarah Chen.

30

HER

SHE HAD LOST all sense of time. The dark had swallowed her whole, blurring the edges between what was real and what wasn't. She had scraped at the wood for hours—or was it days?—her fingers raw, her nails splintered, her palms blistered and torn. The metal fragment in her grip had dulled with use, its once-sharp edge rounded by the endless, relentless motion.

Her breaths were shallow. Every inhale coated her throat with dust, every exhale felt weaker than the last. She had stopped counting how many times she had passed out. Whether it had been minutes or hours, she couldn't tell. Sleep didn't exist there—only unconsciousness.

Her stomach had long since stopped growling, but the thirst never left. It consumed her, an unbearable ache that made her head spin and her thoughts disjointed. How long had it been? How long before her organs started shutting down? And at some point, the hallucinations had begun.

Light flickering at the edges of her vision. Shadows that

moved when she wasn't looking. Voices whispering from the corners of the cabin, just beyond her reach. But the worst had been the singing.

A child's voice, clear and sweet, rising from somewhere beyond the wooden barrier. A tune she didn't recognise, but the melody was soft, carefree, playful. She had frozen, her entire body rigid with shock. The metal fragment slipped from her fingers, clattering against the floor.

No. No, it wasn't real. It couldn't be.

But it had been so clear.

She had barely breathed as she listened, her hands trembling in her lap, skin coated in grime and sweat. The voice wove through the silence like a ribbon, curling around her, pulling her in. Then, just as suddenly as it had started, it was gone.

She screamed.

Lurching to her feet, she had thrown herself at the walls, banging her fists until her bones felt as if they might crack. She had shrieked until her throat was raw, until her voice broke, until she tasted blood in the back of her mouth.

But there was nothing. No response. No child. No sound at all.

A sob wrenched itself free from her chest as she sank to the ground. Had she imagined the whole thing?

Yes.

No.

She didn't know anymore.

The days—or hours, or years—blurred together, bleeding into each other in an endless cycle of scraping, crying, falling into exhaustion, waking up only to do it all over again.

Her makeshift toilet in the corner had become unbearable. The smell turned her stomach every time she moved too close, a sour, putrid stench that clung to the air, thick and inescapable. She gagged just thinking about it. But what disturbed her most was that she still needed to go. How? She had drunk nothing.

Her mouth was dry, her lips cracked, her tongue swollen and heavy, and yet, her body continued to function. Barely.

Maybe it was the hallucinations again. Maybe none of it was real. Maybe she was already dead.

But then—

The metal jarred against the wood. The impact sent a sharp vibration up her arm, rattling her bones, shocking her back to reality. She froze, barely breathing, her grip tightening around the fragment.

Slowly, carefully, she pressed forward again, wedging the metal into the gap she had carved. This time, when she pushed, something shifted. The wood groaned. A small sliver cracked, splintering outward.

She sucked in a breath.

Then—

Light. A thin beam, pale and fragile, cutting through the dust and the dark. For the first time since she remembered, she could see something other than darkness.

Her breath caught in her throat as she dropped to her knees, her face inches from the tiny gap. It wasn't much—just the smallest fracture—but it was daylight.

Daylight.

The dry air seeped through, and she inhaled greedily, taking it in like it was the first breath she had ever drawn. It was warm, carrying with it the scent of something—dirt, maybe? Pine? She couldn't tell.

Tears blurred her vision, spilling down her cheeks, mixing with the sweat and grime that coated her skin.

She wasn't dead.

She wasn't dead.

A sob wracked her chest, but she didn't stop, didn't waste a second.

She dug, scraping at the wood with renewed desperation. Her fingers screamed in protest, the raw skin splitting further, the pain igniting like fire beneath her nails.

But she didn't stop.

Couldn't stop.

The light had found her. And now, she had to find it.

31

HIM

I sat on the edge of the bed, staring at the photo, my breath coming slow and measured.

Laura and Sarah Chen.

Arms slung around each other, their faces bright with laughter.

It wasn't just a snapshot—it was proof of something. Proof of a closeness I was always aware of, proof that Laura doted on her mentor in a way she never did with me.

But that wasn't what chilled me the most.

It was the fact that the photo hadn't been there before.

I was sure of it.

I had put Laura's journal away. Tucked it into the drawer beside the bed. Yet here it was, open, deliberately placed, and that was the image left out for me to find.

Had Laura been back?

The thought sent an icy wave through me. It was the same feeling I had the day before when I noticed her suitcase was missing. That gnawing, irrational whisper at the back of my mind. She was here. She took her things.

But that was insane.

If Laura had come back, she wouldn't be sneaking around like a ghost. She would have told me. She would have stood in that very room, stared me down, and demanded to know what the hell I'd done. She wasn't the type to tiptoe around confrontation. Unless she knew something.

I shut my eyes. No.

That didn't make sense either. If she suspected something, anything, she wouldn't be playing mind games. She would have had it out with me.

So if it wasn't Laura… then who?

Chen?

I doubted it. Laura had gone missing on the very vacation that she had suggested. She wouldn't play games, she'd do anything in her power to prove it had nothing to do with her.

Miguel?

No. Why the hell would he? He barely knew me. We'd met just once. He had no reason to creep into my house, remove Laura's things, leave me a photograph. But nobody knew Miguel. Not even Carmen. So was he involved? Even so, why the hell would he come into the finca and remove Laura's clothes from the wardrobe?

Carmen?

I hesitated.

She was off, I'd admit that. She watched me too closely, touched me in ways that felt like…

I didn't know what she wanted from me, but I knew she wanted something. But I couldn't talk. I'd let her effortlessly into my life.

Still. That wasn't her style. If Carmen wanted to manipulate me, she would do it with her words, her body, her touch.

She wouldn't sneak into my home, rearrange my life piece by piece, and sit back to watch me unravel.

So, that left only one possibility.

The Dutch family.

The boy.

I clenched my jaw.

He was odd, that much I knew. He lingered too long, stared too hard. And he knew about Laura. He knew she was missing. If he was screwing with me, it made sense. He could have stolen her clothes. He could have found the journal, picked the only photograph inside, and left it out—he wouldn't know who Doctor Chen was, but he wouldn't need to. He could have swum in my pool. Left those wet footprints.

My pulse ticked faster.

And the quarry. He had been following me. That little bastard had been watching me.

I swallowed against the dryness in my throat, the walls of the room suddenly feeling too close. My phone buzzed on the bedside table. It was Carmen.

> Can't get over tonight. No cover at the bar.
> Sorry x

I exhaled sharply through my nose. Fine. I had something else to deal with, anyway.

It was time to take a closer look at the Dutch family's finca. They weren't supposed to be there.

The walk down was slow, deliberate. The early evening heat had settled into a thick, suffocating blanket, but I barely felt it. My thoughts were too tangled, my body thrumming with unease. I stopped just before the gates, scanning the property.

Silent.

The same eerie quiet as always.

I pushed one gate carefully, and to my disbelief, the hinges let out the faintest squeak as they gave way. My heart pounded against my ribs as I stepped inside. Why had they left it unlocked when the place was like a bloody prison? But it suited me. I'd wanted to get in ever since I'd arrived. I needed to check.

Closing the gate behind me, I moved cautiously, my ears straining for any sign of movement. But there was nothing. They had to be out still. But then who the hell had been in my pool? Been in my property?

I circled the side of the house, my skin prickling with every step. The farther I went, the more certain I became that something was wrong.

A light breeze swept dust across the dry ground as I took a cautious step forward, scanning the windows. The curtains were drawn tight, as if the house itself had shut its eyes for the night.

I moved farther.

The front of the finca was untidy. A row of terracotta pots lined the porch, their plants brittle and curling at the edges from lack of care. A small wooden table sat to one side, a single glass resting on its surface, as if someone had abandoned it mid-drink.

I hesitated, glancing around. My own footsteps felt intrusive.

Focus, James.

I needed to see more.

Keeping close to the walls, I moved along the side of the house, the narrow gap between the building and the hedgerow pressing in on either side. My shoulder scraped against the whitewashed stone—cooler there—but no less suffocating.

Still no sound.

They were still out. Maybe left for good? Back to wherever they lived.

The passage curved with the shape of the house, opening onto a rougher patch of ground at the rear. The lawn had given up pretending, the earth cracked and sparse, only tufts of brittle grass poking through. Against the wall sat a crooked wooden crate, cluttered with tools and empty wine bottles.

Beyond it—there.

Set back at the rear of the property, almost hidden at the end of the garden, almost as if you wouldn't know it was there unless you went looking. Two low, splintered doors, flush with the earth and almost swallowed by the weeds around them. Not a hut. A cellar.

I crouched, letting my fingers brush the frame. The hinges were corroded to the point of decay. A padlock clung to the metal latch—old but solid. I leant in slightly, careful not to touch my face to the wood, and breathed in.

Nothing. Or maybe something.

I ran a hand along the rusted lock, inspecting the edges, the way the metal had crusted over, the slight tilt of the latch. No recent movement. No one had opened it in a while.

Then…

A sound.

Not loud. Just enough.

The creak of wood. The slow, deliberate groan of the finca's front gates opening. A woman laughing.

I froze, the hairs on the back of my neck rising.

They were home.

And I was trapped.

32

————

SANTOS

Detective Isabel Santos knew she should have gone home hours ago.

The streets outside had long since emptied and the station itself had settled into its usual late-night lull, the hum of the vending machine and the occasional ringing phone the only reminders that the place never truly slept. Most of the other officers had clocked out for the night, leaving only a handful of poor bastards on call or finishing up their reports. She should have been among those departed, packing up, heading out, locking the door behind her.

But to what?

She exhaled slowly, rubbing her hands over her face before leaning back in her chair.

Her apartment was barely more than a shoebox—just a rented space with peeling paint and walls so thin she could hear the neighbour's dog scratching itself in the night. There was no one waiting for her, no one to have a drink with or ask how her day had gone. The only thing she'd be greeted by was a pile of unwashed dishes and a bed that hadn't been properly made in weeks.

Not so long ago, life had looked different.

She had once had a home, not just a place to sleep. A husband too, though looking back, she wasn't sure if it had ever been much of a marriage. He had left her for his secretary, and the betrayal itself hadn't even been the worst part. No, the worst part had been the months leading up to it, the way she had felt it slipping through her fingers but had been too damn stubborn to admit it. She had fought for something that had already been lost, had convinced herself that the long nights and distant stares were just a rough patch and not the prelude to him packing his things and walking out.

And now? Now she had her job. Her cases. The next lead, the next unanswered question, the next sleepless night chasing something that might not even be there.

She had never been much of a drinker—her father had been, and she had learned early on what alcohol did to a man who let it become his whole life—but she wasn't going to pretend that there weren't nights where she wished she could drown it all out. One drink. Just one. Maybe two. But she knew herself, and she knew it would never just be one.

No. Better to keep going. Keep working.

She leant forward again, resting her elbows on the desk, staring at the mess of notes and files in front of her.

James Blackwood.

The name alone made her skin itch.

She had met plenty of men like him before. But there was something about James that didn't sit right. He wasn't panicked enough. He wasn't angry enough.

She tapped her pen against the desk, staring at the timeline she had been trying to piece together.

Chen had been the one to suggest Laura take a break after Megan's suicide. Had that just been out of concern, or had there been something else to it? Had she been manoeuvring something behind the scenes?

And James. James had met Chen before. Maybe only briefly, but they had certainly met. Had it been a passing encounter, as he claimed? Or was there something more to it? She had learned long ago that coincidences were rarely just that. And the way they pretended not to like one another. Was it all a front? Could they be in it together?

Santos sighed heavily. Her boss had already started breathing down her neck.

"Where are you with this missing woman case, Santos? Any leads?"

She had barely restrained herself from snapping back. It's been four bloody days.

Four days since Laura had vanished, and already she was expected to have all the answers. Meanwhile, the department wasted time and resources chasing down some thieves in Nerja, who had pocketed a few low-value items from the tourist shops. It was infuriating, watching them devote manpower to tracking down a couple of pickpockets while she was left untangling what was beginning to look like something far more complex than a simple disappearance.

She rolled her shoulders, trying to shake off the exhaustion creeping in, but her thoughts wouldn't slow down. Something wasn't right. And then her phone rang.

The sound startled her—sharp, jarring against the late-night silence.

She frowned, glancing at the unknown number on the screen. A moment of hesitation, then she answered.

"Santos."

A pause.

Then a voice. Female. Low. Steady. Measured.

"Detective, I have some information you may want to hear."

Her pulse ticked up. "Who is this?"

"That's not important, but you're looking into Laura Blackwood, yes?"

Santos recognised the voice but gave nothing away. Instead, she gripped the phone tighter.

"What do you know?" she asked, more forcefully this time.

33

———

HIM

I DIDN'T MOVE as the floodlight above the house flared into life, illuminating the entire property in a harsh, unnatural light. Shadows stretched long across the ground, and I pressed myself back against the perimeter fence, barely breathing.

The voices, animated but jovial, rippled through the warm night air. I couldn't make out the words, only the rhythm of them. The adults were speaking quickly in Dutch, overlapping, cutting each other off, interspersed with an occasional laugh from the woman.

But the boy. Where was he?

I strained my ears, listening for the lighter footsteps, the higher-pitched voice. But I heard nothing. Was he already inside? In bed maybe.

A loud slam jolted through me. The front gates. Then the scrape of metal, the distinctive sound of a bolt sliding into place.

I closed my eyes for half a second, swallowing the panic that tried to surge up my throat. They'd locked me in. Next, a key turned in a lock, followed by the hinges of a door whining as it swung open. The voices moved inside, muffled now. Then —click—the door shut. Silence.

I exhaled through my nose, willing myself to stay still for just a little longer. My heart drummed against my ribs, loud enough that I swear it could have given me away. I needed to get to the olive tree, where the wall was slightly lower. But the spotlight was still on, lighting up the entire yard. How could I get there without being seen, and if I was, how the hell could I explain myself to the family, and more importantly, to Santos? Another nail in my coffin of guilt.

Still, I needed to move.

Sliding one foot forward, I crept to the rear wall before inching around the side of the house, keeping my back pressed to the rough stone. The ground was uneven, but at least the light offered me some help. I hesitated, listening again.

Nothing.

I moved again, stepping carefully. Pushing forward, I skirted the far edge until I reached the point of escape, my breath shallow. The floodlight buzzed faintly overhead, throwing long streaks of brightness across the yard. Then, the timer shut it off, plunging everything into darkness. The moon took over once more. I could still see the wall.

Hurrying forward, I kept myself low, my legs tensing with every step. Each movement felt agonisingly loud. And then—a shape.

A wheelbarrow, half-rusted, tipped up farther along against the wall. My hands grasped the cold metal handles, my fingers slipping slightly against the surface as I braced myself. It was unsteady, but it was better than nothing. The grazes on my hands were a constant reminder from last time.

I placed one foot on the edge and pushed myself up, using it to reach the thickest part of the vine-covered wall. My fingers dug in, finding purchase between the cracks. I hauled myself up, muscles burning, feet scrambling for support until I could grip the top of the wall and pull myself up—

Then I froze.

Below, in the courtyard, something shifted. A shadow. Small. Still.

It was the boy.

He just stood there, his face half in shadow. His arms hung loosely by his sides, his posture eerily motionless. His eyes, deep and unreadable, were locked onto mine.

He didn't move.

He didn't speak.

He just watched me.

A sickening chill slithered up my spine.

Still, his expression gave nothing away—no surprise, no fear, no anger. Just that blank, unwavering stare.

A warning?

Or something worse?

I didn't wait to find out.

I swung my legs over the wall, clung to the ancient olive tree, and dropped to the other side. I landed hard on the uneven ground. My knees buckled slightly, but I forced myself to keep going, stumbling forward into the darkness.

And I didn't look back. Not until I reached my finca, panting, my hands shaking as I fumbled with the key. Inside, I slammed the door behind me and slid the deadbolt across. And only then did I allow myself to glance back through the window.

The Dutch finca was out of sight, but in my mind, I could still see him. The boy.

Standing there. Watching.

And in my gut, I knew he wasn't just a kid staring at a trespasser.

He was something else entirely.

PART V

DAY FIVE

34

HIM

I'D BARELY SLEPT. Again.

Every time I closed my eyes, I saw the boy. Standing there in the dark, watching me, his hands limp by his sides. I saw his face, still and unreadable. Had he been there *all* the time?

I'd lain on top of the sheets, staring at the fan whirring slowly on the ceiling, turning it all over in my head.

Should I have called Santos? Told her what I saw? But what would I even say? *Hey, there was a kid standing outside his own property, just watching me.* It wasn't a crime to stare. And more importantly, she'd ask why I was over there in the first place. She'd push. Press. Probe. And I didn't like the way she looked at me when she did. As if she already knew something I hadn't said out loud.

I'd thought about calling Carmen too. I even reached for my phone at one point. Maybe she could have helped make sense of it.

But I didn't call her. Because I knew exactly how the conversation would go.

"What were you even doing there, James?"

It didn't matter what I'd say. And if she thought I was keeping things from her—if she thought I was starting to look guilty—then Santos would be here faster than I could blink.

No. I had to think.

And I had to get to the boy. Alone.

By morning, my body was aching from exhaustion. I felt sluggish, slow, like my limbs had been weighted down in my sleep. Outside, for the first time since I'd arrived, thick clouds choked the sky. But the heat hadn't broken. If anything, it was worse. Heavy. Humid. My T-shirt clung to me as soon as I stepped outside.

I took my coffee to the patio, rubbing a hand across my face. My eyes felt gritty and dry from the lack of sleep. I watched the rolling hills in the distance, but my mind was somewhere else entirely.

How could I get the boy alone?

It was a risk—hell, it might be insane—but I had to talk to him. I needed to know if he was just some weird kid who enjoyed creeping around at night, or if he actually knew something.

Santos had already been to see them. If she thought there was anything there, she would've pushed harder. And besides, if she went back again, his parents might keep their son indoors, away from the crazy English guy just along the track. And I'd lose any chance of finding out what the boy really knew. No. I had to do it myself. But how?

My eyes flicked to the pool. If he was the one who sneaked in for a swim, maybe I could use that. Tell his parents they didn't need to worry. He was welcome to come over. Perhaps then he'd relax, let something slip. But I knew the second I spoke to them, it would fall apart. That look the mother gave me. The father making it quite obvious I wasn't wanted anywhere near them.

I took a slow sip of coffee, thinking.

And then, my mind drifted to the spot where Laura's suitcase had been, and a fresh, uneasy feeling twisted in my gut. Could it have been him?

The thought hit me fast. I hadn't really considered it before. But who else could have taken it? The Dutch family were the closest neighbours. He was just a kid, but maybe that made it easier for him to slip in, to move quietly. Maybe it was him playing games.

But why?

Why would he take Laura's clothes?

The blue blouse. I was still no closer to finding out whether it was indeed Laura's. But again, Santos found nothing. It must have been the frantic state I was in at the time.

I set my coffee down, rubbing a hand over my face. My thoughts were starting to spiral, paranoia seeping into the cracks. I needed to focus. I needed—

Rumble.

The low, gravelly sound of tyres crunching over dry earth snapped me out of my thoughts. I hurriedly stepped around the side of the finca and looked up.

A car. Coming down the track.

My stomach clenched, my fingers tightening around the handle of my coffee mug.

At first, I prayed to see our car weaving its way down the hill. But then I recognised it. It wasn't our car, but I knew exactly who it belonged to.

Santos.

She stepped out before the car had even fully stopped, her face set, her eyes scanning the finca. She had a partner with her—a tall, wiry man, mid-fifties with hair greying at the temples. He climbed out from the passenger side, speaking low into a radio.

I stepped forward, trying to keep my expression neutral, desperate to not look too defensive.

"I need to search the house," Santos said. No hello. No pleasantries. Just straight to it.

I hesitated. Not because I had anything to hide but because I knew what it meant. They weren't just poking around anymore. They weren't just checking in. It was serious.

Santos stared at me, waiting.

I nodded. "Fine."

She gave a small, sharp tilt of her head to her partner, who stepped past me and into the house. Santos followed, brushing past me like I wasn't even there.

I stood in the kitchen, arms crossed, my chest tightening with every creak of the floorboards. They moved methodically, room by room, opening drawers, checking under furniture. My mind was racing, trying to track what they were doing, what they might find.

And then…

"Detective?"

Santos' partner's voice carried from the bedroom.

I saw the way her body stiffened. The way her head snapped towards the voice.

I didn't move. Didn't breathe. What the hell had he found? Laura's journal? Good. They might make more sense of it than me.

Santos walked past me, fast, her heels clicking hard against the tiles. I followed, my pulse hammering against my skull.

Her partner stood by the wardrobe, his back straight, his face blank. But the wardrobe had been moved, a few feet to the left.

And then I saw it.

Behind where the wardrobe originally stood, streaked across the white plaster…

Blood.

A deep, ugly stain, half-hidden by shadow, but unmistakable.

My stomach dropped. The room tilted slightly, my breath catching in my throat.

Santos turned slowly, her dark eyes locking onto mine.

I opened my mouth, but nothing came out.

I had no words.

35

SANTOS

DETECTIVE SANTOS STARED at the number on her notepad, the one she'd jotted down following the anonymous call the night before. The caller's voice still rang in her ears, even though she had obviously tried to disguise it. But Santos knew exactly who it belonged to.

Rebecca. The receptionist from Doctor Sarah Chen's practice.

Santos smiled to herself, setting the notepad down on her desk. Rebecca must have thought she was being clever—masking her voice, refusing to give her name—but Santos had spent years tuning into the spaces between words, the pauses, the subtle cracks. It wasn't just what Rebecca said. It was what she didn't. That hesitation. The sudden retreat. As soon as Santos asked what she knew, Rebecca said she'd made a mistake. One moment she was offering something, the next she was shutting down completely. She hung up seconds later, and despite Santos calling straight back, it went direct to voicemail.

So what did Rebecca know? Had she overheard something at the clinic? Had someone—Chen, maybe—let something slip? Whatever it was, it had been enough to make Rebecca reach out. And just as quickly, enough to make her disappear again.

Santos had tried calling Chen first thing that morning, but the woman hadn't answered. Not once. Two voicemails left. No response. That in itself was suspicious. Just as suspicious as when she said she was in the UK.

So while she waited for Chen to crawl out of whatever hole she was hiding in, she needed to do something. And James Blackwood was next on her list.

She grabbed her keys and turned to her partner.

"Álvarez, get your coat. We're going up to Blackwood's finca."

Álvarez was quiet beside her, arms crossed, occasionally glancing her way as though waiting for her to say something. The winding mountain roads eventually gave way to the dirt track leading to James' finca. Santos knew exactly what Álvarez was thinking. Finally, he asked, like he'd been holding his breath all the way. "You think we need a warrant for this?"

Santos exhaled slowly, watching the road. "Technically, yes. But we're not arresting him. Yet."

"He could say no," Álvarez pointed out.

"Then we turn around, come back with one," she replied. "But if he lets us in, that says something too."

Álvarez grunted. "If he's guilty, he's had more than enough time to cover his tracks."

"Yes," Santos murmured, more to herself than in reply. "Five days. More than enough time."

The finca loomed ahead, its whitewashed walls almost

glowing in the morning light. It should have been picturesque, but to Santos, it just looked… empty.

They pulled up, dust kicking into the air as the car slowed to a stop.

James was already standing in the driveway. He still hadn't shaved, and his shirt was wrinkled and damp against his chest. His eyes, shadowed from exhaustion, flicked between them, his expression unreadable.

Santos stepped out first, and she didn't waste time. "I need to search the house."

She expected hesitation. Resistance. Protest, at the very least. But James Blackwood only stared at her for a moment, then nodded. "Fine."

Santos exchanged a glance with Álvarez. That wasn't the reaction of a guilty man. Not outright, anyway. But that didn't mean he wasn't hiding something.

Santos took the living room while Álvarez moved in the direction of the bedrooms.

The house felt different this time. The last time she'd been there, Laura's presence had still lingered, her perfume somehow clinging to the air. Now, the place felt abandoned, stripped of anything that made it a home.

James stood by the kitchen counter, arms folded. His gaze flickered to her now and then, watching but not interfering.

She moved methodically, lifting cushions, checking under furniture, opening cabinets. Nothing.

Then, a voice from the hallway.

"Detective?"

She turned, hearing the note in Álvarez' tone. Controlled, but tight. Santos crossed the room in seconds, stepping into the dim bedroom where Álvarez stood beside the wardrobe.

His expression was unreadable, but he tilted his chin to the wall.

Her stomach clenched as she moved closer.

And then she saw it.

Dark smears stained the plaster. The unmistakable dried residue of blood.

For a moment, the only sound was the faint buzz of cicadas outside.

Then James stepped inside to join them, and she nodded to the wall. His face immediately drained of what little colour remained. His eyes locked onto the stains, and Santos saw it— the way his breath hitched, his balance shifting slightly as he reached for the doorframe.

She moved instinctively, grabbing him under the arm just as his knees threatened to buckle.

"Sit down," she ordered, steering him towards the bed.

He obeyed numbly, fingers gripping at the edge of the mattress. Álvarez disappeared for a moment, returning with a glass of water. James took it, his hands shaking slightly as he brought it to his lips.

Santos crouched in front of him. "Whose blood is it, James?"

James' head snapped up, anger flashing across his features. "I don't know."

"You're sure?"

"Of course I'm sure!" His voice rose. "Do you think I'd be sitting here if I knew?"

She studied him carefully. His reaction felt... real. But then again, if he had done something, he'd had five days to prepare his performance. He took a deep breath, trying to steady himself. Then, quieter, he asked:

"Do you think it's Laura's?"

Santos didn't answer immediately.

That was the question, wasn't it?

"We'll need forensics to confirm that," she said eventually.

James shook his head, gripping his hair. "How long will that take?"

Santos glanced at Álvarez, who answered, "A basic test to confirm if it's human? A few hours. DNA analysis?" He exhaled. "Days. Maybe a week."

James let out a bitter laugh. "A week?"

Santos ignored him, turning to Álvarez. "Get a sample sent to the lab. See if we can expedite the results."

Álvarez nodded and stepped out to make the call. Santos straightened, watching James closely. "There's nothing else you want to tell me?" she asked.

James met her gaze, jaw tightening. "No."

A long silence stretched between them.

Finally, Santos sighed. "We'll be in touch, then. But, James…" She paused until she knew she had his full attention. "Don't go anywhere."

Back in the car, Álvarez drummed his fingers against the dashboard. "So?"

Santos exhaled, staring at the dirt road ahead. "If that blood matches Laura's…"

Álvarez nodded. "Then James Blackwood is screwed."

Santos didn't reply immediately.

She tapped her fingers slowly against the steering wheel, her brow furrowed. "There's very little chance Laura's DNA is on file," she said eventually. "No criminal record. No medical database access unless she's been in hospital for something that triggered a DNA collection, which I doubt."

"So we can't confirm it's hers?"

"Not unless we get a familial match—or unless we find something belonging to her we can compare it to." She paused. "Even if it's not hers, it still tells us someone bled there. It gives us something to work with."

"And James?"

"No point giving him the full picture," Santos said. "I want to see what he does next, now that he thinks we might be close."

Álvarez nodded slowly, then frowned. "So what now?"

Santos stared out at the trees ahead. "Now we wait on the lab. And in the meantime, I need to contact Doctor Chen."

"You think she's connected to the blood?"

"I don't know. But she's connected to Laura. And she's hiding something."

And Santos couldn't shake the feeling that whatever was happening out there hadn't started with Laura disappearing.

It had started before.

Without another word, Santos put the car in gear and drove away.

36

—————

HIM

I DRANK two more glasses of water after Santos left, but my mouth still felt dry, my throat tight. My body was working against me, telling me I needed to get out of there, to move. But I didn't. I just stood there, staring at the blood on the wall.

It had dried, darkened over time, but it was still unmistakably blood. How the hell had I missed it? I thought I'd looked everywhere, covered my tracks, checked every inch of the place. But I hadn't thought to look behind the wardrobe.

Slowly, I dragged the furniture back into place; the legs scraping against the floor with an ugly, grating sound. It felt heavier than before, like I was sealing something away. When it was back where it belonged, I stepped away, staring at it as if it might move on its own.

Santos hadn't looked much farther after she'd seen the bloodstained wall. Maybe she didn't think she needed to.

I sat down on the edge of the bed, my head in my hands. I needed to think. I needed to be smarter than this. My gaze landed on the bedside cabinet, where Laura's journal lay inside. The one thing Santos or Álvarez hadn't bothered to check—or if they had, they hadn't taken it. I reached for it and flipped it open, scanning the pages as though they might suddenly start making sense.

There were lots of names. Familiar names. Her ex-patients, noted in her neat handwriting, some underlined, some with numbers next to them. Small diary-like entries beside them. A record of her thoughts? Or something else?

It meant nothing to me. Maybe I should hand it over to Santos, let her figure it out. If she hadn't already got me by the throat, maybe I could give her something to appease her, get her back on my side, if she'd ever been there. But then again, I didn't trust Santos any more than she trusted me. She was out for a quick win. Blame the husband. He was the last person to see his wife, so it *must* be him.

I tossed the journal onto the bed, rubbing my palms over my face. Sitting around, waiting for the Dutch kid to show up, wasn't doing me any good. I needed to get out.

Carmen should have checked in by now. Two nights ago, she was all over me, bringing wine, pressing close, whispering in my ear. And now, nothing. I pulled out my phone and checked it again. No messages. So, I typed one out.

Why aren't you contacting me?

A minute passed. No response. I exhaled slowly. Maybe it was for the best.

I grabbed my keys and left.

Town was quiet, the midday heat keeping people inside. I didn't know why I was there, not really. But my feet carried me through the streets, following the same route I had taken the day before. Before I even realised it, I ended up at the same bar. I told myself it was because I needed a drink, but I knew that was a lie.

Pushing open the door, I stepped into the dim, cool space. It was lunchtime, but the place wasn't busy; a few locals, a couple of tourists nursing beers at the counter. I moved to the bar, about to order, when a voice came from behind me.

"I'll buy that."

I froze, my skin prickling. I knew exactly who it was without needing to look. Fabián Vargas.

Turning, I found him already on his feet, heading towards me, like he had been waiting until I inevitably arrived.

He hunched over the bar, smelling of stale sweat and old smoke. His fingers were yellow-stained from endless cigarettes and his clothes looked as though they hadn't been washed in weeks.

"I knew you'd be back," he said, his lips curling into something that wasn't quite a smile.

I didn't move, and he was right. "What made you so sure?" I asked, keeping my voice steady.

Fabián lifted a shoulder in a shrug and ordered two beers, anyway. When the bartender set them down, he slid one towards me without looking. "Sit down," he said, as if it were an order.

Lowering myself onto the stool across from him, I studied him carefully.

Fabián raised his glass. "To old friends."

I didn't correct him. I just drank. It was barely lunchtime, and he was slurring his words. What had Carmen said? *"You're listening to town drunks now?"*

I felt the cold beer travel all the way down, settling uneasily in my stomach, before Fabián leant in slightly, his voice dropping just enough so I had to focus.

"Tell me, James," he said. "Have you found what you're looking for yet?"

My fingers tightened around the glass. "What's that supposed to mean?"

Fabián smiled, but it didn't reach his eyes. "I think you know."

The silence stretched between us.

I could have asked him outright what the hell he was playing at, but something told me I wouldn't like the answer. I set my glass down carefully. "Yesterday, you mentioned a missing woman."

Fabián smiled, slow and lazy, but his eyes sharpened. "Did I?"

I ignored his insolence. "Yeah. You said women disappear. Sometimes they come back, sometimes they don't."

Fabián chuckled, shaking his head like I was some naïve idiot.

I should have left. I knew that. But the beer was already slowing my instincts, and I was intrigued by what he might say. Any clue to Laura's whereabouts was in my interests after all, especially with Santos breathing down my neck. But then he laughed again, as if he could read my bloody mind.

I started to stand. "Forget it."

Before I could push my stool back, Fabián's hand shot out and grabbed my arm. His grip was strong. "Sit down."

Leaning in slightly, he lowered his voice again. "They've been coming here. To the town."

I stared at him. "Who?"

"English women."

A chill ran down my spine.

Fabián swirled his drink, watching the liquid coat the inside of his glass. "For the past three years. One, sometimes two at a time."

Something about the way he said it made my stomach tighten.

"And?" I pressed.

"And then, I don't see them again."

"That doesn't mean anything," I said. "You're talking crazy."

Fabián laughed under his breath. "Maybe."

I pushed my stool back, ready to leave. The conversation wasn't leading anywhere good, and I wasn't about to sit there drinking with the local drunk while listening to his riddles.

This time, he let me go, but as I reached the door, he called after me.

"Amigo," he said, his voice laced with amusement. "Why don't you ask that girlfriend of yours?"

I froze.

Slowly, I turned my head. But Fabián was already lifting his glass, grinning like he'd just won something.

I walked out, my pulse hammering in my ears.

37

HER

HER FINGERS BURNED as she prised them into the splintered wood. She had worked at the boards for what felt like hours, wedging her nails between the gaps, pulling until the grain cracked and broke away in brittle fragments. Her hands were a mess—bleeding, raw, packed with splinters so deep she could feel them stabbing into the bone. But she couldn't stop. Not now.

The gap she made was eventually just wide enough to squeeze through. She pressed her body into it, the jagged wood scraping across her shoulders, her ribs, her hips. She twisted, contorted herself into the tight space, her breath coming in shallow gasps. Her vest caught on something, tearing it further, but she barely noticed. Then... she was out.

A blinding sheet of light slammed into her face, and she flinched hard, her whole body curling in on itself as her eyes burned. After days in the claustrophobic dark, the sudden explosion of sunlight was unbearable. She gasped, shielding her face with trembling hands.

The heat was like a living thing. It clawed at her, pressed into her skin, filled her lungs with thick, suffocating air. Even with her eyes squeezed shut, the brightness scorched through her eyelids, and when she blinked she saw red and white flashing lights. She turned her head, tried to force her eyes completely open, but it was impossible.

She waited, breathing through it, until she could finally squint through her lashes.

Everything shimmered under the glare of the afternoon sun, the light bouncing off pale, dust-covered stone. Her vision sharpened slowly, bringing the surroundings into focus —steep rock walls on all sides, like a giant bowl carved into the earth. Rubble littered the ground, broken stone blocks and old machinery parts half-swallowed by dust. It was a quarry. Not the kind of place you stumbled across by accident.

She shifted, forcing herself upright. Pain lanced through her spine and down her legs, every muscle stiff, her skin scraped raw in places. Her knees buckled, and she grabbed the edge of the broken cabin wall behind her, steadying herself as the world lurched again.

She didn't know where she was.

That was the first thing that hit her—that sickening, hollow truth. She had no idea how far she'd been taken; no clue of what direction. But someone had brought her here. Someone had driven.

She looked down at the dusty ground. A dirt track curled up one side of the quarry, with tyre marks faint but visible, baked into the earth. She stared at them, heart thudding. A road meant a vehicle. A vehicle meant whoever brought her could still be nearby.

Her gut twisted.

She didn't trust the track. It was too open, too exposed. If someone was watching, waiting, she'd be a clear target. Her eyes swept the quarry edge again, slower this time. And then she saw it: a narrow footpath, barely more than a thread in the brush, winding between slabs of broken rock and climbing through the undergrowth in the direction of the ridge. Another way out.

Without thinking, she turned towards it.

Her head pounded. Everything before waking in that suffocating wooden box was a blur. She remembered James. She remembered the plan to go to Andalusia. She remembered packing. Then—nothing.

She swallowed. Her throat resembled sandpaper, her tongue thick and dry.

Water.

She needed water.

She forced one foot in front of the other, moving stiffly along the crude footpath. Each step sent pain up through her bare feet, her heels scraped raw, her ankles swollen. She hadn't eaten in—how long? Three days? Four? Maybe more. Her stomach cramped at the thought, but the thirst was worse. It made her dizzy, made her limbs feel weak and disconnected.

Finally, she reached a wire fence, rusted and sagging. It looked poorly maintained. She ran her hands along it until she found a gap where the wire had come loose and curled outward, just wide enough to squeeze through. A few more minutes and she reached what she considered was civilisation.

The road curved, and she stumbled down the incline, catching herself just before she hit the dirt. Her breath hitched, and she paused, pressing a hand against her ribs. Then movement on the hillside caught her attention. She spotted tiny houses dotted along the ridge, nestled into the landscape, half-hidden behind trees. Some were whitewashed with terracotta roofs, others a pale sandstone blending into the dry earth.

Was she near the finca? Near James?

But what if…?

Should she knock on someone's door, plead for help? But she hesitated, looking down at herself. She stank. Sweat, filth, something worse. Her vest was little more than a tattered rag, her shorts stained with dirt, her legs streaked with blood from the splinters in her knees.

She couldn't approach anyone looking like that, smelling so bad. She needed to clean herself up first.

Her eyes scanned the road ahead, searching for anything, anywhere, she could find water.

Then she saw them.

A set of bins sat just off the road, half-hidden behind a small outcrop of rock. Large, green plastic containers, their lids pushed open. A horrible thought struck her, but she shoved the shame down. She had no choice.

She stumbled towards them, her stomach twisting at the rancid smell of rotting food, the sickly-sweet stench of decay. Flies buzzed in thick clouds, darting around her face. She gagged but forced herself to keep going.

The first bin was overflowing with household waste— black bags split open, spilling fruit rinds, crushed tins, scraps of meat already crawling with insects. The second was packed with dry, crumpled cardboard, paper, and plastic.

Plastic.

She reached in, wincing as something slimy brushed her wrist, and fumbled blindly until her fingers closed around the smooth shape of a bottle.

It was clear.

She pulled it out, turning it in the sunlight. A water bottle, half-crushed, but with a tiny trickle of liquid left inside.

She didn't think. She tipped it to her lips and shook it, desperate for even a drop. It hit her tongue, stale and plastic-tasting, but it was water. Swallowing, she wiped her mouth and then dug deeper.

Another. This one barely had anything in it. She shook it, let the last few drops spill into her mouth. It wasn't enough. She knew it wasn't safe—God; she knew it—but her body didn't care. She found a third bottle, this one with slightly more left in the bottom, and drained it too.

Her stomach clenched at the sudden intake, and for a second, she thought she might throw it up. But she forced herself to breathe through it.

And then she heard it. A low hum, growing steadily louder. A car.

She spun, her breath catching as a dark shape appeared on the winding road in the distance. A vehicle, moving fast, kicking up dust behind it.

Her heart pounded.

This was it.

She staggered forward, forcing her weak limbs into action. The car was getting closer. A blue hatchback. She lifted both arms and waved frantically, her whole body shaking.

"Help!"

The word tore from her throat, barely more than a croak. She tried again.

"Help me!"

The car didn't appear to be slowing down, so she moved farther into the road, forcing herself into its path, waving wildly. The driver couldn't ignore her.

She stood her ground as the vehicle sped towards her, the sun flashing off its windshield—until, finally, it began to slow.

38

HIM

I STEPPED out of the bar and straight into the blinding midday sun. It hit me like a hammer, making me squint, my head pounding harder than before. The air was thick, heavy with the scent of fried food and exhaust fumes, and the heat clung to me like a second skin.

I had no idea where I was going, so I just walked.

The town was slow at that time of day. Most of the shops were quiet, and a few people lingered under awnings, fanning themselves as they pretended to window shop. The distant whine of a scooter echoed through the narrow streets, and somewhere, a dog barked loudly.

I moved as if I was underwater, every step heavy, my thoughts thick and slow.

Go ask your girlfriend.

Fabián's words rattled around in my skull.

What the fuck did he mean by that? And why did I feel like I was missing something, like there was a whole part of the town's story that I wasn't privy to?

I passed the same café twice without realising, looping through the same streets, lost in my own head. I barely noticed the sweat pooling at the small of my back, the way my shirt clung to me, the way the world just passed me by.

Eventually, I found myself standing next to my car. I didn't even remember walking there. Without thinking, I got in and turned the key.

Then I drove to Carmen's.

The bar was quiet again, a handful of customers hunched over their drinks. Carmen glanced up as I walked in, but didn't look surprised. She didn't even ask what I wanted; she was already pulling a beer for me.

"Been talking to your friend again?" she asked.

I hesitated. "How do you know that?"

She gave a small nod towards the far corner of the bar. "He was in earlier."

My stomach lurched. How the hell had he got there so fast? Had I really spent that long wandering aimlessly around town? I checked my watch. Two hours since I left Fabián.

"He had to drive up into the mountains to see a friend. He'll be back later." Without waiting for a reply, she slid the beer to me. "Drink up. I'll follow you back."

I didn't argue.

The drive back was slow as I approached the winding dirt road leading to the finca. The landscape stretched out on either side, golden and endless under the afternoon sun. Then, up ahead, a car. It was approaching me fast. A blue hatchback, speeding, its tyres spitting up dust.

I instinctively flashed my lights and honked my horn. Just

before he passed me, the driver stuck his hand out of the open window and gave me the finger.

Twat, I thought, but did I recognise him? He'd driven by so quickly, his face had been a blur, but…

Then he was gone, disappearing behind me in a cloud of dust. I frowned, gripping the wheel tighter.

Carmen pulled in behind me at the finca and cut the engine. She barely had one foot out of the car before I turned on her. "What the hell is going on in this place?" I demanded.

Carmen sighed, pushing past me into the house. "James, not this again."

"No." I followed her inside. "What did Fabián mean when he said, 'go ask your girlfriend'?"

She let out a breath, shaking her head as she made her way to the kitchen. "It's just gossip. You should know what people are like around here, too much time on their hands."

I didn't buy it. "There was a missing woman," I pressed. "A year ago. Fabián said something about English women coming and going…"

Carmen rolled her eyes, opening the fridge. "James." She pulled out two beers, popped the cap off one, and handed it to me. "People talk shit. Ignore them."

I took the bottle automatically, lifting it to my lips. The cold liquid burned down my throat, and before I'd even finished, she passed me another. But I took it without a quibble. I needed it.

I rubbed a hand over my face. "They found blood on my wall."

Carmen finally looked at me properly, and for a moment, there was silence. Then, carefully, she said, "Is it Laura's?"

I didn't even hesitate. "No. It can't be."

She studied me for a second longer, then gave a small shrug. "Then what are you so afraid of?"

I let out a short, humourless laugh. "Because it obviously belongs to someone."

Carmen moved closer. Her hand brushed against my face, her fingertips ghosting over my jaw.

I stepped back.

"Carmen."

She tilted her head slightly. "James, you're exhausted."

I wanted to argue, but I was too fucking tired. She took the beer bottle from my hand and placed it on the table. I should have stopped her. I should have walked away.

My head swam. My body felt too warm, too heavy. The beer had settled deep in my stomach, seeping into my limbs, making me slow.

Carmen stepped even closer, her hands finding my face again. This time, I didn't pull away.

"You need to let go," she murmured.

I was shaking. I didn't even realise it until she pressed her body against mine, stilling me. Squeezing my eyes shut, I could feel her breath against my skin, the warmth of her, the way her fingers traced along my jawline.

I told myself I wouldn't. But the truth was, I was already lost. And then I was kissing her. Or maybe she was kissing me. I didn't know who started it, only that I couldn't stop.

Her hands slid down my chest, pulling at my shirt, guiding me backward.

The bedroom door was open, then closed.

I fought it. With everything I had left, I tried to fight it. But it was futile.

The beer had made me slow. My thoughts were muddled, my body too warm, too weak. And Carmen was everywhere. Her hands, her lips, her breath against my neck.

I wanted to stop.

But I didn't.

Because for the first time in days, I didn't feel like I was drowning.

And for the first time since I could remember, I felt truly wanted.

39

HER

THE SECOND she climbed into the passenger seat, she regretted it. Despite the smell emanating from herself, the stench hit her like a punch—stale alcohol, sweat, something sour lurking beneath it all. A half-empty whisky bottle rolled at her feet, clinking softly against the dusty rubber mats. She hesitated before pulling the door shut, thinking maybe she should have got into the back seat instead, but there was no point. The car was a mess, and so was she.

She stole a glance at the driver, her heart pounding. He was older, maybe late fifties, with a wild, sun-bleached beard that swallowed the lower half of his face. His long, greasy hair curled around his ears, unkempt and tangled, as if it hadn't seen a comb in years. His skin was dark and weathered, deeply lined from too many years under the Andalusian sun. A scruffy, faded T-shirt clung to his frame, stained dark under the armpits, and his baggy shorts were smeared with something she didn't want to identify.

The man grinned, showing off yellowed, crooked teeth.

"What's your name?"

She hesitated. "I got lost," she said instead, her voice hoarse. "I was out walking and fell. Trapped my leg." She gestured vaguely to her filthy clothes, her scraped legs. "Took me days to get free."

The lie came easily. She hated how pitiful she must look. She had always taken pride in her appearance, in being well put together. Now she was a wreck, a complete stranger to herself.

The man said nothing, just slammed the car into gear and took off, the sudden acceleration pinning her against the seat. She barely had time to react before the vehicle lurched over the rough road, kicking up a thick plume of dust in the side mirror.

"Do you have any water?" she asked.

He shot her a sidelong glance, then reached blindly into the back seat. Her stomach clenched. His eyes were scarcely on the road, and they were already flying across the uneven terrain, bumping and jostling hard enough to rattle her bones. She almost told him to forget it, but then he produced a battered plastic bottle, the label long since worn away.

She took it with a mumbled thanks, half thinking what the fuck was in it? But thirst won out over caution, and she unscrewed the cap, tipping it back greedily. The lukewarm liquid spilled down her chin, soaking into her filthy vest top.

The man laughed, watching her instead of the road again.

A horn blasted ahead.

She barely had time to brace before he jerked the wheel violently, swerving back into his lane just as an old estate car drove past.

Jesus Christ. He's a maniac. She hated those twisting mountain roads anyway.

She wiped her mouth, gripping the door handle. "Where are we?" she asked, her voice tight.

He flicked another glance at her, then back to the road. "Coming into town now."

She sat up straighter, heart hammering. Through the grimy windshield, she saw the first buildings of a small town, low, whitewashed houses with terracotta roofs, the kind that blended into the Andalusian landscape.

They rolled past a bar, two occupied tables outside. People sat drinking beer or coffee, chatting in the shade of a faded red awning, making her stomach clench.

She knew the place. Her gaze flicked to the sun-bleached sign above the door.

Carmen's Bar.

Her breath caught. Fuck. Fuck, fuck, fuck.

This wasn't just any town. This was *the* town. The one they were meant to be staying in. Whoever had taken her to the quarry hadn't taken her far after all.

Her pulse raced. "Where are we going?" she asked sharply.

The man grinned again, that same, yellow-toothed smirk. A fresh wave of whisky-breath washed over her.

"Back to my place," he said. "You can at least shower."

Minutes later, they pulled up outside a house that looked like it was rotting from the inside out. The plaster was cracked, peeling away in long curls to reveal the brick beneath. The shutters on the windows hung at odd angles, some barely clinging to their rusted hinges. Filthy net curtains sagged behind the glass, yellowed with time.

The place reeked of abandonment, yet clearly, it wasn't.

She hesitated before stepping out of the car, but the driver was already making his way to the front door. He didn't unlock it. Just shoved it open with his shoulder.

She swallowed hard. Who the hell would bother breaking in anyway?

Inside was somehow worse than outside.

The whole place was a single open-plan room, with a kitchen crammed into one corner. If you could even call it that. A scratched-up counter held a rusted sink and an old, yellowing stove. A fly buzzed around a plate of stale bread, and something in the bin smelled rancid.

Two doors led off from the main space. Both were open.

One revealed a bedroom, if you could call it a bedroom. A sagging mattress, no frame, covered in crumpled, stained sheets. A battered wooden chair stood in the corner, draped with what looked like old clothes.

The other door led to a bathroom. She didn't even want to look inside.

"You can sleep on the couch," he said.

"I don't need to stay," she replied. "I just need a little money to get by."

He laughed—a dry, bitter sound—and said, "Money? You think I have money?" He shook his head, gesturing around at the crumbling walls and battered furniture. "No," he insisted. "I think it's best if you stay here tonight."

She hesitated before saying thank you. She didn't complain. She was exhausted, and at least it was a roof over her head. The place was disgusting, but after a good night's sleep, she could move on and find James.

He nodded. "I'll make you a sandwich. You look famished."

"Thanks," she repeated.

As she pulled out a chair at the table, he turned and smiled.

"Oh," he said. "My name's Fabián. Fabián Vargas."

PART VI

DAY SIX

40

HIM

THE FIRST THING I felt was warmth. Soft skin pressed against mine, the heat of another body tangled up with me in the sheets. For a moment, I was floating between sleep and waking, a weightless, dreamlike state where nothing mattered. Then the reality came crashing in.

Carmen.

I inhaled sharply, my muscles tensing as she moved against me, slow, unhurried, like she had all the time in the world. My mind was screaming at me to stop before it started again, but my body had other ideas.

"Carmen," I rasped, my voice rough with sleep.

"Hmm?" She didn't stop.

I swallowed hard, trying to sit up, but she pushed me back down effortlessly.

"This—" I started, but she cut me off with her mouth on my neck, her teeth grazing lightly against my skin. I exhaled sharply, my hands clenching into fists. "We shouldn't," I tried again. But my hands had already betrayed me, gripping her hips, pulling her against me.

She smiled next to my skin. "You sure about that?"

I wasn't.

And we both knew it.

Standing perfectly still under the shower, I let the hot water run over me, my palms pressed against the tiles. My head was clearer now, but the guilt was heavier.

Six days. Laura had been gone for six days, and the night before, I had buried my grief in Carmen's body. And again that morning. I squeezed my eyes shut. What the hell was wrong with me?

The water did little to wash away the weight pressing down on my chest. No amount of scrubbing could erase the fact that I had been unfaithful. That instead of searching for Laura, I'd let myself fall into bed with another woman. And not just any woman. Carmen.

There was something about her—something intoxicating, impossible to resist. She had slipped so effortlessly into my life, into my home, into my bed; she hypnotised me whenever I was in her presence. I'd been there before, and she knew it.

I turned off the shower and stepped out, grabbing a towel. The scent of coffee and toasted bread drifted through the open door, pulling me back to reality.

She was outside when I found her, sitting on the patio, barefoot, wearing nothing but one of my T-shirts. It was too big on her, falling just past her upper thighs, but somehow, that made it worse.

The morning light caught the curve of her tanned legs, the bare skin where the fabric ended. She sat with one knee drawn up, her coffee cup cradled in both hands, the picture of lazy, effortless sensuality.

I hesitated in the doorway, towel slung around my waist. Why hadn't I dressed? She looked up, eyes raking over me slowly, the ghost of a smile on her lips. "Coffee?"

I forced my feet to move, stepping out onto the patio, taking the cup she offered. My fingers brushed hers, and I ignored the way it sent a pulse through me. Instead, I took a long sip, letting the bitterness ground me. "We need to talk," I said finally.

Carmen leant back in her chair, stretching like a cat, utterly unbothered. "About what?"

I gestured between us. "This."

Her lips twitched, but she didn't speak.

I pushed on. "It was a mistake."

She arched a brow. "Was it?"

"Yes." I set the coffee down, rubbing a hand over my face. "However much I'm—" I caught myself, shaking my head. "Attracted to you, this shouldn't have happened."

Carmen didn't look remotely convinced. "We'll see," she said lightly, taking another sip of coffee.

"Carmen."

"Give it time, James."

I exhaled slowly. "So, you're certain Laura isn't coming back?"

The moment stretched between us. She didn't answer. And that silence told me everything I needed to know.

I paced to the edge of the patio, staring out at the dry landscape. The heat was already building, the cicadas humming in the distance. Behind me, I heard Carmen shift in her chair, and I turned to face her.

"What do you want from me?" I asked.

She tilted her head slightly. "What do you mean?"

"This." I gestured towards her, towards us. "Is this just…" I trailed off, searching for the right words. Taking advantage of my vulnerability sounded too pathetic. A distraction didn't seem right, either. Maybe she was just lonely. Maybe she'd seen an opportunity and taken it.

Carmen didn't answer right away. She just smiled, standing up and crossing to me. Her fingers trailed lightly over my chest before she leant in and kissed my cheek.

Then she whispered, "You think too much."

And just like that, she stepped back inside.

I watched the dust settle long after her SUV had disappeared down the track. I should have felt relieved, but instead, my mind wouldn't stop racing.

Something didn't sit right.

I turned back to the house, trying to shake the feeling off, but the thoughts kept coming.

Her dismissiveness about the blood on the wall.

The way she'd shown up that first day.

I frowned, stepping inside, running a hand through my damp hair.

Something about that first day…

I forced myself to go back through it, piece by piece.

Arriving at the bar.

Carmen behind the counter, but we barely spoke. I just confirmed I was waiting for someone to take us to the finca and then sat in the corner, facing the door, awaiting Miguel.

But then I returned after my argument with Laura. I had sat outside, nursing two, maybe three beers, letting the heat and alcohol sink into my bones.

Carmen had come out once or twice, collecting empty glasses, taking fresh orders, but she never stopped to talk. In fact, I hadn't spoken to anyone. I hadn't told anyone where I was staying.

And yet, later that day, she had shown up at my finca. Checking on me. Making sure I'd got back safely.

I stood there, the realisation tightening around my chest like a slow-moving vice.

If I hadn't told her where I was staying, then how the hell had she known where to find me?

41

SANTOS

THE ROAD STRETCHED ENDLESSLY AHEAD, a ribbon of asphalt cutting through the barren Spanish landscape. Isabel Santos gripped the steering wheel, her fingers aching she'd been clenching it so tightly. The E-902 was long, dull, and unforgiving—just like the case. Five hours to Madrid. Five hours to sit with nothing but her own thoughts.

And yet, she still wasn't certain if she was wasting her time.

She could have called again, but Rebecca would only hang up. And Chen still wasn't picking up at all.

Santos had known it was Rebecca the moment she answered. The weak attempt at disguising her voice had been pointless. Those soft English vowels had slipped through, those slight hesitations between words. Rebecca had been nervous, rattled. And scared people made mistakes.

Santos had recognised that fear immediately.

But what had she been about to say?

"Detective, I have some information you may want to hear," she'd begun, voice trembling on the edges. And then—nothing. The moment Santos pushed, Rebecca clammed up.

So who, or what, made her change her mind?

James? Doctor Chen? Laura, even?

The answer had to be in Madrid. It's why Santos had woken at four in the morning, to get most of the drive out of the way before the unrelenting heat kicked in.

She flexed her fingers on the steering wheel, shifting in her seat. Her lower back was already starting to stiffen from the drive, but she ignored the discomfort. She was used to it. She was used to a lot of things.

Such as waiting.

Such as having no goddamn answers.

She'd been informed that the blood results from the finca wall could take up to forty-eight hours, and even then, it might all be for nothing. The techs had already warned her— the sample wasn't clean. It was already degraded, and they had no idea how old it was. And without Laura's blood to compare, there were no guarantees.

Futile, they'd said. Maybe even pointless. But Santos didn't believe in pointless.

She had to work with what she had, and right then, that wasn't much.

James Blackwood had told her nothing of use. Miguel had vanished off the face of the earth. And as for Doctor Sarah Chen? Santos had left messages, sent emails, even called from an unregistered number. Nothing. Not a damn thing since that call when she heard the ambulance in the background. Why had Chen hung up so damn quickly?

She pushed the thought away, focusing on the road instead. There was still one other thread she hadn't pulled yet; one she had deliberately kept from James.

The other missing woman.

The one from just over a year ago.

It had been a quiet case, barely making the local news.

An English woman, Emma Carter, had checked into a small hostel in the town. The kind of place that catered to travellers who wanted to disappear for a while. No questions, no paperwork.

Two days later, she was gone.

The hostel manager had said she was hanging out until the person showed up who she was waiting for. He reported her missing forty-eight hours later, after noticing her room was untouched. The bed hadn't been slept in, nothing had been taken. The only thing missing was Emma herself.

She had told one of the other guests she was going for a walk but hadn't said where. And that had been the problem. Nobody knew which direction she had gone.

There were dozens of hiking trails leading out of the town. The terrain was rough and unpredictable. She could have been anywhere. The search had lasted a month. But nothing. No sign of her, no body, no trace.

Eventually, the Guardia Civil had written it off.

She must have fallen somewhere in the mountains, they had concluded. Slipped, hit her head, been taken by the elements.

End of case.

Santos hadn't believed it then, and she sure as hell didn't believe it now.

And what made it worse?

Emma Carter had no family. No one pressing to keep looking. No one demanding answers.

No one even knew if 'Emma Carter' had been her real name.

No passport had been found, no ID. Just a name written on a check-in form.

Like a fucking ghost, Santos thought.

And now Laura was gone too.

Santos felt the hair on the back of her neck prickle.

Two English women.

Both vanishing from the same town.

She'd put it down to coincidence. There were no similarities, apart from them both being English and female. But one was a recluse, a solo traveller who just happened to stay in the same town, while the other was a successful professional. A trauma specialist, and highly regarded at that. Laura was affluent, well-travelled.

Her frustrations made Santos press harder on the accelerator.

Maybe she should have told James about Emma Carter.

But she hadn't wanted to hand him an excuse. He was a smart man, clever enough to use the information to his advantage. If he was guilty, he'd spin it. If he wasn't, she didn't want to send him into a panic.

Either way, she knew the town would talk soon enough.

Some old woman in the square would mention it. Some bar regular would whisper it over a drink.

And James Blackwood would find out.

The sudden thought made her stomach twist.

Santos braked hard, veering into a lay-by. The car skidded slightly before coming to a halt.

Dust curled around her, the heat pressing through the windshield, but she barely noticed. The roads were deserted, an endless stretch ahead of her.

Reaching into the back seat, she grabbed a folder, flipping through the pages with quick, practised hands.

There.

The case file from last year.

She scanned the pages, barely blinking.

And then she found it. The last known photograph of Emma Carter, taken the day she arrived at the hostel.

Santos felt a sharp, cold wave wash over her as she realised what she'd missed from the day James Blackwood told her.

Emma Carter was wearing a blue blouse.

42

———

HIM

I KNEW I had to go back to the bar.

I had to get Carmen alone, press her, figure out how the hell she knew where I was staying that first night. The question began to gnaw at me like a parasite, burrowing deeper into my skull, whispering possibilities I didn't want to consider.

She must have followed me. Or someone had told her. But who?

There was only one way to find out.

I turned back towards the finca, already planning where I was going and what I'd say to her when I got there. The house was warm as I walked through the hallway, past the empty kitchen, to my bedroom. The bed was still unmade from the morning, sheets twisted, an empty glass on the nightstand. I removed the towel, tossing it onto a chair, and pulled open the wardrobe.

And that's when I heard it.

Soft at first. Barely audible over the whisper of the ceiling fan.

Singing.

I froze, my fingers gripping the wardrobe door.

The same tune as before.

That same lilting, breathy child's voice, humming a melody I didn't recognise.

I stepped back, my pulse picking up speed, as I moved to the window. Pushing it open, the sultry morning air flowed in, carrying the scents of dry grass, dust, and something akin to distant smoke. But the singing wasn't coming from outside my window. It was somewhere in the garden.

I grabbed a shirt, pulling it on quickly, my fingers fumbling with the buttons. Then I found some underwear and a pair of clean shorts. Stepping out of the bedroom, I made my way through the quiet house towards the terrace doors.

The song continued. Soft. Mocking.

I stepped outside. The singing was ahead of me now. I followed it past the pool, my heart thudding against my ribs. But it didn't appear to be getting any closer. It stayed just ahead, like it was leading me somewhere.

I walked farther, down the narrow stone path to the back of the property. The long garden stretched out beyond the house, bordered by crumbling walls and clusters of wild olive trees. The song drifted on the air, just out of reach. It was definitely a child's voice. Clear. Unmistakable.

The farther I walked, the more I realised I had never been that way before. The garden seemed endless, but this time, I reached a different exit; the land dipping into a clearing, and beyond it, something else. Something I hadn't noticed before. Another footpath. Not one I'd previously taken. Not one I'd ever seen. And then, just like that, the singing stopped.

A sudden silence pressed against my ears, thick and unnatural.

And I saw him. Standing in the path ahead. The boy.

She screamed…

His arms hung loosely by his sides, his dark eyes locked onto me. He didn't move. He didn't speak. Just stood there, staring.

A cold, sick feeling crept through me. Swallowing, I forced my voice to stay steady. "Hello?"

Nothing.

The boy didn't even blink.

I took a hesitant step forward. I'd wanted to get him on his own, but as he stood before me, I only wanted to turn and run. "What's your name?" I forced.

Still nothing.

The longer he stared, the worse it got. The silence was unbearable, stretching too long. A slow, hot irritation began to claw its way up my spine.

"Look," I said, my voice sharper. "If this is some kind of joke—"

Still no reaction. Just that blank, unreadable face.

I exhaled, shaking my head, turning to leave. Then the boy spoke.

"I know the man who brought you to your house."

I stopped dead. Miguel.

The words hung between us, and slowly, I turned to face him. My mouth was dry. "What did you say?"

The boy just watched me.

I took a step towards him, heart pounding. "How do you know him?"

He didn't answer.

His small face was expressionless, his eyes unreadable.

A wave of frustration swelled in my chest. "Who is he?" I demanded. "Tell me."

The boy shifted slightly but said nothing.

I exhaled sharply, my jaw tightening. "I don't have time for this."

I turned again, ready to walk away, ready to leave the unsettling little bastard behind. But then, softly, he spoke again.

"His name is Miguel. Miguel Ruiz."

Something cold and sharp coiled in my stomach. He did know him. He knew his surname too. I turned back. "What?"

He lifted his chin slightly. "He lives on the other side of the town."

The way he said it, so calm, so deliberate, made the back of my neck prickle. I narrowed my eyes. "Can you show me?"

He shook his head. "My parents wouldn't let me."

I almost laughed. Of course they wouldn't. "Please tell me," I said. "You can use my pool whenever you want."

He looked at me as if I was crazy. "I don't want to use your pool."

"But the other day, you went for a swim. It doesn't matter, I don't—"

He tilted his head, stopping me mid-sentence. "I've never used your pool. It isn't mine. Why would I?"

He meant it. I could detect his childhood innocence. So who the fuck had been in my pool? "Okay. But you can if you want." I paused, ensuring I had his attention once more. "Can you tell me where Miguel Ruiz lives, please?"

Then, carefully, he began to describe the way. Road by road. Turn by turn. I listened intently, my breath slow, steady. I knew the way he was talking about. I had walked that way the day before. My pulse picked up.

"Which house is it?" I asked.

The boy smiled slightly. "A white house."

I let out a breath, shaking my head. "Every fucking house is white."

His smile widened. "You shouldn't swear," he said, and I

couldn't help but smile slightly. "But the man's house is the only one with yellow shutters."

Yellow shutters.

I didn't move in case there was more.

Then the boy giggled—an odd, breathy sound—and turned, sprinting back down the path, vanishing into thin air. Gone.

I stood there for a long moment, my thoughts tangled, my skin cold despite the heat. I never did ask him what I'd wanted to ask. About his house. If he'd found anything. But I now had something to go on.

Yellow shutters.

The only house with yellow shutters.

For my own sanity, I had to find Miguel Ruiz.

43

SANTOS

THE DRIVE to Madrid felt longer than it should have; the endless stretch of highway, the dry warmth rising off the asphalt, the radio crackling in and out of static was driving her crazy. But it wasn't the road that occupied Santos' mind; it was the damn blue blouse.

Emma Carter had worn a blue blouse in the photo and James was adamant he'd seen a blue blouse on the Dutch family's washing line. But when she went to check, it was gone. Not in the laundry basket, either. James had also said Laura was wearing a blue blouse the day she disappeared.

Coincidence?

It didn't sit right.

James wouldn't know about Emma Carter. He had no reason to. Was he even living in Spain when Emma turned up in the town?

Fuck.

What the hell was going on? She needed to look into James Blackwood's background a bit more. She knew little about him, apart from his flashes of anger and, at times, lack of empathy for his missing wife.

The closer Santos got to Madrid, the heavier the traffic became. She followed the satnav into the southern suburbs, weaving between cars, her focus split between the road and her thoughts. She needed to find Laura Blackwood. Her boss was on her back, and she was certain the rest of the crew were smirking as every day passed by without development.

She concentrated on the roads and satnav again. The heat shimmered off the tarmac, thick and oppressive, making the city feel even more suffocating than usual. Madrid was fucking chaos.

The mid-morning rush clogged the roads, motorbikes zipping between lanes, taxis cutting in without warning, buses lumbering at a crawl. She inched forward, her car's air conditioning barely keeping up with the sun beating down on the windscreen.

Eventually, she reached her destination. The clinic.

It was smaller than she expected—an understated two-storey building, wedged between a pharmacy and an empty lot. White-painted stucco, a set of narrow windows running along the front, a metal security shutter rolled up over the glass entrance door. No sign outside, nothing to advertise what it was.

She parked a little way down the street and stepped out into the heat.

Madrid was unbearable. The pavement radiated warmth, the air thick and dry. Sweat gathered at the back of her neck almost instantly as she walked towards the building, half-expecting to find it locked. Maybe a sign taped to the door.

Out of office. Call for appointments.

The five-hour drive could be a fucking waste of time.

But there was no sign. And when she pressed the handle, the door pushed open.

A chill ran through her. She hesitated. Who might be inside? She hadn't thought it through and wished she had brought Álvarez after all. Taking a deep breath, she entered.

The reception was stark. White walls, white-tiled floor, clinical and cold like a hospital. It smelled faintly of antiseptic and something else, something chemical; fresh paint or bleach.

Behind the desk sat a woman. She was petite. Mid-thirties. Brown hair tucked neatly behind her ears. She looked up as Santos entered, blinking quickly, her hands still resting on the keyboard in front of her.

It was Rebecca.

Santos knew it immediately.

"Can I help you?" the woman asked, her voice polite but thin, as if it might crack at any second.

Santos gave her a slow smile. "Yes, Rebecca. I'm Detective Santos."

Rebecca flinched. A sharp, involuntary movement, like a rabbit ready to bolt. But there was nowhere to run. Santos watched her carefully. "Is Doctor Chen in?"

Rebecca hesitated. Just a fraction too long. "No," she fumbled. "She… she's not here."

Santos didn't buy it. "Where is she?"

"I'm not sure, honest."

This time, Santos believed her.

Rebecca was a nervous wreck. Exactly what Santos expected and exactly how she wanted her. She softened her expression just a little, making herself seem less threatening. Then she leant against the desk, watching the woman squirm. "Tell me everything you know, Rebecca."

Rebecca swallowed.

It took a moment. A long, painful moment. But then the words started coming. And once they started, they didn't stop.

"I-I don't know what's going on," Rebecca admitted. "I

mean, I do, but I don't. There's so much I'm not told. So much I don't want to know."

Santos said nothing, letting the silence stretch. Waiting for Rebecca to fill it.

"I don't even know if you're looking in the right places," Rebecca continued. "There's nothing here. But I assume this is about Laura?"

Santos' pulse ticked up. "You know where she is?"

Rebecca shook her head quickly. "No. But… have you found her?"

Santos hesitated. Then said, "No. But do you know why she was in Andalusia? Was it just a vacation?"

Rebecca bit her lip, glancing at the closed office door behind her. "There's a safe house there," she admitted. "Somewhere they send the most vulnerable patients. If they're discovered after they arrive in Madrid, if they're at risk… we move them."

We.

That didn't slip past Santos.

"We?" she asked.

Rebecca hesitated. Then nodded. "Doctor Chen and Laura run it. The women here… they're escaping things. Domestic abuse, trafficking. Dangerous situations back in the UK."

Santos absorbed this.

"Did they send Emma Carter there? About a year—"

Rebecca's face gave her the answer without needing to speak.

"And Laura?" Santos asked. "When did she arrive in Madrid?"

"She came over to look after Megan."

Santos narrowed her eyes.

Rebecca had mentioned Megan Walsh before.

Santos made a mental note but dismissed it as conjecture.

"Go on," she said. "You told me before that Megan Walsh was under Doctor Chen's care."

"Yes, as I said on the phone, Doctor Chen had to go back to England to look after her sick mum. Megan was passed to Laura."

Santos kept her expression unreadable.

"You have to understand," Rebecca continued. "It wasn't an easy decision for Doctor Chen. Not just leaving Megan but leaving Spain. She had built the practice from scratch just three years earlier, pouring her heart and soul into it. It wasn't just her livelihood, it was her pride and joy. The idea of leaving it, even temporarily, kind of devastated her. She had barely taken a day off in all that time. She would do anything to protect its reputation, no matter what." Rebecca inhaled slowly. "And when she returned from England, that's when things changed."

Santos leant in. "Changed how?"

Rebecca exhaled sharply. "Laura became… protective. Super protective of Megan. Like she was her own child."

That sent a ripple of unease through Santos.

She nodded for Rebecca to continue.

"Megan was supposed to go to Andalusia too," Rebecca said. "That was the plan."

"But?"

Rebecca looked down at her hands. "She took her own life."

A beat of silence.

Santos let it settle.

"Laura took it real bad," Rebecca added, her voice quieter now. "She was the one who found her."

Santos absorbed that, filing it away, turning it over in her mind.

"But there's another thing," Rebecca said.

Santos straightened slightly.

"Go on."

Rebecca swallowed, glancing towards the door again before lowering her voice. "The women we've sent to Andalusia," she said carefully. "They all had money."

A slow, creeping chill worked its way through Santos' spine. "How much money?" she asked.

Rebecca held her gaze.

"A lot."

44

————

HIM

I FOUND MY SHOES, grabbed my car keys, and left the finca without hesitation. Miguel Ruiz. Finally, I'd found him!

The Dutch boy's words still echoed in my head. He had sounded so sure, as if he knew something I didn't. As if he had been waiting for me to ask.

He still gave me the fucking creeps, mind.

The air was thick with heat as I drove along the winding dirt road in the direction of town. The dust, fine as ash, kicked up behind my car. My windshield was coated in a thin film. I should have been thinking about Laura, about what the hell I was going to do next, but instead, my mind kept drifting back to Carmen.

As I neared her bar, I knew I should have stopped. I had questions. How on earth had she known where I was staying that first day? And what did she actually want from me?

But it wasn't all one-sided, was it? It takes two to play that game.

I could have told her to leave. Could have resisted. I was

supposed to be frantic about my missing wife. So why the hell had I given in to her? And why didn't I feel a hell of a lot more guilty?

The thought sat heavy in my stomach as I passed her bar without slowing down. The wooden shutters were pulled open, and a couple of locals were drinking coffee at the outside tables, smoking. She was in there. Maybe even watching me drive by.

The market square was near-empty, just a few cars, and I pulled into a space near the church and cut the engine.

The town was quiet. The air smelled of warm stone, baked bread, and the faint tang of exhaust fumes. I stepped out of the car, the sun beating down on my shoulders, and started walking.

The route was familiar. I had walked the same way barely twenty-four hours earlier, searching for something, anything, that might make sense of Laura's disappearance. Now I was searching again. I turned left onto a narrow side street.

The farther I walked, the more the place appeared dead. No cars. No movement. Even the balconies, the type where elderly folk would sit watching the world go by, were empty. The silence stretched around me, thick and unnatural. It was as if the entire town was waiting for me.

I swallowed, my mouth dry.

What if the Dutch kid had set me up?

Lured me there?

I slowed my pace, my head flicking from side to side. My heart was beating a little too fast now, the way it did when you knew something wasn't right, but you kept going anyway.

A dog barked from behind a metal gate. The sharp, frantic sound made me jolt, my pulse slamming into my throat.

"Jesus Christ," I muttered, pressing a hand to my chest, willing my heartbeat to slow down. I shook off the nerves and kept walking. Then, finally, I saw it.

The house with the yellow shutters.

I stopped, standing a few paces away, and took it in. The shutters, once a vivid canary yellow, were faded and coated in a thin layer of dust. The stucco walls were cracked in places, patches of damp peeling away at the base. A single clay pot sat on the doorstep, the plant inside long dead, its withered stems tangled over the rim. But there was no car. No sign of Miguel's battered Land Rover. No movement behind the windows. No sound.

I stepped up to the door and knocked. Hard. Then immediately took a step back.

I waited, ears straining for any sound inside. Nothing. I knocked again, louder this time. Still nothing. I glanced up and down the street. The emptiness unsettled me. Something felt wrong.

Then I spotted a narrow side gate to the right of the house. Hesitating, I tried the latch. It wasn't locked.

Pushing it open, the hinges creaked, the sound amplified in the still air. I stepped through, half-expecting someone to yell at me, but no one did.

The back yard was as lifeless as the front. A small, sun-scorched patch of dirt, littered with a few stray stones. A rusted washing line sagged between two metal poles, completely empty except for a single, stiff-looking towel. A few plastic chairs sat beneath a faded sun umbrella, their surfaces cracked from years of exposure. It was no real attempt at a garden, just a space that was neither cared for nor completely abandoned. Quickly, I moved to the back window and peered inside. Again, no sign of life.

About to give up and turn back, I reached for the door. It opened.

Fuck.

I hesitated, glancing around once more. Then I stepped inside.

The kitchen was small, dimly lit. The air smelled of stale coffee and old bread. The place wasn't messy, but it wasn't particularly clean, either. Just… lived in. Like someone existed here but didn't care much for the details.

I took a slow step forward. On the table, an espresso cup sat beside a plate of crusts, as if someone had eaten in a hurry and left.

I reached out and touched the coffee machine.

Still warm.

Whoever had been there hadn't left long ago.

I turned in a slow circle, scanning the room. My pulse quickened.

"Hello?"

Silence.

Then, on the table, I spotted a note. A scrap of paper, the handwriting scrawled, almost frantically:

Q. 11 AM.

45

———

HIM

THE NOTE MADE no sense to me.

Q. 11 AM.

I turned it over in my hand, as if the back might hold an explanation. It didn't.

I checked my watch—10:30 am. So if Miguel had to be somewhere at eleven, that would explain why the place was deserted and why the coffee was still warm.

Should I wait?

The thought crossed my mind, but then what? Stand around hoping he'd come back? That could take all day. And even if he did return, what was I expecting—a confession? Some dramatic revelation about what happened to Laura?

No.

If Miguel Ruiz knew something, I needed to be smart. Exonerate myself from blame. I should tell Santos, leave it to her. She would question him, get the truth.

I walked back the way I'd come, the street still eerily empty. My footsteps echoed against the uneven stone pavement, the silence swallowing every sound. It unsettled me. Where the hell was everyone?

The market square was still quiet when I reached it. The couple of cars were gone. I climbed into mine and started the engine.

I should've been thinking about my next move. About what I'd do if Miguel really did know something. But instead, my mind drifted back to Carmen.

As I pulled up near her bar, I saw the same handful of locals sitting outside, smoking and talking. I parked a little farther up the road, not wanting to draw attention to myself. Not that it mattered. They were already watching. They all suspected the Englishman whose wife had gone missing from the remote Spanish finca.

I pushed open the heavy wooden door and stepped inside. Carmen was behind the counter, talking to a man in what I guessed was his mid-sixties. Her eyes flicked towards me immediately, and she smiled. That slow, knowing smile.

"Sit," she said, gesturing to a table near the window. "I'll bring us fresh coffee."

I sat, conscious of the eyes that lingered on me from across the room. Everybody thought I had done something to Laura. And then, there I was, alone in a bar, waiting for a woman who wasn't my wife. Did they know she'd stayed over? Of course they fucking did.

Carmen returned a moment later with two cups of coffee. She set them down, then leant forward and kissed me on the cheek.

It was quick. Casual.

But it felt anything but.

I tensed, my gaze flicking around to see who was watching.

"Jesus, Carmen!"

Did she not understand how this looked? Or did she not care?

I shifted in my chair, lowering my voice. "You really think that's a good idea?"

She gave a little shrug, sliding into the seat opposite me. "What, coffee?"

I didn't smile, didn't find her sarcasm funny. But she smirked and took a sip of hers.

I leant in. "It's bad enough you stayed over. But showing affection in public? You don't think that might add to the speculation?"

Her smirk didn't falter. "Speculation about what?"

"Come on," I said, shaking my head. "You know exactly what. People already think I—"

I stopped myself.

Carmen tilted her head, her dark eyes full of amusement. "That you what, James?"

I exhaled, running a hand through my hair. "That I did something to Laura."

Carmen sipped her coffee, as if considering my thoughts. Then she leant back in her chair, her expression unreadable. "And did you?"

I met her gaze. "No."

Her lips parted slightly, as if she might say something, but she just nodded. "Good." Then she took another sip, her eyes never leaving mine. "So, what do you want from me?"

I frowned. "That's what I was going to ask you."

She sighed, setting her cup down. "James, why are you being so awkward about this?"

I let out a humourless laugh. "Awkward? Carmen, my wife has been missing for six days. How the hell do you think this looks?"

She shrugged. "I think it looks like you're attracted to me.

And I think you should stop overthinking everything and go with the flow."

I stared at her.

Go with the flow?

As if it was all normal.

I shook my head, then changed the subject. "Do you think Santos is getting anywhere?"

Carmen sighed, stretching her arms over her head. "I doubt it."

"I don't think so either," I admitted. "By the way, I found out where Miguel Ruiz lives."

That got her attention.

Her entire demeanour shifted. Her fingers froze around the coffee cup, her gaze sharpening. She tried to recover quickly, but I'd already seen it. "How?" she asked, her voice casual.

I took a slow sip of coffee before answering. "The Dutch boy told me."

Carmen went still for a second, then forced a smile. "Have you been to Miguel's?"

"Yes."

"And?"

"He wasn't in."

Carmen exhaled, tapping a fingernail against the side of her cup.

I studied her. "Carmen, this is a small town. Everyone knows everyone, right?"

She said nothing.

"So why didn't you recognise Miguel the day he collected me from here and took us to the finca?"

Carmen's face stiffened. She glanced away, taking a slow breath. Then, finally said, "I lied."

I felt my pulse quicken. "Why?"

She hesitated, rubbing the rim of her cup with her thumb.

Then, in a quieter voice said, "Because I was in front of Santos."

"That's not an answer."

Carmen let out a breath. "James, Miguel knows people. And it wasn't in my interests to be the one to tell Santos I knew who he was."

Something cold settled in my chest. "What kind of people?"

Carmen shook her head, suddenly looking uncomfortable. "It's not that simple."

"No?" I snapped. "My wife is missing. And the guy who drove me to our holiday home 'knows people'," I air-quoted. "You don't think that's relevant?"

I could feel my heart hammering against my ribs, a slow, growing panic rising. "We have to tell Santos," I said firmly. "She needs to know about Miguel."

Carmen's expression didn't change. Then, calmly, she reached for her coffee and took a slow sip. When she set it down, she met my gaze, her voice soft but steady.

"If you tell Santos about Miguel," she said, "then I'll tell her about me and you."

The words hit like a slap. I stared at her. She tilted her head slightly, watching me process what she had just said.

"And not just Santos," she continued. "I'll tell everyone."

I swallowed.

Because that would be it, wouldn't it? The final nail in the coffin.

A missing wife. A local woman sleeping in my bed within days of Laura disappearing. People were already whispering. They already suspected. That would just confirm it.

Carmen sat back in her chair, waiting, a slow, knowing smile playing on her lips.

46

SANTOS

SANTOS GRIPPED the steering wheel tightly as the car hummed along the near-empty stretch of highway, the distant outline of the Andalusian hills finally coming into view.

She had told Rebecca to keep in touch if Chen turned up or contacted her. And also, on the slight chance Laura should reach out. Santos added not to mention anything, just to let her know immediately. But deep down, she didn't think Laura was going to make contact. That ship had sailed. Santos feared that Laura Blackwood was indeed dead. However, she was no closer to knowing why.

The Megan Walsh angle had been gnawing at her for days. So what if Laura had taken Megan under her wing? So what if she and Chen had fallen out over it? That was internal politics. Petty. Not the kind of thing people got killed over.

But then there was Rebecca's revelation—the money.

The women who passed through the safe house in Andalusia had money. Not just enough to get by, not just 'emergency funds'. Real money. A lot of it.

That changed everything.

A pile of cash was a hell of a better motive than a disagreement at work. It was a motive people killed for.

The question was—did James know? Had he lied about how well he knew Sarah Chen? Because Santos remembered his face the first time Chen's name was mentioned. The way James had said it, as if it left a bad taste in his mouth. Something closer to hatred. Had they fallen out? Had Chen done something to him? Or vice versa?

And then there was still the missing Miguel. The man who had allegedly shown James and Laura to their finca. Another inconsistency. Carmen hadn't recognised Miguel the day James was picked up from the town. That was odd. Carmen knew everybody around there.

So, was Miguel an outsider? And if he was, who had hired him to take James and Laura to the finca?

Nothing made sense.

She felt the weight of the case pushing against her skull like a migraine.

Sarah Chen. She needed to speak to her again. But that was easier said than done. The woman wasn't returning her calls. Santos recalled the ambulance along the phone line. Where the hell was she?

Santos sighed, pressing harder on the accelerator, willing the distance to close faster. And then her phone rang. Álvarez.

She put the call on speaker, barely slowing. She didn't bother with pleasantries. "Yes. What have you got?"

"Where are you?" he asked. "The governor is asking me."

Bollocks to the governor.

"I'm on my way back to the town," she said impatiently. "What do you want?"

"I've found something out," Álvarez said.

"Go on."

He hesitated.

"Spit it out," she snapped.

"James Blackwood was fired from his job sixteen months ago," Álvarez said. "He wasn't working remotely in Madrid. The only money coming into the house was Laura's."

Santos frowned.

That changed the dynamics of their relationship. She had assumed, like most people probably had, that they were a standard middle-class couple. That James contributed equally. But if Laura had been the sole breadwinner, that created a different kind of tension. Men like James Blackwood didn't enjoy being dependent on their wives.

Her grip on the steering wheel tightened. "You're sure about this?"

Álvarez sighed, as if annoyed she even doubted him. "Yes. His contract was terminated. Officially, it says 'due to restructuring'. But I spoke to his old boss. He was let go. But when I pressed him, he said it was confidential."

"And he didn't get another job?"

"Not as far as I can see. He's just been living in Madrid. There's no record of employment since. God knows what he's been doing with himself all day."

Santos recalled her first meeting with James again.

"You seem under pressure. Is that fair to say?"

He'd hesitated. *"Who isn't?"* he'd replied defensively. *"Work's been stressful. Budgets are tight. Layoffs are happening. It's been a lot."*

Santos absorbed the information. "And Laura?"

"She makes decent money. Her salary alone could support them both."

"Right." Santos tapped her fingers against the wheel.

James Blackwood.

A man who had been fired. A man living off his wife's income. And then his wife vanishes. A story as old as time. But was it really that simple?

Because there was Chen. And there was Miguel, a man no one seemed to know much about.

Santos exhaled sharply. "Anything else?"

Álvarez hesitated again.

"Álvarez?"

"I'm not sure of the relevance, but something odd happened. Laura withdrew a large sum of cash from their joint account the day before they left for Andalusia."

Santos blinked. "How much?"

"Nine thousand euros."

Nine thousand.

That was a significant amount.

Santos let the thought settle. Nine thousand was an amount that suggested intention. Not just vacation money. Not just a fortnight of spending money.

"Could she have been planning to leave him?" she asked.

"Possibly."

Santos chewed the inside of her cheek.

It was all lining up too well. Laura was supporting James financially. She then withdrew a large sum of money before the trip. And now Laura was gone.

James had a motive. But why did she have the money in the first place?

If she was threatening to leave him, there was no proof. But if something had happened to her…

"Alright," she said. "Keep digging. And tell the governor I'll report in when I have something worth saying."

She ended the call and refocused on the road, her thoughts racing.

James might be guilty. But there were too many players in the game.

Sarah Chen.

Miguel Ruiz.

Emma Carter.

The money in the safe house.

And something else.

Something Santos couldn't quite put her finger on.

But it was there.

Who else could have known Laura had nine thousand euros?

47

HIM

I LEFT Carmen's bar in a daze, the weight of her words pressing against my skull.

"If you go to Santos about Miguel, I'll tell everyone about us."

I just couldn't process it. Was she serious? Carmen, the woman who had spent days luring me in, now threatening me? The same woman who had slipped into my bed uninvited, who kissed me like it was her right? The same woman who, just minutes ago, had turned soft again, apologetic, almost tender.

I'd reached my car, fumbling with my keys, when I heard her voice behind me.

"James, don't leave like this."

I turned, and there she was, standing a little too close, her expression shifting into something unreadable. She wasn't just playing games, there was something else beneath the surface. Fear? Guilt?

I exhaled sharply. "Are you actually scared of Miguel, or are you just blackmailing me?"

Carmen's jaw tightened. "You don't know him."

"Neither do you, apparently."

She hesitated. "James, listen to me. He's bad news. He knows people you don't want to mess with. If you go poking around, you won't like what happens next."

I ran a hand through my hair. "Then tell me how you knew where I was staying that first day. Was it because of Miguel?"

Her eyes flashed, and I caught the slightest hesitation before she answered. "No. I have nothing to do with him."

I wasn't sure I believed her.

"You told me yourself," she added. "When you came back to the bar after your falling out with Laura."

She actually air-quoted it, smirking as she did.

Anger flared in my chest. "You think it's funny?"

Carmen shrugged. "Everybody thinks it was you, James."

I took a step closer, lowering my voice. "And what do you think?"

She didn't answer.

I turned to leave, but before I could open the car door, I felt her hand press against the middle of my back. A warm, deliberate touch. I froze.

"Don't go like this," she murmured. "Come inside. Have another drink."

I turned slightly, and she tilted her chin up, waiting. It would've been so easy to kiss her. My pulse hammered at the thought. But something in me—something raw, something wrong—made me pull away.

Carmen's lips parted in surprise.

"You don't have to fight it," she said softly. "Call me later. I'll come to your finca when nobody's around." She smiled, playful and dangerous. "Our little secret."

I got in the car and drove away.

· · ·

Driving back, I took the long way around, deliberately passing by Miguel's house. There was still no sign of life. The shutters were closed, the air eerily still.

Maybe Carmen was right. Maybe I should have left it alone. But if I couldn't tell Santos, and I couldn't go knocking on Miguel's door myself, then what the hell was I supposed to do? At least it answered my question of how Carmen knew where I was staying. Miguel must have called at the bar or contacted her in another way. Maybe she'd called him to find out where I was? But it still didn't answer if he knew where Laura was, or if he…

The road twisted through the hills as I made my way back to the finca. My mind wouldn't settle. Carmen's touch still burned against my back. Miguel's absence gnawed at me. Laura's missing suitcase haunted me.

As soon as I got out of the car, I saw it.

The front door.

It was ajar.

My stomach dropped.

I killed the engine and sat motionless for a second, listening. No movement. No sounds.

The hills stretched out around me, thick and suffocating.

I stepped out slowly, scanning the area. Then, without thinking, I turned and ran—down the dirt track, kicking up dust as I sprinted towards the Dutch finca.

But just as before, there was no movement. All was quiet.

I stood there, panting, waiting for something, anything, to happen.

Swallowing hard, I turned back to my own finca.

My breath was uneven as I stepped over the threshold, easing the door open wider. The air was stale, undisturbed. Everything looked the same. Had I left the door unlocked? It wouldn't be the first time.

I crept through the house, checking each room. Nothing

missing. No signs of forced entry. Just that open door, taunting me.

I exhaled shakily.

And then.

The walls shifted, and the ground tilted beneath me. I reached for the edge of the table to steady myself, but it slipped away like water. The entire room spun, the furniture warping, stretching, twisting. My vision tunnelled.

I staggered, catching myself against the wall, my heartbeat a violent drum in my ears. I tried to focus, tried to make sense of the sudden disorientation, but my mind wouldn't cooperate. I fell into a chair and then I felt—

Felt—

Nothing.

And finally, darkness swallowed me whole.

48

———

HER

DESPITE THE HIDEOUS COUCH, she had surprisingly slept like a baby. Fabián had given her a thin blanket and an old pillow, stained yellow with age, but somehow, exhaustion had dragged her under and kept her there until morning. She woke groggy but a little stronger, the sun already creeping in through the grimy windows.

Fabián was sitting at the table, watching her. How long had he been there?

"There's a towel in the bathroom," he said without pleasantries. "You should shower."

She only had the clothes she had worn for almost a week, filthy and stiff with sweat and grime. She would have to put them back on, but a shower felt like a good idea nonetheless, a way to scrub off at least some of the dirt and fear clinging to her skin. Offering a small smile to Fabián, she stepped into the bathroom.

The water wasn't clean. She could see it swirling in the base of the shower, pooling sluggishly around the drain, tinged grey and brown. At first, she thought it was from her own body—the filth and sweat of days spent locked inside a container—but now, watching it run, she wasn't sure. She hesitated, holding her palm under the weak stream, trying to decide if the grime was coming from her or if the water itself was already dirty before it touched her skin. The thought made her stomach clench.

She reached for a battered bar of soap on the ledge, its edges soft and worn down by months of use. There was a single dark hair stuck in it. She swallowed hard and rubbed it between her palms, forcing herself to ignore the queasy feeling in her gut. It wasn't a time for squeamishness. She needed to be clean, needed to feel human again. But no matter how hard she scrubbed, she couldn't shake the sensation that she was just moving dirt around.

When she stepped out, she dried herself quickly with a threadbare brown towel Fabián had left out for her, purposefully avoiding looking at whatever stains it might have on it. It smelled musty, as if it had been sitting damp for too long. She fought the urge to gag.

In the other room, she could hear Fabián whistling. The sound made her tense. Although he had been kind, she didn't like him. She hadn't liked him from the moment he'd pulled alongside her in his car, the smell of whisky emanating from inside. At first, she'd been too relieved to see a human face to really register the danger, but now…

She slipped back into the only clothes she had, the same ones she'd worn in the container. Her vest top clung uncomfortably to her skin. The shorts were stiff with filth. But it was her underwear she couldn't bring herself to put back on. She stared at them where they lay in the corner, a crumpled, stained reminder of everything she had endured. No. She would go without.

She needed clothes. She needed money. But more than anything, she needed to get out of there.

A way out?

She sat on the edge of the toilet, combing her fingers through her tangled hair, thinking. The only place she knew in the town was Carmen's bar. If she could find her way back there, maybe she could find her way to the finca. Would James still be there? Or had he given up and gone back to Madrid?

Not that there was anything for him to go back to, she thought bitterly. Out of work and spiralling. She almost laughed at the absurdity of it.

She took a deep breath, pushing the thoughts away. They didn't matter right now.

She stepped into the small living area. Fabián was sitting at the table, hunched over two plates of bread and cold meat. The sight of them made her stomach twist painfully. Despite eating when she arrived, her hunger was still a dull, ever-present ache, gnawing at her insides.

"Sit down," Fabián said, pushing one of the plates towards her.

She hesitated, eyeing the bread suspiciously. She didn't want to think about how old it was. But the hunger won. She dropped into the chair and tore into the food with desperate, manic bites, barely chewing before swallowing. Her body didn't care about dignity anymore.

The coffee he handed her was warm and bitter.

When the food was gone, she wiped her mouth with the back of her hand, not caring about manners. A week ago, she never would have behaved that way. But a week ago, she hadn't been locked inside a wooden box. A week ago, she hadn't been there.

She pushed her chair back and stood.

"Thank you," she said, forcing politeness into her voice.

Fabián stood too. "Where are you going?"

She hesitated. He quickly moved between her and the door. "I need to get fresh clothes," she said, trying to keep her tone even. "I need money."

Fabián shook his head. "No. You stay here."

A chill crept up her spine. "I can't stay here," she said carefully. "I appreciate what you've done for me, but I need to go."

Fabián's expression hardened. "You are my guest until I decide otherwise."

His guest. Right. He stepped forward, and she instinctively stepped back.

"I know who you are," Fabián said, his voice eerily calm. "The missing English woman. There will be a ransom for you, for your safe return. People are looking for you."

Her breath caught in her throat. "No," she whispered. "I'll get you the money myself."

He laughed at her incredulously. "I'll go into town," he said. "See what's what."

"No." Her voice was stronger now. She reached out and tried to grab his arm. "You can't—"

She didn't see his change of attitude coming nor the push coming.

His hands slammed into her shoulders, sending her stumbling backward. Her skull cracked against the wall, and for a second, white-hot pain exploded behind her eyes. She gasped, sliding down the rough plaster, her hands flying up to her head. When she pulled them away, her fingertips were smeared with blood.

Fabián was already at the door.

She blinked through the pain, watching as he stepped outside.

"Stay put," he said, and then the door bolted shut.

She sat there, breathing hard, head throbbing, ears ringing.

Then she moved. Trapped. Again.

She forced herself to her feet, staggering slightly. The room spun for a second before steadying.

She crossed the room, grabbed the handle of the nearest window, and yanked. But it didn't budge. She tried again. Locked. But it didn't matter, anyway. There were metal bars on the outside.

She stumbled to the next one. Same thing.

With her heart pounding, she turned to the bathroom. The tiny window was high up, barely wide enough to fit a shoulder through. But at least it had no bars.

She climbed onto the toilet, stretching up, pressing her fingers against the glass.

It didn't move.

"No, no, no," she muttered, pressing harder.

It was sealed shut.

Panic clawed at her throat.

She climbed down, pacing, forcing herself to think. She couldn't stay there. If Fabián planned to ransom her, that could take ages.

There had to be a way out. She had no choice.

49

———

SANTOS

THE TOWN APPEARED in the distance, its whitewashed buildings clinging to the hillside like scattered bones. Detective Santos squinted against the late afternoon glare, feeling the weight of exhaustion settle over her. The drive had been relentless; miles of winding roads cutting through parched countryside, the kind of terrain that helped people disappear all too easily.

She exhaled sharply, adjusting her grip on the steering wheel.

The Dutch family was on her list, but first, she wanted to check on James Blackwood. If he was acting, he was either very good at it or very bad. But now there was the money. A definite motive, especially for someone out of work.

Did he know Laura had withdrawn nine thousand euros the day before they left Madrid?

The likelihood of him admitting it, if he did, was akin to finding a four-leaf clover. But Santos wasn't relying on words. She'd read it on his face.

She descended the dirt track carefully, her tyres kicking up dry dust, the loose rocks skittering beneath her car. The finca appeared at the end of the road, sun-bleached and eerily still. The place had an abandoned feel, and Santos didn't like it.

She pulled up and killed the engine, the abrupt silence pressing in around her. Rubbing her eyes, she forced herself to push past the fatigue and stepped out. Her boots crunched against the dry earth as she made her way towards the house.

But halfway across the courtyard, she stopped.

A shiver crept up the back of her neck.

Was someone watching her?

She turned sharply, scanning the landscape. The trees stood motionless in the distance, the brush still, nothing but the hum of cicadas filling the air. No movement. No one there.

She lingered a moment longer, then forced herself to move on.

The first thing she noticed was that the front door was ajar.

Santos' pulse ticked up. She stepped forward, knocking firmly.

"James?"

No response.

She pushed the door open another inch, the hinges groaning in protest. The interior was dark compared to the harsh light outside, but from where she stood, she could see that the place looked a mess: empty bottles, clothes strewn about, a chair knocked over.

Another step forward.

"James, it's Santos."

Silence.

The sensation of being watched returned, gripping her ribs. With her hand resting near her holster, she backed away from the door and circled around the side of the finca. And that's when she saw him.

James was slumped in a chair, motionless, his head tilted awkwardly. For a brief, horrible moment, she thought he was dead.

Santos quickened her pace, reaching him in seconds. His skin was pale, almost grey, a stark contrast to the sun beating down on him. His fingers twitched slightly against the table, a half-full bottle of water beside them.

"James?" Her voice was sharp.

His eyelids fluttered. A sluggish blink. Relief washed over her, though she didn't show it.

He looked at her with a glassy sort of confusion, his breathing shallow. The tremor in his fingers didn't stop.

"Jesus, James," she muttered, crouching beside him. "What the hell is wrong with you?"

No answer.

She grabbed the bottle of water from the table and pressed it into his hands. "Drink."

James obeyed, bringing it to his lips with some difficulty, gulping it down like a man who had gone days without.

Santos exhaled, glancing up at the sky. The sun was relentless; no breeze cut through the suffocating heat. How long had he been sitting out there? She gripped his arm. "Let's get you inside."

He didn't resist as she hauled him to his feet. He swayed slightly, disoriented, but she steadied him, guiding him back through the open doorway. She smelt for alcohol, but she already knew he wasn't drunk. He didn't look drunk; he looked ill.

James collapsed onto the couch, his head falling into his hands. Santos fetched another bottle of water from the fridge and handed it to him.

"Drink more."

A few sips later, he leant back against the cushions, the colour gradually returning to his face.

Santos folded her arms. "Did you black out again?"

James hesitated, blinking sluggishly. "I don't know."

"You don't know," she repeated flatly.

He rubbed his temples. "I don't remember anything after coming home."

Santos watched him closely. His pupils weren't quite even. Was it dehydration? Exhaustion? Something else?

"Do you have a history of fainting?" she asked.

"No."

She didn't believe him and made a mental note to check into his medical records later. But, for now, she had other questions.

"Did you know Laura withdrew nine thousand euros the day before you both left Madrid?"

James' gaze snapped to hers. The shock was unmistakable.

"No," he said, shaking his head. "That… that doesn't make sense. Nine thousand?"

Santos studied him.

Either he was a damn good liar, or this was the first he'd heard of it.

He ran a hand through his dishevelled hair. "Why would she do that?"

"That's what I'd love to know."

James frowned, his mind clearly racing. "She never mentioned anything about withdrawing that kind of money."

"Would she have kept it in her suitcase?"

James blinked at her. "Her suitcase?"

Santos nodded. "Yes, James. Her suitcase."

The confusion on his face deepened. "I…" He trailed off, shaking his head again. "I wouldn't know."

Maybe he didn't. But that didn't mean someone else didn't.

James exhaled heavily, rubbing his face. "I swear to you, I have no idea what she was doing with that kind of money."

She believed him.

For now.

Santos turned to leave but hesitated at the door.

She glanced back at James, who was still slumped on the couch, exhaustion weighing on him like a lead blanket.

"You didn't tell me," she said slowly, "that you'd been out of work for sixteen months."

James stiffened.

She watched the tension creep into his shoulders.

For a moment, he said nothing.

"I didn't think it was relevant."

Santos let that hang between them. She could see the defences going up, the subtle shift in his posture.

"You didn't think it was relevant that you were unemployed? That Laura has been the only one earning for over a year?"

James' jaw tightened. "That's not—" He stopped himself, exhaling sharply. "I wasn't completely unemployed. I had freelance work."

"But no stable income," Santos pointed out.

James didn't answer.

Santos didn't need him to.

She nodded once, stepping outside into the heavy afternoon air, and as she walked back to her car, she scanned the landscape again. That eerie feeling from before hadn't gone away.

She still felt she was being watched.

50

HIM

I slumped back into the sofa as soon as Santos left, letting out a huge sigh. My head pounded, not with the dull throb of a hangover but something else, something worse. It was a deep, crushing ache that seemed to pulse from behind my eyes, making it hard to focus. I'd had another blackout, and now Santos knew too.

"Do you have a history of fainting?"

She would have made a note of it. She'd go digging. And she was right to.

I lied to her about it. The problem was, I didn't remember anything. I never could. It would come on like a wave, sudden and disorienting, and then I'd wake up somewhere, seconds or minutes or hours later, with no memory of what had happened in between. The first time it happened, I'd convinced myself it was nothing—a momentary lapse, dehydration, stress. But then it happened again. And again.

Laura had caught me once. She found me in our apartment, barely conscious. I told her I tripped and must have banged my head, but I saw the doubt in her eyes.

But I couldn't ignore it. Not when it started to happen too often. Not when I'd woken up in places I didn't remember going. Not when there were entire stretches of time, sometimes whole hours, that were just gone. And it wasn't always blacking out completely. Sometimes I just forgot what I was doing other than where I was going. I'd left the apartment door open in Madrid on a couple of occasions. So did that mean I'd left the finca open too? Is that how someone got in and took the suitcase, leaving the journal out?

Shit.

I went to a doctor in Madrid, in secret. I'd sat in that cold, sterile office while he frowned at my symptoms, scribbling notes in my file. He told me I needed to go to the neurological department at the hospital, that they'd run tests, scans, figure out what was happening. He even made the appointment for me. But I never went. I convinced myself it wasn't serious. That it would pass.

Now, I wasn't so sure.

Because if I couldn't remember things, then how could I be sure I hadn't done something?

Santos suspected me already, and passing out would only make things more difficult. Her and Carmen had found me outside the day after we arrived. Shit, two blackouts in six days. They were getting worse. They never happened like that, so close together. I could go months in between, but it now felt wrong, bad. Really bad.

Santos would think I was hiding something, and maybe, deep down, I was. Maybe there were things locked away in my own head that I wasn't aware of. And even worse, some things I *did* remember, but I could never tell anybody about those.

After several minutes of contemplation, I pushed off the

sofa, shaking the thought away. I needed to pull myself together. I was unravelling, and that was dangerous. I couldn't afford to be careless.

Realising I needed a shower, I soon concluded that there wasn't time. Instead, I made coffee and then changed, throwing on a fresh shirt. My hands were still unsteady, a subtle tremor running through them as I buttoned it up. I forced myself to take a deep breath. I had to focus.

There was something else I hadn't told Santos.

Fabián.

I didn't mention him on purpose. Carmen had already dismissed him as a drunk, and Santos would go to her first. By the time she got around to Fabián, she'd already have made up her mind that he was unreliable, a waste of time. But I wasn't so sure.

Fabián knew about the other missing woman. He'd spoken about her like it was common knowledge, like everyone just accepted that she'd vanished and no one had done a damn thing about it. If he knew something about Laura, I had to find out.

That was, if there was anything to know. If there *was* anything to remember.

I stepped outside, the late afternoon heat hitting me hard. Santos' car was still parked in the driveway. I frowned, wondering where she was, but I didn't have the time or the inclination to find out.

I got in my car and started driving into town.

When I passed Carmen's bar, she was outside, collecting glasses from the tables. She looked up at the sound of my car, smiling at first, lifting a hand to wave. But I didn't slow down. I didn't even look at her.

Out of the corner of my eye, I saw her expression shift— surprise, confusion, something else. But I kept driving. I didn't have time for Carmen. From my rear-view mirror, I saw her stop collecting glasses and instead scurry indoors.

Minutes later, I parked in town, cutting the engine, and stepped out quickly. As usual, in that place, the streets were empty, only a few people lingering outside the shops. I kept my head down as I walked, slipping into the narrow alleyway, my pulse quickening as I neared the bar.

And as soon as I stepped inside, there he was. Fabián.

I spotted him immediately, sitting in the far corner like he'd been there for hours, hunched over the table. Two beers sat in front of him—one half-empty, the other untouched. A vacant chair across from him.

Fuck. He was waiting for me.

I hesitated in the doorway, knowing I should just turn and run. Find Santos, let her deal with it. It was getting out of hand, and I was getting way out of my depth.

But as I turned to leave, Fabián lifted his head, and a slow grin spread across his weathered face.

"Amigo," he said, gesturing to the empty seat. "I've been waiting for you."

51

SANTOS

Santos stood by her car for a moment, watching the front of James Blackwood's finca. She should call on the Dutch family. She had already spent too much time there, and James, despite his health, had clearly wanted her gone. But something still nagged at her. His exhaustion, the way he slumped on the sofa, the sickly sheen of sweat on his forehead—it wasn't just stress. He hadn't been drinking either, but he looked like a man fighting off the mother of all hangovers.

She knew better.

James Blackwood wasn't a well man. And that made her believe he might not even know what he'd done with Laura. Maybe it wasn't good acting. Perhaps he had no fucking idea what he'd done.

She exhaled sharply and reached for her phone, dialling Álvarez' number.

"I'm at James' place. Any news on Emma Carter?" she asked without pleasantries.

Álvarez hesitated. "Same as before. It's as though she

never existed. No one remembers her. No work history, no family, nothing."

Santos rubbed her forehead. Emma Carter was their mystery woman, the one who had disappeared a year ago under suspicious circumstances. But they had exhausted every lead back then. If anything fresh was going to surface, it would have happened already. And yet…

"She had money," Santos muttered, more to herself than to Álvarez.

"What?"

"Rebecca mentioned large amounts of money. If Emma Carter had money, then maybe we've been looking at this the wrong way."

Álvarez sighed. "That's a big if. We don't even know if Emma Carter was her real name. And without financial records, we've got nothing."

Santos knew he was right, but the thought stuck with her as she hung up. The Emma Carter case had always bothered her.

She looked down the hill. The Dutch family was the last place she wanted to go, but she had no choice. The photograph of Emma was etched in her brain.

As she took the short walk down the incline, the sensation of being watched had gone, but that didn't make her feel any better.

She stood outside the gates, the heavy wooden doors looming over her. This remote part of Andalusia was getting to her. It was too isolated, too quiet, too… off.

As soon as she knocked, she heard footsteps behind the gates. Then the sound of a latch being pulled back.

The doors creaked open, and just as before, all three of them stood there—the man, the woman, and the boy. But something felt different.

The first time she'd visited, the man had been open,

friendly even, in that distant way that some people are when they don't want to get involved. Now, his expression was tight. The woman stood rigid at his side, her arm wrapped around his waist. And the boy was still staring.

He hadn't stopped staring at her the last time, either. A deep, unsettling gaze that made her wonder just how much he saw.

The man spoke first. "Can we help you? We're busy packing. We go home tomorrow."

They're going home? So soon, or their vacation was genuinely coming to an end? Either way, he made it clear he didn't want her there.

Santos didn't waste time. "We're still investigating the missing woman. A witness saw a blue blouse on your washing line."

The man's jaw tightened. "Who said that?"

"That's not relevant."

She turned her attention to the woman, who still hadn't spoken a word. "Do you own a blue blouse?"

The woman hesitated, then nodded. "Yes."

"Can I see it?"

A pause. Then, without a word, the woman slipped back inside the house. The man and the boy remained, watching her. Santos offered the boy a small smile, but he didn't smile back.

When the woman returned, she held the blouse in her hands. Santos took it, running her fingers over the fabric. It wasn't exactly new, but it wasn't old either. Not like the woman's other clothes—sun-bleached, worn, lived in.

"How long have you had this?" Santos asked.

"About six months. Last time we were here on vacation."

"Where did you get it?"

"At the market in town."

Santos' gut sank.

If that was true, then the blouse was nothing. Even if it was Emma Carter's from the photograph, how the hell would Santos ever find where it had come from?

Still—

"Do you mind if I take it with me? Just in case."

The woman hesitated. Then, with a nod, she said yes.

The man crossed his arms. "If that's all, I'd appreciate it if you didn't come by again." And with that, the gates slammed shut.

As she walked back to her car, she heard the low rumble of an engine. She turned the corner just in time to see James' car speeding up the hill. Where the hell was he going in such a hurry?

Then her phone rang.

Álvarez.

She answered. "What now?"

"Are you still at the finca?"

"About to leave. Why?"

"We just got a call from a dog walker."

Santos straightened. "And?"

"There's a quarry down the hill from you. You need to get down there. According to Google Maps, it's beyond the Dutch finca."

Santos frowned. "There's a quarry?"

"Apparently. Disused for years."

She didn't hesitate. She hung up and started walking.

The road dipped into a valley, the land opening up before her. And there it was.

A vast, open pit, abandoned and scarred, its edges crumbling with age. Faded warning signs clung to rusted poles. The remains of old machinery lay scattered, half-buried in dust. And farther down, nestled between skeletal buildings and a wooden hut, was a thin column of smoke.

Santos followed the fence, searching for an opening. Then

she found one, an old, rusted gap where the wire had been pulled apart. She slipped through, hurrying down the uneven path.

The dog walker was waiting. An old man, his scruffy dog straining at the leash. He lifted a hand in greeting.

"This way," he said in Spanish.

Santos followed, stepping over broken concrete and loose stones.

And then she saw it.

The car was barely recognisable, its once-sleek form twisted and blackened, but she still knew it was the Blackwood's car. The fire had burned hot, stripping away paint and melting metal. The tyres had exploded, leaving only charred remnants. The air still smelled of burned rubber, of scorched earth.

And inside…

Fuck.

Santos swallowed hard.

The body was little more than a husk; the fire having done its worst. Skin had shrivelled and scorched, the features gone. The arms curled inwards, drawn up by the heat. Clothes had fused to what remained of the flesh.

But as she stepped closer, there was one thing she could make out. A belt. Leather, cracked from the flames. And beneath it, a glimpse of fabric…

A man's shirt.

Santos took a slow step back.

James and Laura's car.

And inside, a dead man.

She turned to the old man. "Did you see anyone else?"

He shook his head.

Santos looked back at the body in the car, her mind racing.

Who the hell was it?

52

HIM

Fabián watched me as I crossed the bar. His hands were folded neatly on the table, his beer untouched. I stopped at the edge of the table, keeping my hands at my sides.

"What do you know?" I asked, my voice flat.

Fabián smiled, revealing teeth yellowed from years of cigarettes and cheap alcohol. "Please, sit."

I didn't move.

He gestured to the empty chair across from him, a second beer already placed in front of it. I hadn't told him I was coming, but he knew. Reluctantly, I slid into the seat. "I asked you a question."

Fabián leant forward, the alcohol thick on his breath. "Calm down, amigo. This is for your own benefit."

I scoffed. "Right. Because I trust a word that comes out of your mouth."

He shook his head, taking a slow sip of his beer, savouring it. "How much money do you have?"

I blinked, thrown by the question. "What?"

Fabián exhaled through his nose, as if irritated he had to repeat himself. "I asked how much money you have."

I pushed my chair back slightly, preparing to leave. "Fuck this."

His hand shot out, gripping my arm in an iron vice. His strength took me by surprise. I froze, every nerve in my body firing at once.

"Your wife," he said, his voice barely above a whisper. "She's at my place."

A laugh escaped me before I could stop it. The sheer absurdity of it. I ran a hand through my hair, shaking my head.

"My wife?"

Fabián nodded, his bloodshot eyes unwavering.

I should've played along, should've pretended shock or desperation. But I didn't. Either Fabián was completely delusional, or he was telling the truth.

I had to be careful. I forced a frown onto my face. "What the hell are you talking about?"

Fabián pushed his chair back and stood. He swayed slightly, catching himself on the edge of the table. Then he leant down, his voice thick with slurred menace.

"Be at my place tomorrow. Ten am. Bring twenty thousand euros." He paused, his eyes narrowing. "And don't come without the money and don't even think about bringing the police."

I stared at him. He wasn't done.

He took another step closer, his breath rancid. "Be very careful, James. I have a gun."

A cold dread curled in my stomach. He wasn't joking. I opened my mouth to respond, but my phone rang, the shrill sound making Fabián flinch.

"It's the police," I said, showing him the screen. Santos.

Fabián's jaw tightened. "Not a word, amigo." He slipped

me a piece of paper, and then, without another word, he turned and left the bar.

His words echoed in my head. Tomorrow. Ten am. Twenty thousand. Or else.

I sat there for a second, gripping my phone so tightly my knuckles ached. My pulse hammered in my ears as I answered.

"Detective." My voice shook. I cleared my throat. "What's going on?"

There was a slight pause on the other end, like she was studying the sound of my voice. "Is everything okay?"

I forced a laugh, but it came out thin. "Yeah, yeah. Just—" I swallowed. Should I tell her about Fabián? But if I did, and he found out, I had no doubt he'd make good on his threat. "Just a long day."

Santos didn't sound convinced. "There's been a development."

My stomach dropped. "Is it the Dutch family? Have you found Laura?"

"No," she said. "It's nothing like that. But you need to come back to the finca. Now."

A shiver ran through me. "What the hell is it?"

"Just get here, James."

She hung up.

I stood abruptly, nearly knocking over the chair. As I rushed out of the bar, I caught a movement in the corner of my eye. Someone darted behind the bushes at the far end of the square.

I froze.

Was it Fabián? Someone else?

I clenched my jaw, staring into the shadows. I didn't have time for that. I ran to my car and started the engine without a second thought.

As I drove back to the finca, Fabián's crumpled address

burned in my hand. Should I go there now? But no. He wouldn't let me in without money, and I wasn't about to test his threat.

Instead, I pushed the accelerator harder. I could see blue flashing lights in the distance as I approached our holiday home. Santos stood outside, her arms folded, her foot tapping.

I pulled up fast, dust kicking up around the tyres. I barely had the door open before I demanded, "What the hell is it?"

Santos didn't move. "We found your car."

I swallowed. My mouth was dry. "What?"

She pointed. "In the quarry."

I turned my head, staring at the darkened space beyond the Dutch finca. "The quarry?"

"There are quite a few officers at the scene," she said carefully.

My pulse pounded. "Why do you need so many officers for a burnt-out car?"

Santos didn't answer right away. She was scrutinising me again, her dark eyes sharp, unreadable. Then she said it.

"Because there's a body inside, James."

Everything inside me turned to ice. My mouth opened, but no words came out. Santos hesitated, no doubt studying my reaction.

I forced my breath out in a rush, shaking my head. "Oh fuck!" I heard how it sounded—too loud, too dramatic. Shit. "Is it Laura?"

Santos' expression didn't change.

"No, James," she said, quietly. "It isn't Laura."

I exhaled sharply, relief hitting me first, but it didn't last.

"We found some ID," she continued. "The body's pretty burnt, but their belt and wallet somehow survived the worst of the blaze."

My pulse roared in my ears. "Who is it?" I asked, my voice barely above a whisper.

Santos met my gaze.

"It's Miguel, James. Miguel Ruiz."

The world tilted. I heard my own breath hitch. I took a step back. My body felt disconnected from my mind, like I was floating outside myself.

Miguel. The man who had shown me to the finca.

And now, he was dead.

Burned. In my car.

A wave of nausea rolled over me.

Santos was still watching me, as if she was waiting for something—for me to break, or confess, or react in a way that would confirm whatever suspicion she already had.

I forced myself to look away, staring towards the flashing lights. Miguel was dead. Burnt to nothing. In my fucking car.

___

53

HER

SHE HAD SEARCHED every inch of the house, behind the rickety wooden furniture, inside the rusted fridge, under the creaky bed frame that smelled of stale sweat and damp. Nothing. No loose boards, no open windows, no way out. The realisation sat heavy in her chest. She would have to wait for him.

The thought made her stomach lurch. Where the hell had he gone? To arrange a ransom, that's what. A fucking ransom. She exhaled sharply, pacing the small living space, ignoring the flies that buzzed lazily around the sink. How long would that take? Hours? A day? She had no sense of time anymore. No clocks, no phone. Just the unrelenting heat pressing in from outside, the cracked walls that pulsed with the late after-noon sun, the stench of herself clinging to her like rot.

She lifted an arm and inhaled—sour, acrid, unwashed skin. Despite showering, the smell hadn't left her. It was in her clothes, in her hair, in her pores. She could almost feel it curling off her like smoke. It made her want to peel her skin off. She flinched as she touched the bump on the back of her head, blood dried where Fabián had flung her against the wall.

She stopped pacing, pressing her forehead against the wooden door, listening. Silence. Beyond it, the world was going on as usual. People walking, cars passing, dogs barking in the distance. Unaware. Unconcerned.

She couldn't stay there. Couldn't be locked up again.

The thought sent a jolt of panic through her, sudden and electric. It tightened her throat, propelled a fresh wave of nausea rolling through her. She swallowed hard. No. She wouldn't break. Not now. Not when she was so close.

But what now?

Her gaze flicked to the kitchen counter. A knife was sitting there. Fabián had left it there after preparing the disgusting stale bread and curled meat.

She took a slow, steadying breath.

Fabián was strong. She'd seen the way his thick fingers clenched into a fist when he lost his temper. She had no chance in a straight fight. If she was going to do this, she had to do it right. Quick. Decisive.

She ran her tongue over her dry lips. She just had to wait.

Minutes crawled by. Or maybe it was hours. She wasn't sure. The heat bore down on her skull, intense and unrelenting, making her drowsy, sluggish. She forced herself to stay alert, moving, keeping the edge of panic sharp enough to keep her ready.

Then, finally, footsteps.

A scrape against the door. A bolt, followed by a key sliding into the lock.

She was already in position, pressed against the wall behind the door, body coiled tight as a spring. She clenched the handle of the knife, her fingers slick with sweat.

The door opened.

A moment of silence. Hesitation. He was looking for her.

Then the shuffle of boots on the floor. The distinct smell of alcohol. He stepped inside and she moved.

It wasn't graceful or practised. Just pure, raw instinct.

Her arm shot out, the knife cutting through the thick air. She barely felt the resistance as the blade sank deep into his throat, just under the jaw. A wet, sickening gurgle filled the space. Fabián staggered back, eyes wide in stunned confusion, his mouth opening and closing like a fish out of water. Blood, thick and hot, spilled over her hands, her wrists, her arms.

He made a sound—half-growl, half-choke—as his legs buckled. His body hit the floor hard. He twitched once, twice, then went still.

She stood over him, panting.

It was done.

Her fingers trembled as she pushed the door shut and wiped the knife against his shirt, watching as the dark stain spread across his chest. She needed to move.

Grabbing him under the arms, she tried to drag him away, but her muscles screamed in protest. He was heavy, too heavy. She had no choice but to leave him where he was.

The smell of blood was thick in the air, metallic and cloying, and she had to press her fist against her lips to stop herself from gagging.

She crouched, rifling through his pockets.

Nothing.

No phone. No keys. Just loose change, the coins cold and damp against her palm. She counted them quickly—fifteen euros, barely enough for anything. But it was something. Enough to get a bottle of water, maybe a cheap T-shirt. Anything to help her blend in.

She couldn't go anywhere looking as she did.

She staggered to her feet, gripping the edge of the table for balance. The room spun. She closed her eyes tight, forcing herself to stay upright. There was no time to be weak. Not now.

Moving quickly now, she squeezed out of the door, pausing just long enough to listen.

Silence.

She pulled it open.

The heat hit her instantly. She sucked in a breath, blinking against the glare. The street stretched out ahead, bathed in golden light. It was deserted. Good.

She took a tentative step outside, then another.

She knew where she was. The town lay just down the hill, a cluster of whitewashed buildings, quiet and unassuming. But she couldn't go there.

No. The town wasn't safe. She knew that now. She'd just been locked up in a fucking wooden hut and taken hostage by a bloody drunk.

Instead, she had to find him.

She had to get to James.

54

HER

SHE RAN, her breath coming in ragged gasps, her legs unsteady beneath her, but she forced herself forward. The late afternoon sun cast long shadows across the cracked pavement, stretching her silhouette into something monstrous. She barely registered where she was, just that she had to get away. Away from the house. Away from him.

Her heart hammered, drowning out the distant sounds of the town, the occasional bark of a dog, the faint hum of a motorbike far off in the hills. She turned a corner and staggered, gripping a rusted fence post to steady herself.

Then she saw it.

The blood.

It was everywhere, splattered across her arms, soaked into the fabric of her already filthy top, clinging to her hands like wet paint. She had been too consumed by the need to escape, too focused on putting as much distance as possible between herself and that house, to even notice before.

Now, with the sun beginning to dip behind the rooftops, it was impossible to ignore.

Panic surged through her.

She couldn't be seen that way. She might as well have been screaming for attention.

She crouched low, pressing herself against the fence, her breath coming in quick, shallow bursts. Her pulse roared in her ears. There was a garden beyond the fence—a narrow strip of land behind a squat, whitewashed house. And there, just beyond a sagging lemon tree, was a washing line.

Clothes.

She scanned the house, searching for movement behind the shuttered windows. Nothing. No movement. No sound.

Keeping low, she slipped through a gap in the fence, careful to keep her footsteps light against the dry grass. The clothes swayed gently in the breeze, the scent of detergent mixing with the citrus from the tree. She reached for the first thing her fingers brushed against—a faded blue T-shirt. Next, she grabbed a pair of cotton shorts, beige with a thin draw-string at the waist. Finally, she spotted a brown hoodie.

She turned them over in her hands.

They'd do.

And luck was on her side for once. They were a size too big, but at least they fit. But the blood; she couldn't put them on like that.

Her gaze darted around the garden, searching. Then she saw it—a coiled hosepipe lying discarded near a cracked, tiled patio.

She moved quickly, unwinding the hose, twisting the tap. The water burst out, ice-cold against her skin, and she let out a sharp gasp as she shoved her arms beneath the spray. She scrubbed at her hands, her arms, anywhere the blood had touched. The water hit the tiles, swirling dark before fading into nothing.

She removed her stained top, wiping at the last of the blood on her stomach before tossing it aside. She did the same with her shorts, then pulled the stolen clothes on, still damp from where she'd splashed herself. The T-shirt was too big, the shorts hung loose at the waist, but they would do. Finally, despite the heat, she pulled on the hoodie.

She dropped the hose and moved back to the fence, slipping through the same gap she had entered, and then she walked.

Fortunately, everywhere was quiet. She found shelter in a derelict building near the outskirts, just a skeleton of what it once was. The roof had partially collapsed, and weeds pushed through the cracks in the floor. It smelled of damp and rust, but it was better than nothing.

She curled up in a corner, pulling the hoodie over her, tucking her knees into her chest. The night air was settling in, biting at her damp skin. She shivered, wrapping her arms tightly around herself. The cold worked its way into her bones, making her teeth chatter, but she forced herself to stay still.

She just had to make it until morning.

She woke stiff and aching, her body curled awkwardly against the hard ground. Light bled through the broken slats in the walls, casting thin beams across the dirt floor.

She'd made it to morning.

She sat up slowly, rolling the stiffness from her shoulders. The town would be waking now. People would be moving. It would be safer to blend in.

She stepped out of the shelter, squinting against the early sun. The air still held the last traces of the night's chill, but the day would soon burn it away. She walked down the street, keeping her head low, but she felt them—eyes. Watching.

They don't recognise you. She told herself that. Over and over. But paranoia had its claws in her.

She crossed into the market square. Stalls were being set up, wooden tables dragged into place, crates unloaded. But not many people were there yet.

She drifted to a stall selling clothing, where a man was unrolling a sheet to display his goods. He barely glanced at her. The baseball caps were stacked at the edge of the stall, some still wrapped in plastic.

She lingered for a moment, scanning the street, then let her fingers brush over the top one—a simple black cap, unmarked. With one smooth motion, she lifted it, slipped it down the side of her shorts, and walked away without a backward glance. A minute later, she pulled it onto her head, tucking her hair beneath it.

Better. Nobody would give her a second look.

She kept walking, past the stalls, past the locals that were beginning to filter into the square, past the town's small collection of shops.

Then finally, she saw it.

Carmen's bar. Its wooden sign swaying slightly in the breeze.

PART VII

DAY SEVEN

55

HIM

I woke with my head pulsing, each heartbeat a dull thud against the inside of my skull. My tongue felt thick, my throat raw. Dehydration. Lack of sleep. It had been another long, restless night.

I swung my legs over the side of the bed and sat there for a moment, pressing the heels of my hands into my eyes. Through the open window, the first streaks of morning light had begun to spill over the hills, turning everything a pale shade of gold. I swallowed, my throat dry as sandpaper.

Santos had left late, but not before she'd drilled me with more questions.

"So let me get this straight; you have no idea who could've taken your car, driven Miguel Ruiz down to the quarry, and set it alight?"

"None."

"And you think it's just a coincidence that it happened so close to the finca you rented?"

"Laura rented it. It wasn't my choice. I had no part in it."

"Right," Santos had said, nodding slowly.

And then, in the silence of the morning, I sat there thinking about it again.

Santos didn't trust me.

And now Miguel Ruiz was dead.

The car at the quarry had been burned to nothing. The body inside was just a charred mass of bone and tissue. Miguel's ID had survived the fire. But the corpse inside? Santos said the police would be working with dental records, maybe DNA if there was anything left, but they were still highly confident of exactly who the remains belonged to.

And that's when I remembered. The note at Miguel's house…

Q. 11 AM.

'Quarry. Eleven o'clock'.

That's where Miguel had gone. That's why his coffee pot was still warm.

I forced myself to my feet, dragging a hand through my hair. I needed caffeine. Strong, black, hot enough to burn.

I moved through the finca in a daze, filling the kettle, setting it on the stove. As I waited, I leant against the counter and thought about Fabián.

The twenty thousand euros.

He'd set the terms. Ten am. His house. No police.

And he had a gun.

But I also believed that Fabián could easily be playing me. He'd seen how desperate I was. He'd waited for me in the pub, gauged my reaction about the other missing English woman from a year ago.

Perhaps, as Carmen said, he was just the local drunk, trying to exploit me for money. Maybe he didn't have anyone at all.

It was the first thought that made any sense. Fabián had been circling the situation like a vulture, watching, waiting. Maybe he'd picked the perfect moment to cash in.

And yet…

The other possibility itched at the back of my skull.

If it was Laura, then where the hell did he find her? Just wandering the streets? But how had she managed that?

The kettle screamed, and I flinched. I poured the water and drank the first cup too quickly, burning the roof of my mouth. It didn't matter. I needed to wake up.

At exactly 9:15, I pulled on my last clean shirt, shoved my feet into my shoes, and grabbed my keys.

The drive to Fabián's place wasn't long, but I didn't want to rush into it blind. If he was bluffing, I had to find out what exactly he knew.

I stepped out onto the gravel driveway, inhaling the warm morning air. Then I slid into the driver's seat, shifted into reverse, and looked in the rear-view mirror.

And that's when I saw him.

A small, pale face standing directly behind my car.

The Dutch boy.

I slammed the brakes so hard that I stalled the car. My heart leapt into my throat.

What. The. Hell.

I twisted around in my seat, panting. He was still there. Still fucking there.

Standing perfectly still.

Watching me.

I could feel my own pulse hammering in my ears.

How had he got there?

I hadn't seen him when I got in the car, and there had been no footsteps, no warning, no sign of movement.

I swallowed hard, forcing my breath to steady. Slowly,

carefully, I reached for the door handle. Then, with a sharp click, I opened the door and stepped out.

Still the boy didn't move. His wide blue eyes were locked on me, unblinking.

I cleared my throat, my voice coming out rough. "What the hell are you doing?"

He didn't answer.

My skin crawled. There was something wrong with the way he stood. Too rigid. Too still. The wind stirred his hair slightly, but his expression didn't change.

I took a step closer. "Where's your mother? Your father?"

Silence.

My mouth felt dry again. What did he want?

Then, finally, he moved.

Not a step forward. Not a shift in posture.

Just his mouth.

His lips parted slightly. Not to speak, not to make a sound. Just enough to show the edges of his teeth.

I felt something cold slither down my spine.

Then, suddenly, he turned. Without a word, without a sound, he walked away. But not back towards the Dutch finca. Not towards the road.

Just into my garden.

I watched him until he disappeared into the shadows. Then, slowly, I exhaled.

My hands were still shaking.

I climbed back into the car, shut the door, and locked it.

I took one last look in the rear-view mirror, expecting to see him standing there again. But he was gone.

I gripped the steering wheel, swallowing hard, then started the car, shifted it back into reverse and pulled away.

I didn't have time for this. Not then. But I knew I had to find the Dutch boy later and deal with him once and for all.

Did he know something?

56

SANTOS

SANTOS SAT at her desk before the sun had fully risen, the office still wrapped in the dim hush of early morning. A half-empty coffee cup rested beside her laptop, the dregs gone cold. She'd barely slept—again.

The case gnawed at her.

Miguel Ruiz. That was the name that mattered now.

His body had been discovered in the burned-out car at the quarry, a gruesome discovery that left little room for doubt. There would still need to be a formal identification, but she already knew. The ID found in his wallet was conclusive.

Ruiz was the man who had driven James and Laura Blackwood to their finca exactly a week ago. A week. Seven days since the couple arrived, and now the guy who met them was dead. She recalled Carmen admitting she didn't recognise him, but was she telling the truth? She'd already instructed Álvarez to carry out searches, see if he had a history and where the hell he came from.

Santos drummed her fingers against her desk, scanning

through her notes. She had questioned James Blackwood the previous evening. He hadn't appeared to know anything. If he was lying, he was doing a damn good job of it.

But then, he hadn't booked the vacation. Laura had. And that led to the real question: how much had Laura Blackwood known?

She was the one who had chosen the location, who had arranged the entire trip. And now, just under a mile from where they were staying, the guy who showed them to their accommodation had been found burned beyond recognition in their car.

And then there was the money.

Laura had withdrawn nine thousand euros in cash the day before they travelled. Why? Who was it for? And had she already handed it over? Or more to the point, had she not, which could be why Miguel Ruiz was now no more than a burnt crisp?

So many questions. No real answers.

Santos leant back, exhaling slowly.

She went through her notes again, for what felt like the thousandth time. If she stared at the same facts long enough, maybe something would shift, something would align in a way she hadn't considered before.

It was a methodical process, but it was getting her nowhere.

She pinched the bridge of her nose and reached for her coffee, grimacing as the cold liquid hit her tongue.

A shuffle of movement caught her attention.

Santos glanced up as Inspector Álvarez approached her desk, a thick folder in hand. He had that look, the one that said he had something but was drawing it out just long enough to irritate her. Why couldn't she have a woman as a partner? Santos realised she didn't particularly have time for any men, didn't trust any of them, since her husband cheated.

Maybe it's why she was so adamant James Blackwood knew much more than he was letting on.

"Well?" she asked impatiently.

Álvarez placed the folder on her desk and crossed his arms. "We've got the results from the blood found on the finca wall."

Santos sat up straighter, her exhaustion momentarily forgotten.

"And?"

Álvarez hesitated.

"That bad?" she pressed.

"No," he said. "Just… unexpected."

Santos narrowed her eyes. "Then spit it out."

He sighed. "It can't be Laura Blackwood's. The sample is too old."

Santos exhaled sharply through her nose. That complicated things. If it wasn't Laura's, then whose was it? However, she already doubted it was Laura's.

"Besides," Álvarez continued, "we don't have a match for her anyway."

Santos nodded.

"But," he added, his tone shifting, "we did find a match."

Santos leant forward. "Who?"

Álvarez tapped the file. "Emma Carter."

Santos frowned. Emma Carter? The missing woman from a year ago. The same one from the Madrid practice where Laura Blackwood worked.

Álvarez flipped open the folder, pulling out a printed report. "British. Went missing a year ago." He paused, then met her gaze. "And before she came to Spain, she did time. Petty crimes—shoplifting, fraud, minor drug offences. The UK authorities had her DNA on file because of it."

Santos sat back, absorbing the information.

Emma Carter had a criminal past. Mind you, that wasn't

a surprise. The women brought to Madrid appeared to have had an awful existence back in the UK. But now, somehow, Emma Carter's blood had been found at the finca where James and Laura Blackwood had booked to stay.

The pieces were stacking up.

She thought of Miguel Ruiz again.

Whatever was going on, he had been mixed up in it too. And now he was dead, burned to a crisp in the Blackwoods' car.

"You think Laura knew her?" Álvarez asked.

Santos looked at him. "Somebody knew her. Either Doctor Chen or Laura Blackwood would have suggested Emma come to Andalusia. But how does her blood end up at that finca? She stayed at a hostel in town. But then she left, told another guest she was going for a walk…"

Santos considered her next step.

Ruiz had been more than just someone who showed people to their holiday homes. She was certain of that now. Whatever had happened to Laura, whatever this mess was—he had been involved. And now someone had made sure he wouldn't talk.

Coincidence? No chance.

She closed the file with a snap. "Good work."

Álvarez didn't move.

"There's one more thing," he said.

Santos raised an eyebrow. "Go on."

He hesitated again.

"Álvarez!"

"We did some digging into James Blackwood."

Santos frowned. "We already know his background."

"Not all of it," Álvarez said. "He was married before."

That stopped her.

She tilted her head slightly. "Married?"

Álvarez nodded, passing her a slip of paper. A name and a

phone number were scrawled across it in his neat handwriting.

Santos took the sheet, staring at it.

James Blackwood had an ex-wife.

A wife he hadn't mentioned.

Was it relevant? Santos doubted it, so why couldn't she stop looking at the piece of paper in her hand?

57

———

HIM

I DROVE SLOWLY, my fingers tapping against the steering wheel as I passed Carmen's bar. I glanced at my watch. Still over an hour until Fabián had told me to call with the money. I almost laughed.

What money?

Even if I had it, there was no way I was handing twenty thousand to a drunk, but I was still more than interested in what he'd been talking about—and who he had at his house.

I pulled into Carmen's, ignoring the part of me that told me I should be putting distance between us. There was something about her I just couldn't shake. She had mesmerised me from the first time I'd set eyes on her, yet I couldn't explain why. It wasn't just her looks, though she was striking, all dark eyes and effortless curves. It was the way she carried herself, how she seemed to see through me in a way no one else ever had. Like she knew exactly what I was thinking before I even said it.

A spell. That was the only way to describe it.

A hypnotist picking on a poor bastard from the audience and making everybody laugh at their expense, bending them to their will, getting them to bark like a dog or forget their own name.

And I was the fool on the stage, waiting for the next command.

It was early, and the bar was empty, apart from Carmen. She was wiping down the tables, a strand of hair falling in front of her face as she worked. I had the sudden urge to step over and tuck it behind her ear, but I forced myself to stop.

There it was again—that fucking spell.

She looked up and smiled when she saw me, her entire face lighting up. She crossed the room in a few quick strides and pulled me into a hug, her arms strong, her body warm against mine. She smelled like vanilla and something floral, something I couldn't name but wanted to breathe in forever. Before I could even think about pulling away, she pressed the softest kiss against my cheek, lingering just a second too long.

"I heard about the car fire," she murmured, pulling back just enough to look at me.

I couldn't help but smile. "Of course you did. Everybody knows everybody around here." I paused, but she didn't say anything. "It was that Miguel guy," I added. "The one who drove us to the finca."

She didn't look surprised.

She knew.

Maybe I was being paranoid, but how would even the worst gossip-mongers have that information so quickly? The fire had barely gone out.

"You knew him, didn't you?" I asked.

Carmen shook her head. "No."

I studied her. She was lying.

I exhaled sharply, raking a hand through my hair. "I'm done looking for Laura. I'm sure something bad has happened now."

Carmen didn't look surprised at that either.

"I'm sorry," she said softly. Her hand brushed against mine. "I want to come over later and stay." She looked me up and down, frowning. "You're losing weight," she added. "You need a good meal."

I let out a dry laugh and glanced around. "I can stay here instead," I said. "I don't want to be at the finca. Not after everything. Not after the body. And that Dutch family still freaks me out."

Carmen pulled away so abruptly I barely had time to react.

"No," she said quickly, wiping the closest table with her damp cloth.

I frowned. "Why not?"

"You just can't."

"Why?" I pressed, looking around. "Why can I never stay here?"

"It's not safe."

I let out a hollow laugh. "Safe from what?"

But she didn't answer. She turned away instead, walking behind the bar. "Coffee?"

I shook my head. "No, thanks."

I walked to the door, not bothering to say goodbye.

"I'll see you later," she called after me, but I was already halfway outside.

Back in the car, I looked up at the upstairs windows of Carmen's bar. Why wouldn't she let me beyond the bar? What the hell was she hiding?

I sighed and turned the key in the ignition, driving slowly to the address Fabián had given me. The crumpled piece of paper sat on the passenger seat, the ink smudged from where my damp fingers had clasped it. I pulled up just along the street and killed the engine.

The place looked deserted. Like everywhere else in that godforsaken town; a place time forgot.

As I stepped from the car, I suddenly recalled that Fabián said he had a gun.

I scanned the ground, searching for something, anything I could use, just in case. My fingers brushed against a broken piece of wood. It was heavy, about a foot long, the edges jagged where it had splintered off from something larger. It was nothing against a gun, but at least it was something. I gripped the wood tightly as I walked towards the house.

The footpath was overgrown, weeds spilling over onto the cracked concrete. The front door was closed, but something smelled off. A putrid stench that curled in my nostrils. Sweat, filth, something worse.

I knocked.

No answer.

I knocked again, harder this time, and the door creaked open. The smell hit me like a wall, thick and sour and rancid.

"Fabián?" I called.

Nothing.

The silence pressed against my ears.

I pushed the door open farther, but it stopped halfway. Something was blocking it. I frowned and pushed harder, shoving it with my shoulder. The resistance finally gave way, and I stumbled inside.

And then I saw it.

Fabián's body slumped against the door, blood soaking his clothes, his neck twisted at an unnatural angle. A knife jutted from his throat, buried to the hilt, the blade catching the dim light. His eyes were open, clouded, unseeing.

I froze.

For a moment, all I could hear was my own breath, ragged and uneven.

Fabián was dead.

And as I looked down, I saw my footprints in his dried blood.

58

HIM

I held my breath metaphorically. Then literally.

Fabián Vargas' body was sprawled across the tiny living room, eyes wide, frozen in a final moment of terror. The blood around him was thick, congealing, and my shoes—Jesus, my shoes—were covered in it.

Shit.

I stepped over him carefully, the movement slow and deliberate, as if anything too sudden might wake him up. I could feel my pulse hammering against the inside of my skull. This wasn't happening. This couldn't be happening.

But it was.

Fabián was dead.

And I had been drinking with him. More than once. There would be witnesses. People in that grimy bar would remember me—remember us. And worse, I'd raised my voice. I'd got angry.

I could hear my own words now, thick with frustration. *"Fuck this."*

And Fabián, smug and leering. *"Be at my place tomorrow. Ten am. Bring twenty thousand euros."*

I swallowed hard.

They must have heard it. Every single person in that fucking bar had watched me argue with a man who was now lying dead in his own house with a knife sticking out of his throat.

I crouched down instinctively, as if making myself smaller could undo my presence there. As if I could rewind the last five minutes and never have stepped foot inside.

I needed to move. Reaching down, yanking off my shoes, I carried them in one hand as I stepped across the room. My bare feet made no sound against the cracked tiles. The place was suffocatingly small, the air thick with the smell of rot, sweat, and now, death.

I had no idea what I was looking for, but I pushed open the bedroom door anyway.

The mattress sagged under its own weight, its sheets balled up in a filthy knot. A couple of empty beer cans littered the floor, crushed and discarded, and the whole place stank of stale alcohol and something even worse underneath it.

I almost laughed.

Not from amusement, but from something darker, something twisted and on the edge of hysteria.

For a split second, my imagination conjured an image of Laura tied to that filthy bed, a gag shoved in her mouth. But there was nothing. No signs of a struggle, no signs of her at all. Just more filth, more squalor.

I turned away, stepping carefully towards the tiny kitchen.

Dishes were stacked in the sink, thick with congealed grease and old food. Flies hovered lazily in the stagnant air. An empty bottle of cheap whisky lay on its side on the counter, a small trail of liquid seeping down onto the surface.

Still nothing.

I forced my breathing to steady, willing myself to focus. If Fabián really had had a woman there, I needed proof. Something, anything, to tell me he wasn't lying.

The only door left was the bathroom.

I hesitated.

Then, before I could talk myself out of it, I kicked it open.

The smell hit me first.

Damp, mildew, and something cloying underneath. The toilet seat was up, stained yellow. A cracked mirror hung above the sink, its reflection warped. And in the far corner…

I stopped.

A bra.

And a pair of knickers crumpled against the dirty tiles.

Fuck.

Fabián *had* had a woman there.

It had to be Laura.

My stomach twisted, bile rising in my throat. Fabián had said he had my wife. He'd demanded money for her safe return.

I didn't let the thought finish. I turned and bolted.

Shoes still in my hand, I threw myself out of the front door, lungs burning. Outside, the sun was too bright, the air too thick, the world too fucking loud. I slipped my shoes back on, smearing blood into the dust beneath my feet, trying to scrub away any evidence I'd been inside.

Then I ran back to my car.

Thankfully, the street was just as deserted as when I arrived, and I climbed inside, slammed the door shut and pressed the lock.

Gripping the wheel as I drove, the landscape blurred past me, dry earth and distant hills, the road twisting back to the finca. I had no plan, no next step. My thoughts were fractured, tangled.

But one thing was obvious.

Fabián Vargas was dead.

And if anyone found out what he'd said to me last night, if they knew he'd told me he had Laura, then I was fucked.

I pulled up outside the finca, my heart still racing. I barely registered turning off the engine before I was out of the car and moving. Then I remembered the Dutch kid and what was in that house.

I turned and sprinted down the track, my feet pounding the earth. When I reached their gates, I didn't hesitate. I banged on them with my fist.

"Hey!" My voice cracked. "Come out! I know you're in there!"

Silence.

I banged again. Harder.

Nothing.

I backed up, scanning the perimeter, then darted to the side, scrambling up the bank to see over the fence. My breath caught.

The place was deserted.

No sun loungers. No chairs. No signs of life.

It looked as if no one had ever lived there at all, just as I'd originally thought when we arrived. Seven long days ago.

My stomach twisted into knots, but I didn't even think. I moved on instinct. With my hands gripping the top of the wall, I heaved myself over, landing hard on the other side with a dull thud. But this time, I didn't try to be quiet.

Instead, I ran through the courtyard, past the empty terrace, scanning the windows. All the shutters were closed. No movement. No sounds. Everything was gone.

A chill rippled down my spine.

I forced myself to breathe, pushing on to the back of the property.

The cellar.

What would it smell like?

I fumbled in my pocket, fingers shaking as I pulled out my keys.

Come on, come on, come on.

I shoved one into the rusty padlock, twisting.

It clicked open.

I hesitated only for a second.

Then I yanked the door open.

59

____

SANTOS

SANTOS GRIPPED the steering wheel as she drove, berating herself for not thinking of it sooner.

The safe house.

She should have checked it days ago.

Her thoughts had been so tangled in James Blackwood, Laura's disappearance, and the inconsistencies between everyone's stories she had overlooked the obvious. If Laura had got away—if she was running, desperate, and knew about it—would she have gone there, or was it _too_ obvious?

The issue was, Santos didn't know where the safe house was.

She had only been told that there was one buried somewhere in the town. But that wasn't exactly helpful. If she was going to find it, she needed information. That's why she was going to see Carmen.

Carmen was sharp. She played dumb when it suited her, but Santos had been in this game too long to buy it. The woman had eyes on James, and more than that, Santos suspected she had feelings for him. That complicated things. It also made Santos wonder how the hell she had fallen for him so quickly.

Did James Blackwood have that much of an effect on women? Santos didn't think so, but Santos didn't care for men anymore. She shifted gears as she navigated the winding roads to the town. She had other things to consider too.

Such as James' ex-wife.

Álvarez was handling that. She'd given him instructions to track her down, ask all the right questions. It was a long shot, but maybe there was something in it; something that would give Santos a better idea of what kind of man James really was behind closed doors. On the surface, his divorce had looked clean. A mutual separation, no dramatic court battles, no accusations. But Santos didn't believe in clean breaks.

People left breadcrumbs, and it was her job to find them.

Then there was the other issue.

James' medical record.

Santos had told Álvarez to dig into that as well. Did he have a history of blacking out? Forgetting things?

And if he did…

What kind of things had he forgotten?

The thought unsettled her more than she cared to admit.

She pulled up outside Carmen's bar and was about to get out of the car when she caught sight of someone slipping inside ahead of her. A woman. She was wearing an oversized brown hoodie and a black baseball cap pulled low over her face.

Santos raised an eyebrow.

She looked ridiculous.

Who the hell wore something like that in this heat? If anything, she stood out more, trying to blend in.

As Santos reached for the door handle, her phone rang.

Álvarez.

She sighed and leant back into the seat before answering. "Yes," she said. "Have you got in touch with his ex-wife yet?"

"Not yet, boss." His voice was clipped, urgent. "But you need to go into town. Now."

A beat of silence.

Santos frowned. "Why? What the hell is it?"

Álvarez rattled off an address. There was something in his tone that made her sit up straighter. "What's going on?"

He hesitated, then said, "There's a body. Just get there."

Santos cursed under her breath, casting one last glance at Carmen's bar before throwing the car into reverse and speeding back into town.

The squad car was already there when she arrived, red and blue lights slicing through the morning air.

The house itself was a wreck, set back from the road, its exterior sun-bleached and cracking, vines creeping up the walls. The pathway leading up to the door was fractured, weeds forcing their way through broken concrete.

She barely had to step out of the car before the stench hit her. A thick, putrid wave of decay. Santos swallowed against the instinct to recoil.

She took a slow, steady breath through her mouth as she walked towards the house. The front door hung ajar, listing slightly on its hinges, and one of the officers stepped out to meet her. His face was pale, his jaw tight. "It's not good," he muttered.

It rarely was good.

"His name is Fabián Vargas."

Santos exhaled through her nose and stepped inside.

The smell was worse in there. It clung to the air, thick and suffocating. Then she saw him.

His body sprawled across the floor, his shirt soaked

through with blood, the fabric clinging to his stiffening skin. A knife jutted from his neck, the handle slick with red.

Santos inhaled sharply, forcing herself to take in every detail.

The blood pool beneath him was wide, dark and dry. He'd been dead for hours.

There were no signs of hesitation on the knife wound. It had been deliberate, forceful, meant to kill.

A struggle? Possibly. His hands were curled, fingers half-clenched, as if he'd been grasping for something before…

Her gaze flicked to his face. His eyes were open. Wide.

Frozen in terror.

Santos felt something cold settle in her stomach.

Fabián Vargas.

The name meant nothing to her, and she turned to the officer. "Who is he?"

"We've asked a couple of neighbours, and it appears he's a bit of a drunk. We can't find any history of him working, no tax records, no official employment. Not even a social security number registered in the system. One thing though, he's lived here most of his life, apparently."

Santos frowned. "Then how the hell was he getting by?"

The officer shrugged. "Odd jobs here and there, one neighbour said. Repairs, a bit of gardening, that kind of thing. No one really knows much about him. He kept to himself, mostly."

That made things even harder. Without a digital footprint, tracking down his connections would be slow. If there was anything to find at all.

She let out a gradual breath and turned back to the body. The stiffened limbs. The blood, deep and congealing.

"Get a photo of those footprints in the blood," she instructed the officer. "They look fresh."

Whoever had done this hadn't hesitated. And the most

important question: was it related to Laura Blackwood's disappearance? But how could it be? Laura and Chen's organisation wouldn't even know of him.

Santos was about to ask more when another officer stepped inside.

"Found something," he said hesitantly. "Not sure if it's relevant."

Santos turned to him. "Go on."

"One of the neighbours just mentioned something strange to me. They had some washing go missing off their line last night."

Santos narrowed her eyes. "Washing?"

"A T-shirt. A brown hoodie and a pair of beige cotton shorts."

Her pulse picked up.

A brown hoodie.

Beige cotton shorts.

She saw it in her mind instantly; the woman stepping into Carmen's bar, ridiculous in her oversized outfit and the cheap black baseball cap pulled low over her face.

Santos had laughed to herself at the time, thinking how absurd the woman looked. But now…

She turned back to the officer. "Did the neighbour say exactly when the clothes were taken?"

"Just sometime overnight. They hung them out in the evening, and they were gone this morning."

Last night. Santos guessed around the same time Fabián Vargas had been murdered.

She straightened. "I need a full report on Vargas. Whatever we can dig up—any priors, any records, even unofficial ones. And I need to know if he had any visitors in the past few days or if he's been spotted with anyone in public."

She didn't wait for a response. Her mind was already racing ahead. She needed to get back to Carmen's bar.

Because if her instincts were right, the woman in the hoodie wasn't just some random drifter.

And if she was involved in Fabián Vargas' death, then Santos might have just seen a murderer walk right through Carmen's front door.

60

HER

She froze outside the bar, mid-step, her fingers twitching at the sleeves of her hoodie. The sound of tyres crunching against gravel sent a flicker of unease through her, and instinctively, she turned her head slightly, just enough to catch sight of the vehicle.

There was a woman behind the wheel. Dark hair. Watching her.

The woman's lips curved; was that a smile?

She tensed. Was she imagining it?

The heat in the hoodie was suffocating now, and she wanted to shrug it off, to be rid of the feeling of being trapped inside it. But instead, she clenched her fists under her sleeves and lowered her gaze. Fuck her, she thought, jaw tightening, but even as the thought crossed her mind, she felt an odd twist of gratitude when the engine revved again and the car peeled away, kicking up dust and gravel as it sped off along the street. Exhaling, she pulled open the door to the bar and slipped inside. Darkness swallowed her whole.

The air was thick with the scent of old wood, stale beer, and something faintly citrusy; maybe a cleaning product that had failed to mask the decades of sweat and smoke embedded in the walls. The door creaked shut behind her, muffling the outside world. The place was empty, deathly quiet except for the low hum of an old ceiling fan that rotated lazily above her.

It was smaller than she expected. A long, polished wooden bar stretched across the right-hand side, lined with six empty stools. A handful of small tables sat in the dim corners, their chairs pushed in neatly. The walls were faded, painted in a once-warm terracotta now dulled by time. A row of dusty liquor bottles gleamed in the faint light from the bar's single overhead lamp. The place felt… forgotten.

Then a door at the side of the room opened, and a woman stepped through.

Carmen.

She was beautiful. Even in the dim light, her presence filled the space with something sharp, something aware. Five and a half feet of quiet confidence, with dark brown eyes that held secrets she would never freely offer. Her dark hair, just past her shoulders, framed high cheekbones and full lips that parted slightly as she took in the stranger before her. She wore a fitted T-shirt, shorts that showed off tanned legs, and simple leather sandals. She looked as if she belonged there.

For a moment, Carmen simply studied her, gaze flicking over the brown hoodie, the faded shorts, the tired stance of someone who had been moving too long without rest. Then her expression shifted, subtle but there. Her shoulders straightened, her fingers twitched slightly against her sides.

"Can I help?" Carmen asked. Her voice was smooth but held a definite note of suspicion.

She didn't answer immediately. Instead, she took a step forward, aware of Carmen's gaze darting past her, towards the door she had entered through. Checking if she was alone.

"Weren't you expecting me?" she asked with a hint of sarcasm.

Carmen's brow furrowed. "Expecting you? Why? Who are you?"

She smiled. Slow. Calculated.

"Oh, come on, Carmen."

The bartender's face changed.

Just for a second. A flicker of recognition, then something else, something deeper, something skimming dangerously close to panic. It was gone in a blink, but she had seen it.

She tilted her head subtly, watching the way Carmen's lips parted, the way her hands hovered slightly away from her sides as though unsure whether to reach for something. The silence between them stretched.

Then, finally…

"You know about the safe house."

Carmen's eyes narrowed, the panic on her face replaced by something harder. "What safe house?"

She let out a breath and shook her head. "You know very well." She paused, looking around. "But I just need to clean up first."

Without waiting for permission, she turned and strode into the hallway at the back of the bar, guessing where the ladies would be.

Carmen didn't stop her, but she didn't look happy about it. She could feel the stare boring into the back of her head until she closed the door behind her.

The light inside the ladies flickered twice before settling into a dull, yellow glow buzzing lightly overhead. The mirror was cracked along one edge, and the sink was stained from years of hard water. A single small window near the ceiling let in the faintest breath of air.

She gripped the edge of the sink and leant forward, staring at her reflection.

The hoodie was suffocating. She peeled it off, tossing it onto the metal rail beside her. Underneath, her skin was damp from the heat. She ran the tap, splashing cold water onto her face, her neck.

Her hands trembled.

Get a grip.

She stood there, breathing deeply, pressing her damp palms against her thighs. A sharp knock at the door made her jump.

"You okay in there?" Carmen's voice.

Her heart was hammering. She clenched her teeth. "I'm fine."

A pause.

Then Carmen's voice again, more forcefully this time. "I need you to come out now."

She took another steadying breath, grabbed the hoodie, and pulled it back on.

When she opened the door, Carmen was waiting. She followed her back into the bar.

Sliding onto a barstool, she watched as Carmen moved behind the counter, keeping a careful distance. The bartender leant against the back wall, arms folded, eyes sharp.

"You going to tell me what this is about?" Carmen asked.

She drummed her fingers against the wood. "I just did."

"A safe house."

"That's right."

Carmen exhaled slowly, her expression unreadable. "Who sent you?"

"No one had to send me. You owe us, Carmen."

Something flickered across Carmen's face—guilt maybe, or frustration. Then she straightened, shaking her head. "I don't owe you anything. In fact, you owe me money."

She tilted her head. "I don't have money."

Silence. Heavy.

She watched as Carmen's jaw tensed. "Then I don't know what you expect from me. You can't stay at the safe house. Not without…"

She leant forward slightly. "You need to do what you promised Doctor Chen."

Carmen hesitated, then grabbed a bottle from behind the bar, pouring herself a shot. She downed it fast, barely flinching, then met her gaze again.

"Without money," Carmen said finally, "you're not staying anywhere."

The woman smiled as she silently thought, we'll see.

"You need to drive me there, Carmen."

61

———

HIM

I PULLED the cellar doors open, bracing for the gut-churning stench that had haunted me since that night. But instead of the putrid assault I expected, I was met with a musty dampness—the thick scent of old wood, mildew, and something almost metallic, like rusted iron. It reminded me of childhood summers spent exploring abandoned barns, the air heavy with decay, but this was different. This was worse.

Panic twisted through me. If the smell had changed, did that mean something else had too? My stomach clenched. Had I miscalculated? Had something, someone, been down here? Did the Dutch family know all along?

I swallowed and pulled my phone from my pocket, thumb fumbling to switch on the torch. A thin beam of light cut through the darkness, illuminating the steep wooden steps that led down into the abyss. My pulse pounded against my temples as I descended, the air growing colder with every step. The hairs on my arms stood on end. It wasn't just the chill; it was the feeling of being watched.

I kept expecting the Dutch kid to come lunging out of the shadows. Or worse, for the doors above to slam shut, trapping me inside. The thought made me hesitate on the last step, my breath coming in short, sharp bursts. *Get on with it. It's too late for second thoughts.*

The cellar stretched out before me, a cavernous space that mirrored the entire footprint of the finca above. My torch flickered over stacks of firewood against one wall, dust-covered crates, and the rusted remains of an old bicycle leaning at an awkward angle. A wheelbarrow with a flat tyre sat abandoned near the centre of the room, its handles coated in a thick layer of grime. A torn sheet of tarpaulin sagged over a pile of forgotten junk: broken furniture, shattered glass, and a long-discarded radio with its wires spilling out like exposed veins.

But none of that mattered.

I turned towards the far corner, my heartbeat hammering in my ears. And then I saw her.

Slumped against the wall, exactly where I'd left her.

I gagged as I stepped closer. The torchlight caught the edge of the blanket, still wrapped around her body, but it had loosened slightly. My hands shook as I crouched and reached out. The fabric was damp beneath my fingers. With a deep breath, I pulled her forward—just a little. And then the blanket fell open.

I jerked back, bile rising in my throat. I couldn't look.

A choked noise escaped my mouth, something between a gasp and a dry heave. I squeezed my eyes shut, fumbling to re-wrap the blanket, tying it tighter, making sure nothing could slip free. I was already sweating, the back of my shirt clinging to my skin, and I hadn't even started the hard part yet.

Getting her across the floor was harder than I thought. The stone was uneven, catching at the blanket, making every inch feel like a mile. My arms burned, my shoulders screaming in protest, but I didn't stop. Couldn't stop. The weight of her—of what I'd done—pressed down on me, suffocating.

By the time I reached the steps leading up to the open cellar doors, my entire body was trembling. The hot air drifted in, taunting me with its intensity. Almost there.

I turned my head away, trying not to think about what I was doing, and slipped my hands underneath, gripping the bundled form as if I was holding a sleeping child. A sick parody of something tender.

Lifting her was harder than I expected. My legs wobbled as I hoisted her through the opening, nearly losing my grip as I stumbled onto solid ground. I laid her down carefully, if that even mattered anymore, and turned back to shut the cellar doors. My fingers fumbled with the latch, my mind racing.

Now the real challenge.

The wall.

I stood staring at it, breathing hard. It wasn't high, maybe five feet, but getting the bundle over it without making too much noise was another thing entirely. I flexed my hands, rolling my shoulders back. I had no choice.

Grabbing the bundle, I hefted it up, gritting my teeth as I lifted it above my head. The strain made my arms shake. With one last push, I shoved it over. It landed with a dull thud on the other side. My knees nearly buckled from the relief.

I took a moment to gather myself, wiping the sweat from my forehead, glancing around to make sure I was still alone. The house loomed in the distance, a dark silhouette against the sky. I waited, listened, heart hammering. Still no sign of the boy. Just get back.

Scooping the bundle back up, I made my way to my finca. Every step felt like wading through quicksand, my limbs slow and heavy. By the time I reached the door, my arms were on fire.

I took out my keys and unlocked the door along the corridor. The one Miguel Ruiz had dismissed so easily.

"What's in there?" I'd asked when he showed us around.

Miguel had hesitated. Just for a second. "Storage," he'd said, voice too casual. "Nothing interesting."

I smiled to myself.

Miguel Ruiz had no idea. And now he was dead. Burnt to a fucking crisp.

I pulled the door open, dragging the bundle inside. For now, this would have to do. I'd get rid of it properly later—after dark. I shut the door behind me, locking it again.

The exhaustion hit me like a freight train. I stumbled into the kitchen, grabbed a beer from the fridge, and twisted off the cap, taking a long, desperate gulp. The icy bitterness barely registered. My mind was still spinning, adrenaline refusing to let go.

Then I heard it.

The low growl of an engine.

I rushed outside and heard a car coming down the hill.

Shit.

I stiffened, setting the beer down as I moved onto the patio. The engine cut through the silence, bouncing along the dirt road. My pulse spiked.

Who the hell could it be?

62

SANTOS

THE DETECTIVE PARKED outside Carmen's bar and stepped out, slamming the car door harder than necessary. She hurried across the uneven pavement, pushing open the wooden door and stepping inside.

A couple of elderly men sat hunched at the bar, their wrinkled hands curled around their drinks. They turned to look at her, eyes flickering with the slow, sluggish curiosity of those who had seen too much but still liked to watch.

Santos ignored them.

A woman appeared from behind the bar, wiping her hands on a rag, but it wasn't who Santos had gone to see.

"Where's Carmen?" she asked.

The woman's eyes flickered with uncertainty before she shrugged. "Gone out somewhere. She called me to cover."

Santos clenched her jaw. "When did she leave?"

"About twenty minutes ago. Maybe less."

Shit.

"Did she say where she was going?"

The woman shook her head.

"Is anyone else here? A woman in a brown hoodie?"

The woman frowned, but didn't give her reply much thought. "Not that I know of. Just me and them." She nodded at the two old men. "Oh, and there's a guy out the back fixing the cooler."

Santos wasn't satisfied. She produced her badge and said, "I need to look around."

The woman hesitated but eventually gave a small nod. "Go ahead. I just help out here. It's not my business to say no."

Santos was already moving when her phone rang.

Álvarez. Again.

She cursed under her breath but knew she couldn't ignore it. Pressing the phone to her ear, she stepped away from the bar and answered.

"What have you got? But be quick."

"Relax, Santos. I have something for you."

"If it's not Carmen's location, I don't have time."

"It's not Carmen. It's James Blackwood's ex-wife."

Santos stopped. That got her attention.

"She didn't want to talk at first," Álvarez continued. "But when I told her his current wife was missing, she changed her mind."

"And?"

"She left him because he got violent."

Santos shut her eyes briefly, inhaling through her nose. "Define violent."

Álvarez sighed. "Not just the occasional argument. It escalated. Pushing. Grabbing. Things being thrown. She said there were nights she locked herself in the bathroom. Told me she once woke up with his hands around her neck. Said she thought he was dreaming."

Santos opened her eyes again, scanning the bar as she listened. "Did she report it?"

"No."

"Why not?"

"The usual. He always apologised. Always promised it would never happen again. Then one day, she packed a bag and left."

Santos exhaled slowly. "Does she think he could hurt Laura?"

There was a pause. Then he said, "She doesn't know. Said James wasn't always like that. That something changed in him. He became depressed, and extremely jealous."

Santos didn't answer right away. Her mind was already racing ahead.

"Alright," she said finally. "Good work."

She hung up before Álvarez could say anything else and turned back to the bar.

She needed to find Carmen.

The place wasn't large, but she did a thorough search. The back room was mostly storage: old crates, cases of beer, and a faulty fridge a man in an orange work shirt was grumbling over. The kitchen was small, a basic setup for serving simple bar food, but empty.

The hallway leading to the back rooms smelled of damp wood and cleaning products. There were two locked doors, presumably offices or supply closets, and a stairway leading up. Santos took the stairs two at a time, heart pounding.

Upstairs, she found a row of rooms, likely once used as rental accommodation. Each one had a numbered brass plate on the door, and most were empty, though one had a messy, unmade bed and a half-full bottle of water on the nightstand. The window was slightly open, a breeze stirring the thin curtains.

But there was no sign of Carmen, and there was no sign of the woman in the brown hoodie.

Eventually, she gave up and returned to the bar, frustration building in her chest.

"Are there any secret rooms or tunnels in this place?" she asked.

The woman behind the bar frowned at her. "What? No. At least, not that I know of."

Santos studied her, trying to decide if she was lying, but the woman just shrugged again. "As I said, I just help out here. I don't know anything about the building."

Santos tapped her fingers against the bar, then exhaled sharply. She had nothing.

With a final glance around, she turned and walked out.

The air was thick, cooler than previous days, but still hot. Walking to the car Santos pulled her keys from her pocket, then she noticed someone standing next to it.

A woman.

Her dark hair was neat but not overly styled. Slim build. Hands resting lightly at her sides, composed. But it was the posture that struck Santos first. This woman wasn't waiting. She was expecting something.

Santos narrowed her eyes and stepped closer. "Can I help you?"

The woman tilted her head slightly. "Detective Santos?"

Santos stiffened.

She knew that voice.

She didn't need any further introductions.

It was Doctor Sarah Chen.

63

———

HIM

THE SUN HAD BEGUN its slow descent, sinking lower in the sky, but the heat refused to loosen its grip. A slight breeze rolled through the valley, barely enough to stir the dust on the road. It wasn't relief. It was a cruel reminder that the temperature would remain unbearable for hours ahead.

I stood at the edge of my driveway, beer bottle in one hand, my free hand wiping sweat from the back of my neck. My gaze drifted down the hill in the direction of the Dutch finca.

Still empty. No movement. No voices. No sign of life at all. It was as though they had never been there.

But they had been. I had seen them, spoken to them. That kid: what the hell was wrong with him? And why did they vanish like that?

I felt a prickling unease crawl up my spine.

They wouldn't have gone into the cellar. They couldn't have.

I had locked it myself with a new padlock and I was the only one with a key. There was no other way in. And yet, something gnawed at me, an anxious whisper that refused to be silenced. Where the hell were they?

The low hum of an engine snapped me back to the present. Turning, I stared up the hill, tracking the sound as it grew louder, the engine rounding the last bend. And then Carmen's SUV came into view.

A knot in my chest loosened, but I wasn't sure if it was relief or something closer to resignation. It was as though she was the only person I had left to rely on, but I didn't trust her anymore. Not really.

She pulled up fast, gravel skidding beneath her tyres, then killed the engine. The door swung open, and she was moving before I could take another breath.

She ran to me, throwing her arms around my waist. Her skin was warm, damp with sweat like mine, and I felt her breathing fast against my chest.

"Something is really wrong," she whispered.

I tensed.

She pulled back, eyes locked onto mine, her fingers still gripping my arms.

"That drunk you've been talking to? He's dead. Murdered. Fabián Vargas. The talk is all over town."

I didn't flinch and Carmen leant back slightly, studying my face, her expression shifting from concern to something colder. "How do you know?" she asked.

I swallowed. Too slow.

Her brows pulled together.

"You had something to do with it, didn't you?"

"No. Fuck, no."

But it came out too fast. Too sharp. My voice cracked slightly at the end.

Carmen's gaze dropped to my hands. I realised then I was gripping the beer bottle too tightly, my knuckles bone-white. I forced myself to relax my fingers, took a slow swig of the beer, then offered it to her.

She ignored it.

"You're lying," she said, taking a step back.

I glanced down at my shoes. The memory of blood flashed before my eyes, thick and dark. I had scrubbed it off, but in my mind, I still saw it.

"I had nothing to do with it, Carmen. You have to believe me."

Unbelievably, my words seem to placate her, so much so, I questioned if she knew who killed him anyway.

"Are the police there?" I asked. "Santos?"

"Yeah," Carmen said. "And she's been hanging around my bar too. Pulls into the lot, waits a few minutes, then drives off. She's onto something."

A fresh wave of nausea rolled through me.

Carmen sighed and shook her head. "There's something I haven't told you, James."

I looked up. "What now?"

"Sit down, please."

I hesitated, but she gestured towards the terrace table with an insistence I couldn't ignore. Slowly, I lowered myself onto the seat.

"This finca you're staying in," she said, glancing over my shoulder. "It's the safe house where Laura's practice sends their most vulnerable women."

I exhaled, shaking my head. "Carmen—"

"Jesus Christ," she interrupted. "You knew."

I hesitated just long enough to make it look as though I was thinking. "Maybe Laura mentioned something once, but I didn't—"

"You're something else, James," she said, with a slight smirk twinging at the corner of her mouth. We both had secrets that possibly weren't quite as secret as we thought. "It doesn't matter," she continued. "Nobody knows except me, Laura, and Doctor Chen," she paused. "But of course, you know as well."

We'd never spoken about it.

The finca wasn't just a holiday retreat. It was something else, something neither of us could admit out loud.

Carmen and I had kept the safe house to ourselves for obvious reasons. It was part loyalty, part fear, part unspoken promise to Laura—and to Chen too. Whatever had been agreed back then, it was easier for Carmen to act like she didn't know I knew, and for me to pretend the same. That way, neither of us had to say it out loud. Neither of us had to acknowledge what that place really was. But at least it answered my question of how Carmen knew where to find me the day I arrived.

I turned to her now. "Is that why I could never stop at your bar?"

Carmen nodded once, slowly. "You think I was being coy?" She let out a bitter laugh. "No, James. I was protecting this place. If anyone had seen you stay at the bar, maybe they would have followed us back here."

I stared down at the ground, trying to make sense of everything. There was one thing I had to know.

"What about Emma Carter?" I asked, glancing up. "Did you know about her?"

Carmen blinked, surprised. "Laura told me she was coming. Said she'd arrive late and was staying at a hostel in town that night. The plan was for me to meet her here the next day, introduce her to the place, help her settle in."

"But you never met her."

"No." Carmen's voice had gone quiet. "I was waiting. Then Laura messaged and told me not to come. Said something had changed."

I felt the hairs on my arms rise. I'd been here then. "I was here too," I said slowly, watching her reaction.

Carmen's eyes narrowed. "What are you saying?"

"Nothing."

A moment's silence fell between us. Carmen glanced back at her car.

"You're owed a lot of money by the practice, aren't you?" I asked.

Her gaze turned cold. "Yes, James. I am"

"And it's Laura who hasn't been paying you?"

Carmen's mouth twitched. "Chen signs everything off, but it's Laura who's in charge of the money for this place."

I leant forward slightly. "Is that what this is? Some kind of twisted revenge? You got close to me so you could… what? Get back at her?"

"Don't flatter yourself, James," she said. But she didn't deny it.

My throat tightened. "Did you have something to do with her going missing?"

Carmen didn't answer right away. She just stared at me, her expression unreadable. Finally, she sighed and shook her head. Somehow, I believed her.

"There's somebody in the car to see you, James."

She smiled faintly. Then, without another word, she turned and walked back to the SUV.

I stood, watching.

She pulled open the back door.

A woman stepped out.

Brown hoodie. Pale shorts. Baseball cap pulled tight over her head.

My entire body locked.
My vision narrowed. My breath hitched.
I staggered back, hand slamming against the table.
I knew that shape.
The woman smiled.
"Hello, James."

64

————————

SANTOS

"Doctor Chen."

Santos said it flatly, without any further introduction.

Sarah Chen flinched slightly at the sound of her name, her expression composed but alert. She was dressed neatly: tailored trousers, a lightweight blouse that seemed unaffected by the thick Andalusian heat. A woman who never let herself appear ruffled.

Santos wasn't sure she liked that.

The two of them stood in the parking lot outside Carmen Ramos' bar. Chen had been leaning against her car, arms by her side, waiting.

"You've been quite elusive," Santos said. "Why haven't you been returning my calls?"

Chen hesitated, glancing at her shoes before her eyes looked up at the bar, as if the answer lay somewhere else.

"I'm sorry. When I heard Laura had gone missing, I kind of panicked."

"Go on," Santos instructed.

"I came from Madrid after Rebecca told me you'd paid a visit."

Santos held her gaze. The ambulance in the background during the phone call. "So you were in Spain all along?"

Sarah Chen nodded like a guilty schoolchild.

"And you tracked me here?"

Chen exhaled, glancing past Santos at the bar's entrance once more before answering. "That bit was easy." She tilted her head towards the building.

Santos' eyes narrowed. "Carmen?"

Chen nodded. "I thought she would be involved. I've just missed her, apparently. Then when your car pulled up, I knew from Rebecca's description who you were."

"So why do you think Carmen is involved?" Santos asked.

Chen's lips pressed together, considering. "She runs the safe house."

That made Santos pause. "The safe house?" she repeated.

"Yes," Chen said, eyes sharp on Santos' face, as if watching her reaction. "But she's refused to take on any more women. The practice owes her money. Laura hasn't paid her for much longer than I knew."

Santos let out a slow breath, piecing things together. "How much money?"

"A lot." Chen's voice was clipped, matter-of-fact. "Enough that she's bitter. Enough that she told me a few months back that she'd get her revenge on Laura for it one day."

That made Santos' stomach clench.

"You think Carmen would hurt her? That she's had something to do with her disappearance?"

Chen exhaled, shaking her head. "I'm not sure, to be honest. But she's been warning Laura for months to pay up, and yet the money never arrived. Not just Carmen's payment, but other funds. Money was disappearing."

Santos frowned. "What money?"

"From the practice." Chen's gaze sharpened. "We only send extremely vulnerable women to Andalusia, Detective. Women who need to vanish for their own safety. But Laura started sending a different kind of patient."

Santos remained silent, waiting.

"The kind with money," Chen continued, quieter this time. "Rebecca noticed it first."

Santos silently kicked herself for assuming it was Chen behind the wealthy women being sent to southern Spain. Why the fuck hadn't she asked Rebecca herself? She couldn't let anybody back at the station know. They'd eat her alive for such a rookie mistake.

Chen carried on, oblivious to Santos silently rebuking herself. "The women coming to the safe house weren't just escaping abusive husbands or violent ex-partners anymore. They had assets. Some of them were in the middle of divorce settlements. Others had inherited money. A few had simply been wealthy women in terrible relationships."

Santos frowned, shifting her stance. "But why was Laura choosing them?"

Chen's mouth pressed into a thin line. "I don't know."

Santos wasn't sure she believed that. James was out of work, and although Laura earned decent money, maybe she wanted more.

"But after Rebecca told me, I saw a pattern," Chen continued. "The money in their accounts would be moved around. Not all of it, just increments, small enough to go unnoticed at first. But when I brought it up with Laura, she brushed it off. Said it was just the cost of their relocation that they had agreed to it. That it was necessary."

Santos crossed her arms. "How many women?"

"Four, maybe five, over the past eighteen months or so."

"And what happened to these women?"

A silence settled between them.

A beat too long.

Chen looked down, her shoulders stiffening slightly. "I'm not sure. I assumed Laura had found them somewhere to relocate. I trusted her. She's very good at her job."

Santos studied her. "But you suspect something."

Chen exhaled through her nose. "I guess I became suspicious after the Megan Walsh case," she admitted.

Santos tilted her head. "You mean when she refused to leave Laura's side?"

Chen gave a humourless smile. "I was angry at first. You're right about that. I thought Laura had manipulated her —an extremely vulnerable patient, one that should never have formed such an attachment."

"But you changed your mind?"

Chen hesitated. "Not immediately," she admitted. "But something didn't sit right."

Santos' jaw tightened. She had known there was more to that case. "What about Emma Carter?" she asked.

Chen's brows drew together. "Emma Carter?"

"Her blood has matched a sample found on a wall in a finca nearby."

There was a shift in Chen's posture, a flicker of something unreadable in her expression.

"The safe house?" Chen asked.

Santos frowned.

Then it clicked.

The breath left her lungs in a slow exhale.

"The finca is the safe house?"

Chen's gaze flickered to the horizon, where the hills rolled away into the distance. She muttered something under her breath. Santos didn't catch it all, just one word. "Shit."

She exhaled, pinching the bridge of her nose. "Tell me more about Emma Carter. What else do you know?"

"Not much," Chen admitted. "But she had money too.

She was meant to be divorcing a man in finance. I didn't handle her case, but I remember Rebecca mentioning her name. She wasn't the type of woman we usually take in."

Santos felt a headache coming on. She looked back at the bar, then at Chen, trying to piece together the timeline.

"You're not involved in this," she said, almost to herself.

Chen's brows lifted slightly. "You sound sure."

"I am," Santos said. "You're calculating, but you're not a criminal. And you wouldn't be here if you had anything to hide."

Chen let out a quiet breath, as if relieved, though she hadn't asked for Santos' reassurance.

"I'm sorry for lying about where I was," Chen finally admitted. "The practice is my pride and joy. I've built it from scratch. I had to try to find out for myself what was happening when Laura went missing. It was me who suggested they use it for their vacation, after all."

The detective looked towards the bar again, her mind turning over everything she had just learned.

Carmen. The money. The missing women. Where were they? Maybe she'd never know.

She turned back to Chen, her expression unreadable. "Thanks for your time," she said.

Chen nodded, but her gaze lingered, as if debating whether to say something more. And then she did.

Eventually, Santos turned and unlocked her car. She slid into the driver's seat but didn't start the engine. Instead, she sat there, staring ahead, the weight of the conversation settling over her.

It was what Chen had told her...

That changed everything.

65

———————

HER

SHE WATCHED as James staggered back, his foot catching the edge of the table. He gripped it for support, his knuckles turning white, his breath coming in shallow gasps. His eyes—those cold, calculating eyes—now stared at her as if he had seen a ghost. For a moment, she thought he might faint.

"You look surprised, James," she said, savouring his shock.

Across the patio, Carmen took an instinctive step forward, her hand hovering near James' arm, as if afraid he might collapse. She studied her, noting the subtle shift in her posture—the way her body tensed, the way her eyes darted between them, trying to make sense of what was happening.

"Megan?" James whispered, his voice barely audible. "Megan Walsh?"

"Yes," Megan smiled. "You thought I was dead, didn't you?"

The silence stretched between them, thick and suffocating. The only sound was the chirping of cicadas.

"Megan?" Carmen said, her voice sharper now. "You're Megan Walsh?"

She turned to James, who had gone completely white. Carmen's expression shifted from confusion to something resembling horror. "What the fuck's going on, James?"

Megan took a step closer, her eyes locked on James. "Tell her," she urged. "Tell her where I've been."

James swallowed hard. His mouth opened, but no words came. He shook his head slightly, as if trying to wake himself from a nightmare.

"I... I don't know," he stammered. "I thought you were dead. Laura... Laura went to your funeral."

Megan let out a short, bitter laugh. "Laura never went to my funeral, James. I was never dead. And you knew."

James blinked, his breath hitching in his throat. He looked genuinely lost.

Carmen glanced between them. "Somebody start explaining. Now."

Megan kept her gaze on James, drinking in his unravelling composure.

"You came to see me that night in Madrid," she began, her voice controlled but edged with fury. "Told me I was influencing Laura. Said I was destroying your marriage. You knew I had money too. And then, after you half-strangled me..." She tilted her head slightly, watching the way his body stiffened. "...you slit my wrists."

Carmen sucked in a sharp breath.

Megan didn't take her eyes off James. "You were good. Careful. You wore gloves, made sure not to leave a trace. You even positioned me so it looked like suicide." She exhaled, shaking her head. "And then you just... left."

James shook his head violently, his hands trembling. "No. No, I—"

"You left me in a pool of my own blood." Megan's voice

hardened. "But you weren't as thorough as you thought, James. I didn't die."

James stared at her, his breathing ragged.

"I was still alive when Laura found me," Megan continued, her voice dripping with accusation. "She came to my apartment, knowing you had followed me. And she found me just in time, clinging to life."

Carmen stood frozen in place. "Laura found you?"

Megan nodded, glancing at her briefly before fixing her gaze back on James. "And instead of calling an ambulance, you know what she did?"

James didn't answer. His lips were pressed together, his body visibly trembling.

"She cleaned me up," Megan said. "Said she had a safe house for me, a place where I'd be protected. All I had to do was wait for a while and follow her instructions."

James' eyes somehow grew wider still. He looked behind him at the gleaming white finca.

Megan continued. "She gave me a time, this address," she said, taking a slow step forward. "Told me exactly when to show up. She even booked me a taxi." She cocked her head. "But when I arrived"—her lips curled into something that wasn't quite a smile—"you were here."

James looked at her now, full of something beyond panic —true, bone-deep horror.

"I thought it would just be Laura, and when I let myself in, you jumped me from behind, James. You knocked me out cold," Megan said. "And then dragged me to some godforsaken wooden crate in the middle of nowhere and left me for dead. Again."

James stumbled back against the table, his breath coming in sharp, uneven bursts.

Carmen turned to him now, her expression unreadable. "You… you did this?"

James shook his head wildly, sweat forming along his hair-line. "No. I... I thought she was dead, I swear. I thought..." He turned to Megan, his voice raw. "I didn't... I thought you were dead."

Megan studied him carefully. He looked desperate. Maybe even sincere. But she knew just how good he was at lying.

Carmen watched the exchange, her fingers curled into fists at her sides. Megan could almost see the doubt creeping in.

"Don't believe him," she warned, voice sharp. Then, after a pause, her lips twisted into something cruel. "Oh wait. Are you two an item?"

Carmen flinched.

Megan chuckled. "Does Laura know?"

Another heavy silence.

Then James said, his voice hoarse. "Laura is missing."

Megan stilled.

James swallowed, glancing at Carmen before turning back to her. "She disappeared the day we arrived here." He paused, thinking. "It must have been Miguel. He must have hit you. Laura too."

Carmen exhaled sharply. Then, turning to James, she said, "But now Miguel is dead. Was it you, James?"

James ran a hand through his hair, looking utterly lost. "How could it be?" he pleaded. "After what happened with Megan... I thought that was..."

Megan folded her arms. "So where's Laura now?"

James' face was full of anguish. "I don't know."

Megan watched him as his head turned towards the finca. "Is she in there?"

James opened his mouth, then closed it again.

"You've killed her, haven't you?" Megan said softly. "She's dead in there, isn't she?"

James' entire body jolted, his face twisting. "No."

Megan didn't look away. "You bastard. And what about Emma—"

James cut her off. "No!"

Then everything fell so silent, Megan could hear the pounding of her own heart. Carmen shifted uncomfortably beside James, her gaze flicking between them.

And then…

A sound.

Faint at first, but unmistakable.

Sirens.

The distant wail of police vehicles descending the hill, growing louder. The pulse of blue lights flickered against the windowpanes, flashing like an omen.

James turned in the direction of the sound, his face draining of whatever little colour he had left.

Megan watched him, savouring the moment once more. The realisation. The fear.

"No escape now," she whispered.

James looked at her, eyes pleading. "Megan, please…"

But Megan just watched as the blue lights washed over his face.

66

HIM

I couldn't breathe.

Megan Walsh stood before me, alive.

But she shouldn't have been.

I staggered back, barely aware of Carmen's presence beside me. My body felt detached, my limbs foreign. I'd experienced this once before—the day I did it. The night I pressed down hard enough on Megan's wrists that the blood flowed across the apartment floor like the scene of some tragic overdose.

But it wasn't a tragedy. It was justice.

It had to be.

I blinked, trying to process the impossible. She was dead. I left her for dead.

"I thought you were dead. Laura… Laura went to your funeral," I muttered.

Megan took a step forward, her lips twisting into something almost playful. She let out a short, bitter laugh. "Laura never went to my funeral, James. I was never dead."

Carmen shifted beside me. "Somebody start explaining…"

I barely heard her. My mind was ripping through the past, frantically stitching together the truth I hadn't let myself face until now.

Megan Walsh had destroyed my marriage.

From the moment she wriggled her way into Laura's life, I'd known. She was dangerous—manipulative. She'd lived a hundred lives before she met Laura, each of them dirtier than the last.

Drugs. Fraud. A violent background. And she was clever. I knew if she ever went to Andalusia, she would find out what I did.

I tried to warn Laura. I begged her to see Megan for what she was. The way she twisted people, how she played the victim, how she made people need her. But Laura wouldn't listen, despite what I'd done for her a year before.

And the more I pushed, the more she resisted. The more she clung to Megan. Until one night, she came home and told me she was leaving.

"I can't do this anymore, James."

I'll never forget the way she looked at me. Like she'd already made her decision. Like she had had help making it.

I knew then; Megan had persuaded her. Megan had won.

I had no choice.

Take Megan out of the picture, and I'd get my wife back. And then our secret would be safe forever. It was that simple.

That day, I went to her apartment. She was alone—drunk, high—who knew? I didn't ask. She let me in without thinking, that same sly, knowing smirk on her face.

"James," she'd purred. "Come to beg me to leave your wife alone?"

She already knew.

I'd done it without thinking, without planning. My hands

had moved on their own, my fingers pressing against her skin. Holding her in place, I took the knife from my pocket and slit the blade across her wrists, and then I watched the colour drain from her face until she was gone.

And then, silence.

I stood over her, breathless, free.

I even had the audacity to tell her what I'd done to her precious *friend* Emma Carter.

I knew Laura would come back to me.

But she didn't.

Instead, she grieved. She spiralled. She struggled.

I should've seen it coming. Megan had worked her way into Laura's mind like a parasite, feeding on her thoughts, twisting her emotions. Even in death, she wouldn't let go.

I had to get her out of Madrid.

I had to fix things.

So after the *funeral*, when Laura suggested a vacation, I jumped at the chance. The idea of staying at the finca surprised me, but I also knew who was there.

And I knew Laura wanted to go back. She'd always loved the town, always said we should revisit one day.

But then we arrived, and Miguel Ruiz was waiting, I thought something was wrong. I instantly didn't trust him. He wasn't some friendly local. But still, somebody had to let us in.

And then another thought clicked into place as I stood staring at Megan, slotting neatly into all the other pieces.

Doctor Sarah Chen.

It could have been her all along.

Chen could easily have known everything. The real story. And she would desperately want to clear the name of the practice. Her baby. She'd do anything to save its reputation.

And Chen knew we were going to the finca. That was why Ruiz had been waiting, and when I left for the bar, leaving Laura alone, Megan arrived, and Ruiz struck.

I clenched my fists.

And then Chen killed Ruiz before retiring to dispose of Laura. All to wipe the slate clean. To make sure her secrets, Laura's secrets, stayed buried.

Everything made sense. I had a genuine get-out clause.

Everything except for two very real problems.

One: Megan Walsh was still alive. And I had tried to kill her.

Two: There was a body in the locked room inside the finca.

Fuck.

I barely registered the distant sound at first. Then it hit me.

Sirens.

Wailing through the hills. Getting closer.

I swayed. My vision blurred. I had to move. And I bolted inside.

"James!" Carmen shouted, but I was already through the finca door, my mind racing.

The police wouldn't believe anything I said. Why would they? I'd tried to kill Megan, and my wife was missing. There would be no trail to Chen, and they'd find the body in the spare room. And Megan would tell them everything.

I shoved the bedroom door open, heart hammering, and tore open the wardrobe, yanking up the loose panel where I'd stashed Fabián's gun. My fingers closed around the cold metal grip and my chest heaved.

I barely remembered taking it. When I found him dead, the blood cold and congealed, I hadn't thought. I had just taken it.

And now…

Now it was my only chance.

I whirled towards the window, my pulse thundering in my

ears. Blue lights flickered through the trees, bouncing off the walls, casting everything in cold, violent flashes.

This is it.

I gritted my teeth, gripping the gun tighter. My options were narrowing fast.

Outside, Carmen's voice rang out, sharp and panicked.

"I don't know what the hell is going on, but you need to—"

A second voice cut her off. Megan.

"You have no idea what he's capable of."

I exhaled shakily.

She was right.

They had no idea.

But they were about to.

My gaze flicked to the locked door.

The body.

I felt sick.

Everything had been spiralling since the moment I arrived there. Since the moment I stepped foot in that damn town.

But I had done all of it for Laura.

To save my marriage.

To keep her with me.

And now?

Now Laura was gone. Megan was alive. And I was standing there, in a darkened room, clutching a gun like the man everyone had always suspected I was.

The sirens grew louder, piercing the night.

There was no time left.

I swallowed, tightening my grip.

I had one move left.

And I had to make it count.

67

SANTOS

SANTOS SAT IN HER CAR, her pulse a steady, heavy thud in her ears. She was waiting for backup, but her mind raced ahead, fitting puzzle pieces together faster than she could process them.

Doctor Sarah Chen was gone now, walking away into the night after their conversation, but what she had revealed just before she left made Santos' skin crawl.

Megan Walsh wasn't dead.

And so Laura Blackwood had never attended her funeral.

Santos gritted her teeth, furious at herself for not checking, for not even considering the possibility. They had all assumed Megan Walsh had been buried, but in reality, Megan Walsh wasn't even her real name.

"We never really knew who she was," Chen had said, her voice sincere, almost apologetic. "We smuggled her into the country, hid her in plain sight. And Laura would have done anything for her."

Santos had asked one final question before letting Chen leave. Did James Blackwood know any of this?

"No," Chen had said. "I'm not sure why, but he was convinced she was dead."

Which led to the most pressing questions of all.

Where the hell was Megan now?

And did that mean Laura was still alive?

The crackle of a radio interrupted her thoughts, followed by the crunch of tyres on gravel. Álvarez had arrived.

She stepped out of her car and waved him over. Two additional officers emerged from a second vehicle, their expressions grim as they fell in beside him. The air smelled of dust and dry grass, the early evening unnervingly still. Santos briefed them quickly, keeping her voice low and clipped.

"When we get there, we need to approach with caution," she said. "If James Blackwood is at the finca, we don't know his mental state, but he might be dangerous."

The officers nodded in unison.

Santos climbed into her car and started the slow descent to the finca. The blue lights flashed behind her in the rear-view mirror, casting long, eerie streaks across the dirt road as they snaked their way down.

As they pulled up outside, she spotted two figures standing near the entrance. Carmen. And the woman in the brown hoodie. Santos stepped out cautiously, eyes locked on the hooded figure.

"Megan Walsh, I presume?"

The woman met her gaze, but before she could answer, Santos turned to Carmen. "Where's James?"

Carmen swallowed hard, her jaw tight, and nodded towards the house.

And then the front door flung open violently, and before anybody could react, the sound of the gunshot exploded across the valley.

Santos watched in disbelief as Megan jerked forward, a strangled gasp escaping her lips before she crumpled to the ground. Blood bloomed instantly across her chest, dark and thick, staining the front of her hoodie.

Santos' body reacted before her mind could catch up. She ducked, drawing her gun, adrenaline surging through her limbs.

"James!" she shouted. "Drop the weapon!"

He stood in the doorway, arm outstretched, gun still trained on Megan's body. He was breathing heavily, eyes wild, unhinged.

Slowly, he turned his gaze to Santos.

A smirk. A small, twisted one.

"Where did you get the gun, James?"

"Off Fabián," he said, shaking his head with a soft laugh. "Didn't even have to try hard."

Santos' grip on her gun tightened. So it was James who stabbed Fabián Vargas. And now he'd killed Megan Walsh. And Laura too?

"Put it down, James. Now."

He ignored her. Instead, he took a step forward.

"Tell them to put their guns away," he ordered, nodding at the officers behind her. "Do it, or I put a bullet through you next."

Santos hesitated.

She had no choice. If she didn't comply, he'd pull the trigger.

She lifted a hand, signalling Álvarez, and the others to stand down.

The officers exchanged wary glances but obeyed, their guns lowering slightly but still ready.

James exhaled, then turned to Carmen. "Come with me," he said.

Carmen stiffened, inching backwards, shaking her head.

"No."

James' face twisted. "Carmen, just come with me," he pleaded, his voice almost desperate.

"No," she whispered again, a little louder this time. "You've killed Laura, haven't you?" Carmen's voice trembled, her eyes burning into his.

James flinched.

"Where is she?" Santos asked, and James made the mistake of glancing back inside the finca. Santos knew she was in there.

"You killed Miguel Ruiz," Carmen continued, stepping back. "And Fabián too. And now Megan. Who the hell are you?"

James' expression darkened. He raised the gun again. This time, pointing it at Carmen.

"If you don't come with me, I'll kill you too," he said.

Carmen let out a sharp breath.

"James, don't," Santos warned.

James ignored her. His finger hovered over the trigger, and Santos knew she had only seconds…

And then…

BANG.

A deafening gunshot rang out.

James' body jolted violently as a bullet tore through him.

His eyes widened in shock, his mouth falling open slightly. His knees buckled, and he crumpled to the ground like a marionette with its strings severed. The gun slipped from his grasp, landing with a dull thud in the dirt beside him. Santos whipped around, heart pounding.

Álvarez stood a few feet away, his gun still raised, unwavering. His jaw was tight, his eyes cold, locked on James' unmoving form.

Silence.

Then a single, shallow breath rasped from James' lips. He was still alive. But barely.

Santos exhaled sharply, then rushed forward, kicking the gun farther away before crouching beside him.

His chest was rising and falling in uneven jerks, his lips parting slightly. His eyes, glazed with shock, flickered up to meet hers.

He tried to speak, but only a small, gurgle came out. Blood pooled beneath him, soaking into the dry earth.

Santos heard sirens in the distance, closer now, the world snapping back into motion. She'd asked for an ambulance, foresight telling her things would turn nasty.

She glanced at Carmen, who was staring at James' crumpled form, her hand covering her mouth.

Megan lay motionless on the ground and Carmen rushed to her, pressing trembling hands to the wound in her chest, whispering something; whether a plea or a prayer, Santos didn't know.

Álvarez stepped beside her, gun still at the ready, his expression unreadable.

Santos turned back to James. His breath hitched. His lips parted again.

And then, finally…

His body stilled.

The sirens wailed, but James Blackwood would no longer hear them.

68

———

LAURA

FORTY-EIGHT HOURS LATER

LAURA SAT at the bar in central Madrid, her fingers curled around a cold beer. The dim light reflected off the glass, distorting her features in the mirror behind the rows of liquor bottles. Her hair was cut short, dyed blonde, and tucked beneath a faded baseball cap. The clothes on her back—jeans too tight, a loose sweatshirt, sneakers she would never normally wear—felt foreign, but that was the point. Reinvention required discomfort.

Madrid was loud, chaotic, and indifferent to her presence. Perfect.

Behind the bar, a muted television flickered with breaking news. She didn't need sound to understand. The screen showed the finca, its whitewashed walls gleaming in the Andalusian sun. The footage cut to a sequence of faces: first James, then Miguel Ruiz, then Fabián Vargas. And then the picture of Megan Walsh appeared like a ghost. Laura took a long gulp of her beer. At least she was dead, but Laura had thought she'd taken care of her herself.

Otherwise, she had planned it all to perfection.

The police would still be scrambling to identify Megan's real name, her real background. But that would be impossible. After all, Laura had been the one to give her a new identity before she even left the UK. Even Doctor Chen didn't know she'd done it. And Laura had contacts, people who could forge passports and driver's licences, helping her disappear from England and into Spain. But that was the easy part.

The hard part had come later.

Megan had started asking too many questions. About Emma Carter.

At first, Laura hadn't thought much of it. Megan and Emma had known each other back in England—not close friends, but familiar enough. Megan had found out about the practice through Emma. She had needed an escape, running from the wreckage of her life. But once she was safe, she began digging. She asked Rebecca for files. She wanted to know where in Andalusia Emma might have gone.

That was the moment Laura knew she had a problem.

She had to ensure nobody, nobody, ever found Emma Carter.

That was why she had insisted on keeping Megan under her wing, despite Sarah Chen's protests.

A little over a year ago, she had convinced James to take a vacation to the finca. That was the excuse. The real reason? To get rid of Emma.

James had been on the verge of cracking for months. He'd lost his job, and alongside it, his self-esteem. He couldn't carry the weight of it, the way Laura made all the money. The way she buried herself in her work. He'd threatened her, and that made him dangerous. And so, she manipulated him.

She had already taken the majority of Emma's money, put

it in an account for which only she knew the whereabouts. But then Emma began to suspect her. Laura told Chen Emma didn't have money after all, and that disappointed Chen, who quickly lost interest. But with the promise of being set up for life, she convinced James that he didn't need to worry about work, as long as he did one thing. Kill Emma Carter.

It hadn't been difficult. James had always been too eager to please her, too desperate to keep their marriage intact. He had a reputation for violence with his ex-wife. She knew she could get him to do it.

He had taken her to that cellar beneath the abandoned finca, just down the hill from the safe house, and done what needed to be done.

But months later, Megan began to ask questions. She wanted to know where the safe house was, where Emma was last seen.

And then, on the alleged day of Megan's funeral, she dropped the bombshell. James had bragged that he'd killed Emma Carter too.

Laura wished she'd left Megan to die after all.

So, she had been forced to improvise. To get over the apparent suicide, Chen fortunately suggested a vacation at the finca, and that suited Laura fine. She arranged the trip and told Megan to meet her there. She even paid for her taxi ride.

Laura found Miguel's number on a Facebook Group. One set up by Enrique Gálvez. Miguel was just another person who helped with changeovers, and Enrique didn't care because he knew the agency was stretched to the limits. First, Laura contacted Carmen, asked about a Miguel Ruiz. Of course, Carmen knew him. Everyone knew everyone in that town. Carmen told Laura not to mess with him. He knew people in places you didn't want to go. Perfect. So, she contacted Miguel, and offered more money than usual, as long as he kept things quiet.

Once they arrived, Laura staged an argument with James, riling him up just enough to send him storming off to drown his sorrows at the bar. Then she'd waited, knowing Megan was arriving any minute—pre-planned, as always. Miguel had already returned.

When Megan turned up, Miguel struck her on the head, dragged her into his car, and drove her down to the quarry. Laura heard the damn car alarm going off once or twice, echoing around the entire valley. Had James heard it? Would he have been on his way back from the bar? But she'd had no time to consider the negatives.

So, as planned, Miguel left Megan in an old wooden crate, one Laura had come across during a hike a year before. Megan Walsh, locked inside, was left to die.

From there, everything had been about pointing the blame at James. So, she disappeared herself. She'd already booked a nearby hotel in a small village under a false name. She couldn't be too far away.

During the week, she even returned to the finca, bold as anything, to grab her suitcase and fresh clothes because she was beginning to smell. Hell, she had even taken a swim in the pool to clean up, left her journal and photo of Chen on the bed to make James doubt his own mind. However, the day he walked into the supermarket, she had to run for her life. But she soon found the funny side. His blackouts had been coming much more frequently. Entire stretches of time, gone. One moment he'd be the bedroom, the next outside with no recollection of how he got there. Conversations he couldn't remember having. Objects moved. Messages sent. He'd just put a woman fleeing from a shop down to his growing paranoia.

But then Miguel contacted her. Said he wanted more money to keep quiet. So, she told him to meet her at the quarry. Ten o'clock. And this time, she had to take care of things herself. All it took was a single strike to the skull before dragging him into her car. And then she set it on fire, again knowing suspicion would fall onto James. She drove Miguel's battered car away and dumped it down a lane that time had forgotten. And it all seemed related to her own disappearance. Only one person could be responsible. Her stupid husband.

She had planned to leave him long before the trip. He was too weak, too unreliable. He had been breaking apart, talking about Emma Carter too much, questioning their choices. Then, when he messed up Megan's suicide, she knew it was only a matter of time before he lost control completely.

She had found Megan just in time. And Megan, barely clinging to life, had told her everything.

James had done it. He had staged it to look like she had taken her own life. And then he told her about Emma Carter. That changed everything.

Laura couldn't let him know she had saved Megan. Instead, she had faked her funeral, surprised at how easily she found the false tears.

But Laura had another problem.

Carmen.

The woman was a leech. Laura owed Carmen money—a lot of money. But the year before, Carmen had made advances to James, staking a claim. That ensured Laura would never give her a single penny.

So, she had arranged this trip with a purpose. She would disappear. She knew James would unravel without her. He was weak. He needed her to hold him together. Without her, he would self-destruct.

And that was exactly what had happened. Or, at least, appeared to have happened.

Laura glanced at the television again.

Detective Santos was being interviewed. The subtitles filled in the blanks: James Blackwood shot Megan Walsh. The police were also in no doubt that James Blackwood killed Miguel Ruiz and Fabián Vargas. Santos even mentioned footprints matching James' shoes in Vargas' blood.

They had also discovered a skeletal body in the locked room of the finca. And although still awaiting confirmation, they were convinced it was Emma Carter, and James' DNA would be all over it.

Laura smirked.

She ordered another beer, pulling a thick wad of euros from her pocket to pay the bartender. She still had over seven thousand euros left of the nine she'd withdrawn a week or so earlier, enough to sustain her until James was fully buried beneath the weight of the charges.

She had been patient, waiting in the hotel, biding her time.

She raised her glass to the television screen as Santos delivered the final line. "Laura Blackwood is still missing. Presumed dead, and only James Blackwood would know where."

Laura grinned.

Perfect.

She drained the last of her beer and left the bar without a backward glance.

'The Family' Psychological Thriller Trilogy

Have you read the series everybody is talking about?

Available in eBook, Print & Audio

*EACH BOOK AVAILABLE SEPARATELY OR AS A BUNDLE -
Just search for 'Jack Stainton Books'*

'I was amazed at the twists and turns in these books... brilliant... impossible to put down'

'Had to finish it quickly so I could get my heart rate back to normal...'

'I love a good psychological thriller and I have just found my new favourite author!!'

'I like to think I read enough thrillers to be able to suss them out before finishing, but this one kept me guessing until the very last sentence!'

'Two's Company' Domestic Thriller Trilogy

Don't miss out on these three heart-stopping domestic thrillers!

Available in eBook, Print & Audio

*EACH BOOK AVAILABLE SEPARATELY OR AS A BUNDLE -
Just search for 'Jack Stainton Books'*

It all starts with THE BOSS'S WIFE….

★★★★★ 'Loved every second of this. Didn't think it was possible to beat his "Family" series but this is the best one yet.

★★★★★ 'I have read all of Jack Stainton's novels and **he is now my FAVOURITE author**! His ability to capture the reader… and hold on to you until the never disappointing ending is amazing! **Anxiously awaiting his next book.'**

★★★★★ 'Wow! I thought the first book was good, but **it just gets better and better…'**

★★★★★ "What a read! **The plot is just ingenious.'**

ACKNOWLEDGEMENTS

If you've made it here, thank you—for sticking with me through every twist, every red herring, and every moment you weren't quite sure who to trust. Writing this book was a journey I *loved* taking, and I hope it kept you hooked right up until the final page.

And the finca is real. Just outside a place called Competa in the Andalusian hills. I took a vacation there two years ago, and as soon as I arrived, I knew there was a story!

To my incredible **Advanced Reader Group**—your early eyes, sharp instincts, and thoughtful feedback helped shape this book into something I'm truly proud of. You catch things I miss, push me where it matters, and most importantly, remind me why I write.

To my **editor**—thank you for your insight, your ruthless red pen, and your uncanny ability to spot when I've been too nice to a character who really deserves to suffer. And to my **cover designer**—once again, you've captured the eerie, unsettling spirit of the story with a single image. You make it look effortless.

And finally, to **you**, the reader: your support means everything. Whether you read this in one sitting or over stolen moments, your time and trust are never taken for granted. Your reviews, messages, and word-of-mouth recommendations keep this strange, solitary craft of writing alive. I couldn't do it without you.

Until next time—stay curious, stay suspicious, and remember: nothing is ever quite what it seems.

Jack

If you want to learn more about me and my books, please sign up to my FREE newsletter below…

---

www.jackstainton.com/newsletter

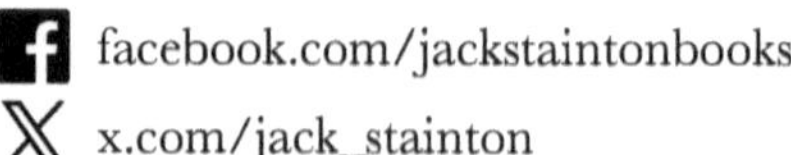

facebook.com/jackstaintonbooks

x.com/jack_stainton

instagram.com/jackstaintonbooks

REVIEWS

Enjoy this book? You can make a big difference

Honest reviews of my books help bring them to the attention of other readers.

If you've enjoyed this novel I would be very grateful if you could spend just a few minutes leaving a review (it can be as short as you like).

Thank you very much.

A GUEST TO DIE FOR

Jack Stainton's debut Psychological Thriller

Available online in both eBook and Print Versions

...I bought the book and read it in two sittings. Very good, lots of twists and red herrings.

This does exactly what a thriller should; it keeps you guessing until the end...

Excellent book full of twists and turns. The characters are brilliant... The ending was totally unexpected...

Sucking you in with a dreamy hope of a better start, the fear of what might happen next will keep you turning the pages!

A fantastic, gripping debut!